Make it Real

GENNY CARRICK

content

Be advised this book deals with themes of grief, emotional abuse (past), and a loved one's medical emergency in-story.

For all the sunshines out there

jed

I WAS USUALLY SMARTER than this, I swear.

My family might object, depending on the day, but I liked to think of myself as a pretty sensible guy. I paid my bills on time, I hadn't been in trouble with the law since a couple of speeding tickets in high school, and I never wore socks with sandals. But every now and then, I managed to do something that showed a disturbing lack of judgment or sense.

Agreeing to meet Callie Matheson for coffee fit squarely in that category.

Waiting at a table in The Busy Bean where she'd suggested we meet up, I scanned the street outside. I'd arrived early because sometime between yesterday's innocent "Would you get coffee with me?" text and this morning, I'd realized I had no idea why she wanted to get together.

Or that she had my phone number.

At first, I'd assumed it had something to do with the kindergarten class she taught. Since she'd become friends with my family over the winter—and turned out to be my nephew Dylan's teacher—she'd invited a couple of us to visit the school and speak to her little students. From all I'd heard, my cousin

Eden had charmed them with a presentation on the public library, and my brother Wade's talk about fire safety had been a smash hit. I'd figured my turn had come to tell the kids about local farms or, I don't know, how many servings of fruit they should have every day, something along those lines.

But around seven this morning, I'd remembered school's out for the summer. Unless Callie was trying to get a jump on next year's guest speakers, it seemed unlikely she wanted to ask about an opportunity for her students to Meet the Farmer.

Which left an uneasy weight in my stomach about what she might actually want from me instead.

I couldn't think of a lot of reasons she would ask me to meet her. I usually only had the one motivation when I asked a woman to get together, but I probably wasn't the best example there. Other, purely platonic, reasons to invite someone to coffee must exist, but at the moment, I couldn't think of anything.

Five past ten, and still no Callie. I drummed a light beat on the tabletop, my eyes on the café's doors. Rigid time constraints were one of the first things I'd gladly let go of when I got out of the Army and came home to Magnolia Ridge, but I would have welcomed promptness today just to ease my mind I hadn't stumbled my way into a date.

Not that I didn't like to date. I did. Believe me, I did.

And not that I didn't like Callie, either. The times our paths had crossed, I'd only had positive impressions of her. My sister and cousins wouldn't have become so chummy with her if she weren't good people, and they adored her. A little on the young side, she tended to chatter and could come across as trying too hard, but she pretty much radiated sweetness and enthusiasm.

Exactly why I hoped she hadn't invited me here with romance on her mind.

I wasn't a romance guy. I dated plenty, but that was about

the extent of it. I didn't have a whole lot of experience with anything more serious. Guaranteed Callie would want something serious. Nothing about her struck me as someone who dated just for fun.

If that was even why she wanted to meet me. Getting ahead of myself here, but that question mark looming over this coffee date turned my stomach in on itself as minutes ticked by. How many lessons had I learned about using my head and avoiding an ambush, and here I'd gone and walked straight into the unknown.

Finally, I spotted her doing a hurried little skip past The Busy Bean's front window, rushing to make our appointment.

Would *not* call it a date until I had confirmation. Possibly not even then.

She burst through the door, head swiveling to scan the café. She wore a white T-shirt and a pair of cut-off overalls that managed to both ease my fears this was some kind of a formal date, and simultaneously ramp up the coil of tension I had going on. When her eyes hit me, a huge grin sprang to her face, twisting a tiny little something in my gut.

Regret, maybe. Did I *want* to be here on a date with her? Best not to think too much about it.

I stood from the table to greet her. A good foot shorter than me, she tilted her head back and the grin disappeared, taken over by a subtle frown.

"Sorry I'm late. That's so rude when you agreed to meet me on such short notice."

"No problem." Didn't think I should open by admitting I'd agreed to the meet-up because I'd thought she needed a favor, and only later connected she might have had other ideas in mind. Other ideas I was currently trying to force from *my* mind.

We moved to the counter, ordered our drinks, and I paid for my Americano and her iced something-or-other. She bounced on the balls of her feet while we waited, her bright blue Converse tapping away with nervous energy. Not a great sign for a non-date explanation. But despite its name, The Busy Bean wasn't too crowded this morning, and we returned to my table a couple of minutes later, drinks in hand.

She took a seat across from me and pushed a lock of dark hair behind one ear. She'd gotten it cut since we first met at Christmas, and it now hit just below her chin in soft waves that seemed destined to get in her way. Not that I was cataloguing her hair. After twelve years in the Army, I'd learned to notice my surroundings, that's all.

Although, a pretty woman's hairstyle had never been part of field training.

"So, what can I do for you?" I took a sip of coffee. Not the best opener, but probably a good idea to keep things a little distant here.

Callie paused a beat as if holding her breath. "I want to proposition you."

Hot coffee shot down my windpipe. I coughed and spluttered, eyes stinging with tears, throat burning. *Not* what I'd expected her to say. So much for keeping things distant.

"That came out wrong!" Her brow tugged together, her mouth twisted up in horror. She pulled a few napkins out of the dispenser on the table and thrust them my way. "I've been practicing how to say this all morning and then I go and lead like that. Ugh! Obviously, I meant to say I had a proposition for you, but it got all garbled in my mind and I said the wrong thing and now you're all—"

She waved the napkins at me as though coffee had shot out of my nose like a Las Vegas fountain show. Should probably count myself lucky there.

I took the napkins and dabbed at my face, but my composure for this mystery meeting had exploded in a cloud of Americano.

She smiled weakly. "I'm sorry. Maybe I should have practiced more."

"I'm fine." I cleared my throat one more time. "What have you been practicing to say all morning?"

Like that didn't pile on more dread. Maybe not as much as the word *proposition*, but close enough.

She laid her palms flat on the table, glancing once around the café before her eyes fell back on me. After a beat, she leaned forward like we were telling secrets, her deep brown eyes brimming with a touch of embarrassment and a whole heap of excitement.

"I was wondering if you'd pretend to be my boyfriend for a while."

I froze.

Her mouth pulled into an exaggerated smile, her eyebrows lifted comically. Couldn't tell if this was a show of nerves or an attempt at a joke. Both, maybe?

"So, you *do* want to proposition me?"

She rolled her eyes as though *I* were the one not making sense. "Forget I said that. I don't want to date you."

Huh. Starting off strong. "I'm getting real mixed signals here."

"Okay, I know. I should explain. See, I live with my granny, it's just the two of us."

I'd heard something about that through my sister, that Callie's dad was long gone and her mom had passed away when Callie was in high school, but I didn't know anything more. I hadn't thought we'd really reached the *personal confidences* stage, but apparently, we were zooming ahead.

"She has three best friends, they've known each other forever.

They're like bonus grandmas for me, which is actually really awesome until their affection goes completely off the rails and they overdo it and everything turns into death by meddling." She took a breath and flashed another awkward smile. "Sorry. Babbling. Anyway, they've been talking about moving to Florida to live that Golden Girls life for years. They're finally ready to do it, they have a condo picked out in Sarasota and everything, but now, my granny's not sure she can leave me on my own. She thinks..."

Callie cringed, a tiny furrow forming between her eyebrows. "She thinks I need a man to take care of me."

I guess that justified the cringe. "How very 1950s of her."

Not that my pop was so different. He'd been dropping similar hints as subtle as a kick to the back since I'd first come home from the Army almost three years ago. He didn't approve of my social life, and made his hopes for me settling down known at every turn. He had no notion I'd long ago ruled out settling down. I wasn't meant for that life.

"Yeah, it's not the most modern view. She and her friends keep setting me up on these awful blind dates, but since none of them are leading to second dates, Gran's not sure she can move to Florida after all."

Seemed a lot to put on Callie's love life. "And you want her to move to Florida."

"Of course I do. She deserves it, after everything we went through with my mom, and how she stepped up to help me through high school and college." She ticked her head to the side, her mouth curling down. "I mean, it's not all about me being generous. When Gran moves, I can do whatever I want with the house."

"You want to decorate it?"

"I want to sell it. But now, she's acting like she won't go if I'm not satisfactorily entangled with a man."

Didn't sound like the greatest situation, but it had an easier solution than...whatever she was proposing. Propositioning.

"Just tell her you're fine on your own."

Tucking that stray hair behind her ear again, she shot me a look like she wanted to thump me on the head.

"Obviously, I've tried talking to her about this, but she won't listen. She's convinced it'd be the best thing for me. Mostly, it's just been annoying, but now, it could ruin everything. Last weekend, I heard her telling her friends she might have to back out of their Florida plans entirely because she feels so guilty about leaving me alone. So I thought, what if I wasn't alone?"

Ah. Thus, the proposition. I finally caught onto her scheme, however convoluted, and the dread from earlier worked its way higher up my chest. "That's where I come in."

"Exactly. If she thought I had a boyfriend, maybe that would be enough to convince her to go spend her golden years on the beach with her buddies."

Maybe, but it also sounded like the makings for a sticky mess.

"I don't think I'm the right guy for this." For so many reasons, none of which I especially wanted to outline for her. My dating history could best be described as surface-level. Romantic attachments—even pretend ones—weren't in my wheelhouse.

Callie moved to grab my hands but shifted and wrapped them around her plastic cup at the last second. My skin tingled as though she'd touched me, but I shushed that away. I didn't need to be thinking about missed opportunities here.

"No, but you are. We've known each other a while now and have spent time together as friends, it's not totally crazy that we might start dating." She raised a hand. "Which we wouldn't be, let's make that clear. But Gran would buy it. Plus, I trust you. And the girls speak really highly of you."

Kind of liked hearing that, not going to lie. I'd never been accused of having a shortage in the confidence department, but I liked knowing the women in my family had positive things to say about me. I couldn't be sure I deserved it all, but it still sent warm fuzzies through my chest.

"And I figure neither of us is going to take things the wrong way and lose our heart in *this* combination." She gestured between us making a face that said nothing could be more unlikely.

Those warm fuzzies turned to snow flurries. She didn't mean anything by it, but something about her writing us off didn't sit right. I couldn't say which side of it bugged me more —that she didn't consider me *lose your heart* material, or the hint that maybe I didn't have a heart to lose.

"It's flattering that you'd ask. Kind of." All things considered, she wasn't going out of her way to butter me up. "But I don't think pretending to be your boyfriend is such a great plan."

I hadn't been boyfriend material in a long time—if I ever really had been—and wasn't looking for a crash-course. Convincing my pop he could fully retire and hand the family orchards over to me took up my free time already, plus we were smack-dab in the middle of harvest. I didn't have room in my days for pretending to woo Callie.

"It wouldn't be for very long, just a couple of months. Gran's friends are planning to move at the end of summer. If I can convince her to join them, we can drop the act after she's gone."

The encouraging smile she shot my way left too much unsaid.

"And if she doesn't leave?"

Her expression fell. "Well...we would fake break up, I guess."

Sounded like a good way to shatter whatever glowing opinions the women in my family had about me. However you cut it, both scenarios ended with me as the bad guy. I didn't care about my reputation around town all that much, but ending a relationship with a girl like Callie would permanently put me in the doghouse with my pop, and probably my sister and cousins, too. Not to mention my stepmother and aunt, who had latched onto her like hens to chicks.

This plan might help her—emphasis on *might*—but it would certainly create giant problems for me.

"Don't you have another guy you could ask?"

She sipped at her iced coffee and pulled a face. "Not really. I don't know that many guys. The ones my grandma and her friends have been setting me up with are part of the problem. They think because I'm agreeing to set-ups, I must be desperate, and they, uh, have certain expectations I'm not willing to meet."

I didn't like the sound of that. "So don't go on the set-ups."

"Wow. What a plan." She rolled her eyes again. It might have been cute if it weren't so full of disdain. "You've never dealt with four insistent grandmas skilled at emotional manipulation, have you? They named a whole wing after my granny at the University of Guilt Trips. If I could just avoid the set-ups, I wouldn't be sitting here asking you to pretend to be my boyfriend."

I tried to put myself in her shoes. My pop's nudges hadn't escalated to blind dates, but if they did, I'd resent it, too. I still couldn't imagine a scenario where playing pretend ranked as the best option. How would that even go?

She sank her chin in one hand, flicking the straw in her coffee with the other. "There's always the divorced fifth grade teacher who was extra friendly to me last year, but he's in his forties and has a daughter almost as old as me. So that's a no-go."

Couldn't blame her—wait. "How old are you, anyway?"

She straightened up as though she could gain height on me seated at the table. "Twenty-five."

Yeah. Not going there.

Her shoulders slumped, and she blew out a breath, eyes darting to the side. "In three months."

"Nope. Absolutely not. This is a bad idea."

"What, because of my age? You're, like, thirty-one."

"Thirty-three, and it's not just the age difference." Although that had jumped to the top of my *Reasons Why Callie's Fake Dating Plan is a Terrible Idea* list. I might not have been looking for long-term, but I never took advantage, and that kind of age difference skated too close to the line. "This is never going to work."

"Why not? We'd just pretend to date for a little while."

"You keep saying that. Are you good at lying? Personally, I've got no problem with it, but you strike me as a very straight-arrow type."

Her gaze narrowed. "Why do I feel like that's not a compliment?"

"Because you're perceptive. You think you can convince your grandma that you're crazy about me? In whatever various methods that entails?" I raised my eyebrows, driving my hint home. No way her grandma wouldn't expect some affectionate displays as proof of our supposed romance.

Her expression shifted like she'd caught the smell of rotting fruit. "I hadn't thought too much about that, I guess, but I'm willing to make a few sacrifices for my granny's sake."

A second later, a triumphant smile curled along her mouth. *Oh. I see how it is.* Her teasing almost got me smiling, too, but I needed to keep my head on straight here.

"The biggest problem is that it sounds like your grandma doesn't want you dating someone, she wants you *married*. No amount of pretending is going to fix that."

Unless a fake engagement turned out to be Callie's next request, in which case, I should have stayed on the farm this morning.

She sank against the chair back, her confidence fizzling out. "Urgh, maybe you're right. It's a crazy plan. I just thought if she believed I was happy with someone, she'd go off and be happy, too."

I couldn't fault her motivation—just wasn't a fan of her methods. Especially when they involved me.

"Try talking to her about it again. I bet she'll come around."

"You've never met my gran." She sighed, seeming smaller than ever. "Maybe I'll ask Damon to be my fake boyfriend, after all. I could be a good stepmom to a twenty-year-old, don't you think?"

I frowned, a big old boa constrictor of distaste squeezing around my insides.

"I'm just kidding. He's totally not in consideration." She took a big, heartening breath, puffing back up again. "Okay, well...this was fun."

I couldn't stop from exhaling a laugh. "That's one way of putting it."

"I know, it was pretty weird. I'm sorry. I don't always go around asking guys to pretend to date me, I promise. This is a one-time thing."

Warmth flared to life in my chest. Was I *proud* of that? Terrible of me to turn her down and then be secretly glad she hadn't asked anyone else, but there it was. "A likely story."

"Do you mind not telling anyone about this? I don't want my friends to think I'm loony-toons."

"Are you kidding? I'm going to tell everyone how you propositioned me."

She burst into laughter, chasing away her embarrassment. "Me and my big mouth."

I much preferred her like this, relaxed and smiling, to the woman trying to make herself small just a minute ago. But I couldn't date either one, real or fake.

I mimed zipping my lips. "Your secret's safe with me."

"Thanks." Her smile slipped a touch. "I should really have paid for your coffee since I brought you out here and subjected you to my bizarro ask. I have some cash."

She started digging around in her purse, but I raised a hand. "It's not a problem."

"Okay. I'm…" She paused, her mouth twisting, eyes squinting at the edges until I suspected she regretted every moment of this meeting. "Yeah, I'm going to go now. Sorry for all of this. And thank you for the coffee."

"You're welcome."

"And thank you for your silence." She raised a finger between us, her smirk ruining the implied threat.

"You've got it."

She slung her purse over her shoulder and stood from the table, and I did the same out of old habit. She flashed a half-smile, ducked her head, and made a quick escape out of the café.

Watching her go, I exhaled a long breath. I figured I could take another minute or two to finish caffeinating before I went back to the orchards, and sat down to drink the rest of my coffee.

That had been…something else.

I'd fielded plenty of strange requests from women in my time, but that one hit a new level of odd. Fake dating to deceive her grandma? I didn't even know where to start. I'd heard of schemes like that, of course—you wouldn't believe how many people married a soldier for reasons other than romantic—but never thought one would come to my doorstep.

Still, I didn't like turning her down when she only had good intentions for keeping her grandma happy. I'd much rather be the guy to swoop in and save the day, but her proposal was straight up bananas. It just asked for trouble and misunderstandings and chaos.

Usually, I subscribed to the theory that a little chaos could be a good thing. Mix it up and keep things interesting. But getting involved with Callie, even just for pretend, would amount to a whole heap of chaos I wasn't prepared to wade through. No, thank you. Better she go off and tell her grandma the truth, or better yet, find somebody to date for real.

Lord knew, that man would not be me.

callie

WELL. Royally embarrassing myself in front of Jed Evans wasn't how I'd thought my morning would go.

Oh, who was I kidding? I'd known going in the odds weren't high he'd agree to my idea. The man was supposedly up to his ears in real dates—why would I think faking a few with me would sound appealing to him? Especially when I was the weirdo who *asked him to fake date me.* Ugh.

I guess I'd figured a short-term relationship would be right up his alley, but no. Not interested. *"Absolutely not."* Just the words a girl wanted to hear when she asked a man to date her, even in a strictly imaginary way.

We weren't exactly close friends, but he'd always been nice to me, friendly and fun, and now, I'd probably obliterated that almost-friendship forever. At least I didn't see him all that often. Maybe the next time we ran into each other, he'd have forgotten all about it. Better yet, maybe *I'd* have forgotten all about it.

Ha. Fat chance. I'd be reliving that coffee date in my night-mares for months.

I let myself into the one-story home I shared with my

grandma. A cardboard box filled with knick-knacks and items she'd deemed non-sentimental sat by the front door waiting to be donated. Other half-filled boxes dotted the living room—books, pictures, and mementos stuck in the space between staying and going.

Granny had been whittling her belongings down for the last year as she and her friends' plans became more serious, and she'd started packing essentials a month ago. But then came her big hesitation, and she'd put a pause on the whole production. So now, it all sat half-in, half-out. Waiting.

Just like me.

Gran, Carmen, and Rita played cards at the dining table, their laughter seeming to fill the whole house. Like today, the friends weren't always together—Linda must have been off doing her own thing somewhere—and they rotated where they hung out, but it still felt like they spent 125% of their time in this room.

Since the school year had ended and I was around during the day more, these women had become inescapable. I loved them, but being with them every waking moment was like using four weighted blankets at once. Comforting but smothering.

"There's our girl," Rita trilled. "Where have you been? We could have used a fourth."

Card games were one of their milder hobbies. Pottery, learning to play the ukulele, making homemade taffy—they seemed determined to try everything under the sun in their retirement. Most of it right here at our dining room table.

"I'm sure Linda wouldn't like me taking over her spot." I walked over to check out their choice for the day. Cards with various shapes, colors, and patterns lay in neat sets in front of each woman. "I'm no good at this game, anyway."

"Neither are we." Carmen laughed, drawing a card from the

deck and examining her hand through purple reading glasses she wore around her neck. "Suzie just likes to toss this one in the mix whenever she's on a losing streak at something else."

Gran pursed her lips into a flat line, eyes intent on her cards. "It has nothing to do with winning or losing. I happen to like a little variety."

"Variety, my behind," Rita said. "I never met such a sore loser."

"Yet, you keep playing games with me." Gran smirked, revealing the last of her cards.

Tossing their hands on the table, Rita and Carmen complained about their loss. Granny gathered up the cards to put back in the box, a smug little smile playing on her mouth. Smart as a whip, she dominated most of the games they played. I usually lost to her, too—I'd inherited a lot from her, but strategy wasn't among my gifts.

Clearly, or I would have figured out a solution to Gran's *Find Callie a Man* quest by now.

"Have I told you I adore that haircut, Callie?" Rita mimed fluffing her hair. A former hairdresser, her gray-blond hair curled in a chic, perfectly blown out bob. "Really brings out your eyes."

"What were you up to this morning?" Gran asked before I could thank Rita for the compliment.

"Just met a friend for coffee."

"Oh?" Carmen spoke, but they all lit up with interest. "Which friend?"

They stared at me as if I might bust out wedding invitations. Maybe I should have been more grateful they cared so much, but living under a microscope had lost its charm.

"Harper." *See, Jed Evans? I can tell lies. Not so straight-arrow now, am I?*

They deflated liked I'd crushed their dreams in my bare

hands. Looking around the table, they seemed to urge each other to say something. I didn't believe in telepathy, but they'd been friends long enough that half their conversations were just meaningful looks and insistent eyebrow motions.

"Speaking of meeting up with friends…"

Rita's eagerness gave her away. Nothing casual about this pivot.

Inwardly, I sighed so hard, my soul briefly left my body. On the outside, I feigned polite interest as if I didn't know what they had in store for me. Kind of cute they thought they were being sneaky. Also horrifying to contemplate what they'd consider *direct*.

"I was talking with my friend Nora the other day," Rita said. "Her grandson is in town on business for several months, he does sales for one of these big-time agricultural outfits. She said he's looking to meet more people in the area, and I told her I knew just the girl to introduce him to."

Everyone these women met must think me the most socially decrepit woman in history for the way they shoved me off on any available man. Gran once tried to set me up with the grocery clerk's nephew as we went through check-out. I stood two feet away, wishing I could ride the conveyor belt to freedom. Or at least a cringe-free future.

Given my behavior of the morning, I could get into plenty of cringey situations on my own.

"I'm probably not—"

"He's twenty-eight, tall, blond, never married." Granny rattled off his stats like reading the back of a baseball card. "Very fun-loving—Nora said he's always posting things like *'Down to party'* on his Facebook page."

Holy red flag, Batman.

"I don't think that means what you think it means."

Carmen shook her head. "I tried to tell them."

"Maybe you could take him to a party in Magnolia Ridge," Gran said.

I practically choked on my own laughter. I probably looked a bit like Jed after my whole proposition fiasco. These women were a menace. They could at least learn some current slang if they were going to try to get involved with my love life.

"I'm not that much of a partier."

"Start small, then. How about you meet him for dinner and then decide?"

Ugh, here we go.

I went into the kitchen and took my time pouring a glass of water, ignoring the half-packed box of china on the countertop that'd been sitting there for weeks. I tried to channel Jed and his easy *"Don't go on the set-ups"* answer. I could do this. Sure, I'd done it before without results, but I could do it again. Maybe this time, it would stick.

Turning to face them, I tried to look sad but firm. Immovable. Resolute. "It's sweet of y'all to think of me, but I really don't need you to play matchmaker for me. I can get dates on my own."

Granny raised an eyebrow, looking around. "Where are they? I don't see anybody. When was your last date that we didn't do the matchmaking for you?"

Of course, she already knew the answer to that. She knew the answer to everything. Perks of being a grandma, I guess.

"College." I'd laid pretty low since coming back to Magnolia Ridge. I liked to think I'd been focused on work and Gran, but it didn't quite explain away my lack of a real social life. The point remained, I could have gotten dates on my own if I'd wanted them.

I wasn't testing that theory or anything, but I could.

Gran nodded, probably mentally ticking off a point for her. "That's not a great track record, little Cal."

"When was your last date?" Carmen asked her.

Gran shot her a silencing look. "You hush, this isn't about me."

To my knowledge, she hadn't dated since my grandpa died of a stroke the year I was born. Having a social life of her own might have distracted her from mine, but it seemed like she'd decided against trying for anything romantic again. Her friends fulfilled her need for companionship, and if she ever wished for more, she hadn't let on in twenty-five years.

But somehow, I'd become the strange one for being on my own. I couldn't get that to make sense.

"I had a date last weekend." Rita's mouth turned up into a satisfied smile. "Stan is quite the dancer."

"This isn't about *you*, either. You've never had a problem finding a man." Gran turned back to me, all of her joking gone. "We're trying to look out for you. You know I hate the idea of you here all alone in this old house."

I wouldn't be in this old house for long once Granny moved. After I had her happily settled in Florida, I would sell this house and find a place to make all my own. In six months, maybe a year, I'd find someplace free from the bad memories and heartache that greeted me around every corner here.

I'd somewhat obsessively been checking real estate sites since she first seriously considered moving. Searching for the exact right house where I could start fresh, a place to fill with friendship and love and laughter. Preferably with a wrap-around porch and closets bigger than a lunchbox, but I would keep an open mind.

I hadn't admitted any of that to her yet, though. Gran had moved in with us when Mom got sick, but technically, the house had been left to me when she died. Telling Gran I wanted to sell would feel too much like evicting her, and I didn't have it in me. Yes, I wanted her to move to Florida, but I wanted her to do it for herself, not because I had my own selfish agenda.

For now, I kept all of those house dreams to myself.

"I'm a grown woman, Gran. I can handle living here on my own."

Her expression didn't change. "Rita's already given Nora your number to pass along to her grandson."

I drew in a deep breath, hoping the fourth—or was it fifth?—time would be the charm. I'd repeated myself so often, it all ran together. "I don't really want to go on another date with a stranger. It makes me uncomfortable."

"Nora says he's a fine young man."

Not exactly irrefutable proof. Nobody's grandmother described him as a spoiled man-child who expected to go home with a woman on the first date. But since every last set-up had come from a friend of a friend, I couldn't burst their bubble and tell them the truth. I'd found vague but true excuses to feed to Gran and her friends for why those first dates had never led to second ones, but clearly, *"We're just not on the same page"* hadn't gotten the message across.

"I'm not looking for a boyfriend right now."

My college boyfriend had pretty well seen to that, but again, I hadn't looped any of them in on that mess. I wasn't sure knowing the details would make a dent in their eagerness, anyway. They were more of the *There's plenty of fish in the sea* camp than *One bad apple spoils the whole bunch* like me.

"It's because of all your romance books," Carmen said. "Your expectations are too high because you think the men you go out with should be like the men in those books. They're not realistic."

Oh, she did not come for my romance novels. "If that were true, I'd expect the men I go out with to be seven-foot-tall blue aliens with horns on their heads and who worship the ground I walk on."

Rita slid a notepad and pencil across the table. "I need titles."

Granny ignored her. "You know I don't ask for much. I just want to be sure that my grandbaby is taken care of when I'm gone. If I go to Florida, or...wherever."

Oh my word, not this. Nothing like the threat of her supposedly imminent death to twist the knife in my back. Or front—she wasn't subtle with the guilt.

"Gran, you're going to go on kicking for a long time," I soothed. "And you *are* going to Florida. You think your friends will let you stay behind?"

"Not for one minute." Rita's enthusiasm earned another *shut your mouth* look from Gran. She wiped away her smile and tried for a more conciliatory expression. "But of course, we'd understand if you feel you need to stay for Callie's sake."

"Callie will be just fine on her own." I hated how petulant this argument always made me sound, like a little girl stomping her foot mid-tantrum. "I don't know how many times I need to say it."

Gran stood and put her hands on my cheeks. "Callie Louise, you'll understand one day. You'll have someone who can look out for themselves, but that won't stop you from wanting to love on them and take care of them, too. Your heart will be torn between giving someone your love, and giving them their freedom, and then what will you do?"

"I expect I'll give them love *and* freedom." A girl could dream.

Her smile held so much affection, it snapped my will to argue right in two. She'd been my whole world for years, I loved her with everything I had—I didn't want to keep letting her down over this. Even so, a small, selfish part of me needed to get out from under her firm embrace. I hated the battle that raged inside me, between appreciating her for all she'd done and been in my life and wanting to find my way on my own.

"It won't be as easy as you think," she whispered. Letting me go, she walked into the kitchen and pulled out a frying pan. "Eggs for lunch today, ladies?"

Carmen and Rita joined us in the kitchen, ready to help out. Rita sidled up next to me, waving her phone in my face. The photo on the screen showed a blond young man on a boat somewhere, smiling into the camera. He looked like the kind of guy who'd be named Preston or Montgomery and used the word *summer* as a verb. I still couldn't figure out where they found all these guys. Maybe they had a secret app for pairing off grandchildren.

"Is this Stan?" I crossed my fingers for a miracle.

"Oh, I'm not sharing *him*." She bumped her hip against mine. "This is Greg, Nora's grandson."

"Gregory Alcott the third," Gran clarified.

"Doesn't really sound like he's from Magnolia Ridge." Not a lot of *the thirds* around here who went by anything other than Bubba.

"He was raised in Southlake, he's just in town for work," Rita said. "Pretty cute, right?"

"Pretty cute." He was no Jed Evans, but so few men were. Hard to live up to a six-foot-something former soldier who looked like he'd been chiseled out of granite and had a laugh that could bring out the sun on your cloudiest day. But who was keeping track?

"It would really make me happy to see you out with a nice man like that."

Gran didn't have to look at me to lay on her guilt nice and thick. She did it all with her tone of voice, the mix of pleading and commanding she'd perfected and patented. Maybe all grandmas had this skill, but I'd only ever known the one.

Well. Along with her three closest friends, two of whom watched me with giant puppy dog eyes, waiting for me to cave. Rita waggled the phone again, a hopeful little smile on her face.

I loved them. I wanted to make them happy, and they only wanted to make me happy. What else could I do?

My shoulders slumped, but I managed a smile. "I'll meet Greg."

Cheers erupted as though I'd announced our engagement. Gran smiled to herself as she got out bread for their lunch. More often than not, their lunches looked an awful lot like breakfast.

"You want something, too, Callie?"

"No, thanks." Between my weird coffee date with Jed and this guilt-fueled conversation, I didn't have much of an appetite. "I'm going to stitch for a while."

Stabbing something a thousand times sounded like a great idea.

I escaped to my part of the house and shut myself up in my bedroom. I flipped on the ceiling fan to add a little circulation and grabbed the nearly-finished embroidery off my nightstand. Sinking onto the mattress, I got ready to clear my head. Focusing on thread and stitches had become a kind of meditation, and boy, did I need some Zen now.

Greg. Ugh. I wouldn't judge the guy on just his name and a single photo, but I didn't have high hopes. Who could say, though? Maybe this time, my granny's tinkering with my love life would lead to a perfect match.

Seemed more likely I'd wind up with one of those blue aliens.

jed

WAS it wrong to shout *What took you so long?* at an engagement party? Probably wrong, yeah.

My sister June and her now-fiancé Ty Hardy had invited a bunch of us to his house to celebrate his recent proposal. I considered it a pretty modest collection of family and friends, but for a guy like Ty, more than a handful of people seemed like a big concession. He wasn't a recluse, but he kept his social circle small.

Say what you would about the guy, I liked him—always had. He kept his word, didn't make drama, and treated my sister right. June had lit up like a firefly since they'd reconnected last year, and I loved seeing her so happy. Gave her a hard time about it now and then, but I loved it. Still, even her happiness paled next to our pop's at the moment.

"You ever seen two people so in love?" He'd joined me where I stood in Ty's living room, his eyes on the couple at the center of the festivities.

Their grins could have powered the whole county for how they shone. They'd been fielding congratulations snugged up close together, already a package deal. June laughed at something our uncle Joel said, resting her hand on Ty's chest as she gazed up at him like she was staring at a dream come true. He pulled her even closer, if any space had been left between them, giving her googly-eyes right back.

"Sickening," I said with a grin.

Pop's unimpressed look told me my joke hadn't landed.

"Come on, you know nobody's more ready to see them walk down the aisle than I am. Frankly, I can't believe Ty held out this long."

He'd been so lost over June, I'd expected him to drop down on one knee months ago. The man loved her so much, it almost pained me to watch them interact. Every little moment between them felt like something intimate I really shouldn't have seen.

Like the way Ty's hand currently rested just south of my sister's hip. Didn't need to see that.

I turned back to Pop. "To answer your question, I haven't seen two people so in love since a couple of months ago in the courthouse downtown."

His stern look softened, his eyes automatically finding his new wife Marilyn in the group of well-wishers. A soft smile flashed on his face, and two pale spots of color shone on his cheeks. Seeing my pop blush would have made me laugh if it weren't so damn earnest. As infatuated with his wife as any twenty-something newlywed, his affections were spelled out in every look and word. After the heartbreak of losing my mom three years ago, he deserved this kind of happiness again.

That turned my thoughts to Callie, and my eyes did the same on reflex. She stood in the dining room with Eliza and Harper in a little yellow sundress as bright as a ray of sunshine. I was glad she'd been invited to join in the celebrations, but couldn't help noticing she hadn't so much as looked my way tonight.

Maybe I'd been too blunt when I shot down her suggestion the other day. I hadn't meant to make her uncomfortable around me, I just couldn't see my way to agreeing to her plans. Whatever she hoped it might accomplish, fake dating would surely stir up more problems than it solved. Had she had that talk with her grandma yet, or did she have more blind dates on the horizon? Or had she asked someone else to step in and pretend to date her?

That option sat in my gut like I'd swallowed a peach pit.

Slipping past my aunt and uncle, Marilyn joined us. A couple of years younger than Pop, she had a warmth about her that proved hard to resist. "These two aren't wasting any time, are they?"

For all Ty's dragging his feet to ask my sister to marry him, once she'd said yes, they'd set a date just two months away.

"When it's right, you don't wait around."

Pop watched me with a little too much hope in his eyes. Wasn't sure who he thought was waiting on me. I hadn't been on a date in months and sure wasn't looking to rush to the altar with anyone.

"I'm surprised they don't follow your example and just run down to the courthouse." Wade and I had almost put money on it. I'd thought for sure June and Ty would turn up at family dinner one night with wedding rings already on. Good thing I wasn't out five bucks.

"Oh, they want a little ceremony out on Ty's property. It's where they fell in love, you know." Marilyn sighed as if her thoughts had turned into giant cartoon hearts. "It'll be the most romantic thing."

"It's good to see them settling down, starting a life together. Making a family of their own."

Again, Pop stared at me with more intensity than I liked. I couldn't say exactly what he was expecting, but I figured I'd be disappointing him for the foreseeable future. Settling down wasn't on my horizon. I had a hard enough time seeing myself as the head of Evans Orchards for the rest of my life, couldn't very well add romantic commitments into the mix, too.

One impossible thing at a time.

"They'll probably be next on the baby train."

Now that brought a sparkle to his eyes. "I'll take as many more grandchildren as I can get."

Okay, that one was on me. Every conversation with him lately had become a minefield of tricky subjects, mostly to do with either marriage or babies, and I'd gone and thrown myself across a tripwire.

"You could spend a lot more time with the grandkids you've got if you cut back your work in the orchards." Passing the baton to me had been his idea, but I couldn't turn around without finding him inspecting trees or supervising in the store. I had mixed feelings about taking on the family business, but I'd rest easier when I knew *he* was resting.

"It's a big job for you, I can't just turn it all over in one go."

He hadn't turned much over to me at all. I didn't like the nagging feeling he didn't trust me to handle it.

"Besides, it's good to have a partner." He lifted his eyebrows as though his meaning could possibly be lost on me.

Thankfully, June and Ty joined us and put an end to Pop's one-sided staring contest.

Reaching across June, I shook Ty's hand. "You sure you know what you're getting into? She's a real handful."

He chuckled low. "Wouldn't want it any other way."

Ignoring my sister's mock-indignant glare, I threw one arm around her shoulders in a quick hug. "Happy for you, Junebug."

"If you don't watch yourself, I'll put you to work as a flower boy," she said.

I straightened invisible lapels. "I prefer to be called a flower man."

She grinned up at me. "You'd look so cute with a flower crown and a basket of petals."

"My masculinity isn't threatened by that."

"Almost makes me wish we weren't keeping things simple." She slipped back to Ty's side like a magnet, her arm locking into place around his waist. "I actually do want to put you to work, though. We're going to have the reception in Ty's big vehicle barn, but we'll need to move some things out to make space."

"No problem. How much are we talking?"

"Mostly tools we'll relocate to the garage, a few larger things I'll need a hand with," Ty said. "It's the cleanup that will take longer. I never planned to host events in my barn."

He met June's eyes, but he sure didn't seem like he regretted his choices. Talk about a look I didn't need to see. They oozed with so much love for each other, pretty sure they'd forgotten the rest of us in the room.

"It's going to be perfect," she told him. "We just need a little help to get it there."

"If you need more volunteers, I have someone I could ask," Marilyn piped up. "A friend of one of my daughters. She's a real sweetheart, I think she'd be just perfect for..."

Her eyes cut to me for a second, just long enough for a tiny spike of dread to stab through my chest.

"A project like that," she finished.

That dread twisted, spiraling deep and locking in tight. Had we finally come to this? I'd thought she was on my side when it came to Pop's pushing, but turns out she'd just been waiting for the right moment to strike. Appreciated the thought, but—no, I didn't really appreciate it. Couldn't think of anything I needed less than optimistic introductions to family friends.

"That's awful generous of you, Marilyn, but it sounds like

Ty and I have this handled. We'll call Wade or Booker if we need to."

"Now Jed, there's no harm in—"

A baby's angry cry interrupted Pop's wheedling.

I tossed a thumb over my shoulder. "Maisie's calling me. Let me know when you sort out the date for the work party." I pointed at June. "And remember I called dibs on the flower man job. Don't go giving that to the boys."

June and Ty laughed, but Pop and Marilyn's twin frowns proved their disappointment. They could go right on being disappointed. I saw no good reason to turn my sister's wedding prep into an opportunity to be forced into a blind date. I hadn't even planned on looking for a real plus-one, sure wasn't about to let them choose a stranger to do the job.

Callie's request for a fake relationship was starting to sound almost sane.

I spun around, heading away from the meddling twosome, but collided with the woman herself on her way someplace fast. She hopped backward, nearly falling against my uncle Joel before I took her shoulders to steady her.

"Sorry!" She looked up, her eyes tangling with mine, and her cheeks went pink.

"I'm the one who needs to watch where I'm going." It took my brain a second too long to realize I still held her shoulders, her bare skin soft and warm beneath my fingertips, and I dropped my hands. "Are you cutting out already?"

"Ha, you're not getting rid of me that easily." She forced a laugh and tucked a stray lock of hair behind her ear. "I mean, don't worry, you're rid of me. I'm not going to stalk you or something."

I lifted an eyebrow at that random piece of reassurance.

"Not that I could stalk you," she went on, the color in her cheeks darkening to a delightful red. "You probably learned a whole bunch of evasive maneuvers in the Army. I bet you're totally un-stalkable."

She lightly punched me on the shoulder as if congratulating an old pal, then looked at her hand in horror and moved it behind her back. "I shouldn't joke about stalking you, that's weird. I'm not a stalker, despite strange requests in coffee shops. Which would have been more like pre-arranged stalking which isn't even a thing and—you know what? I'm going to stop speaking now."

I smiled over how she kept digging away at that hole she'd made. She sometimes let conversations get away from her, but this one took it to a whole new level. Kind of liked it.

I leaned a touch closer to her. "Just to confirm, it's impossible to stalk me. My stealth military skills would never allow it."

Her mouth twisted into a smile. "Called it."

We stood there a beat like neither of us had anything better to do than smile away at each other, but she snapped out of it first. "I was going to get something from my car."

"Right. Well—" I stepped aside, clearing her way to the door. "I'd better let you do it."

She nodded and slipped past me to make her way outside. For a minute, I considered going with her since it was already full dark out and Ty's place was in the middle of nowhere. But before I could act on the impulse, she'd snuck back through the door with a thin box in her hands. Deftly dodging me this time, she rejoined my cousins on the other side of the room.

I didn't love all the avoidance tonight.

Maisie wailed again, reminding me I'd been in the middle of something that had nothing to do with yellow sundresses or awkward smiles.

Wandering over to where Wade struggled with his youngest, I had to laugh at the scene. The pudgy baby had a fistful of his hair like she wanted to rip it from his scalp, her slobbery mouth pressed up against his cheek. Couldn't tell if she was kissing him or biting him. Probably a bit of both. Meanwhile, my brother's worn-out expression said he'd survived similar situations a few times already today.

"Looks like you're being attacked by a slobber monster."

At the sound of my voice, Maisie swung her head to me, releasing her death-grip on Wade's hair. Forgetting about the angry tears in her eyes, she grinned, showing off all six teeth. She kicked Wade's stomach in a happy little dance, her butt wiggling where she sat on his forearm.

"Teething's giving her a real attitude." Despite his poor assessment, he smiled at his baby, kissed her chubby cheek, and ran a hand over her hair. If you could call it that.

The poor thing had the most ridiculous hair I'd ever seen. A downy fuzz covered most of her head, with a puff of longer dark hair on the very top, like a terrible baby toupee. Sometimes, they put it in a tiny ponytail standing straight up in the center of her head, but tonight, it was just a cloud of strands sticking out willy-nilly. Pop called it her halo, but she didn't often live up to the rest of that image.

"I like her fiery spirit." I held my hands out, and she lunged into them, the little acrobat. Wade passed her over, and I cuddled her close, swaying back and forth automatically. "What'd you do to tick her off this time?"

"I wouldn't let her eat the bouquet of flowers on the table."

"Worst dad ever." I bobbed her around, her infectious giggles making my day. She patted my face, pinching at my cheeks. Babbling up at me in pure adorable baby mode, nobody would guess this cutie had a secret aggressive streak. Any minute now, she'd hook a finger into my mouth or scrape a nail across my eye. I had to enjoy her sweetness while it lasted. "Who loves her Uncle Jed?"

She gurgled back, her conversation gibberish to everyone but her. Her big blue eyes killed me a little for all the trust and joy they held.

"If her first word is 'Jed,' so help me."

Wade's implied threats hadn't stopped me from coaching her to say my name when nobody was looking.

"I can't help it if she has good taste." Scanning the people moving around in Ty's house, I came up three short. "Where are Annie and the boys?"

"She took Beau upstairs for a potty break. Dylan went along to supervise."

"Didn't realize that was a two-man operation."

"Beau needs a lot of coaxing in that department." Wade gave me a look like he'd seen some things.

While I would eat up Maisie's snuggles and glory every time the boys rallied around me like my own little fan club, encouraging them in the bathroom didn't fall under Fun Uncle duties.

"I don't know how you do it, man."

"One day, it'll be you up there singing potty songs to your kid, and when that day comes, I will laugh my ever-loving head off."

"You really know how to sell parenthood." Didn't need to know about the existence of potty songs, to be honest.

"There's a trade-off." He nodded at the little munchkin in my arms.

"Yeah, yeah." I tickled her sides until she squealed with laughter. After a minute of squirming and kicking, she laid her head on my shoulder in a rare moment of calm. Exhaling like an old man after a hard day at work, she rubbed her face against me as if she might fall asleep in my arms. Probably just wiping snot on my shirt, but the moment tugged at my heart anyway.

"*That's* how you sell parenthood."

"This part's not so—no—son of a—" Maisie dug her teeth

into my shoulder, breaking through our sweet moment of bonding, and quite possibly my flesh. Trying to pull her away only made her bite down harder, a little crocodile refusing to release her prey.

Wade stepped in and got her to let go. He took her from my arms, giving her a scolding about biting people, but her grin proved she wasn't too torn up about it. If anything, she'd probably gotten a taste for it, like a bear or a piranha. The little stinker.

"Sorry about that."

"Good Lord, kids bite hard." I rubbed my shoulder where I probably had a perfect impression of Maisie's dental progress in a circle of welts. "I thought we were friends, Maze."

She gurgled away at me, proud as anything.

"What was all that about liking her fiery spirit?" Wade asked.

"When it comes to injuring *you*, yes. When it comes to me, I'd appreciate a little less tooth-oriented fire."

He adjusted Maisie so she faced out, wisely keeping her chompers away from him.

"Pop's so proud, he looks like a tick ready to burst." He nodded back the way I'd just come. "I'd be careful, if I were you. Only a matter of time before he starts pressuring you to settle down in earnest."

"I assure you, the pressure he's applying now is real enough. I just dodged Marilyn's plans for a set-up, and he didn't look too happy about it." Temporarily dodged, anyway. Seemed unlikely either of them would let that subject drop without a fight. A gently disapproving fight, but I'd be in for one all the same.

"What do you expect of him? There's a lot of love going around."

Wade gestured around the rooms packed with couples. Our

sister and cousins had all fallen in love in the last year or so, every one well on their way toward marriage. Even Harper, who'd told me in no uncertain terms she wanted nothing to do with her high school boyfriend again, had an engagement ring on her finger from him.

"Hope it's nothing catching."

Wade's chuckle didn't carry all that much sympathy. "You'll regret your words one day."

Callie's laughter drew my attention across the room. Smiling over some story from Eliza, she was arresting in a way I couldn't quite define. Beautiful, certainly. Trouble, one hundred percent. I watched her for a minute, that little twist of regret pinching at me all over again.

"Not anytime soon."

callie

THIS GATHERING at Ty's was like the *Brady Bunch* meets *Modern Family* plus a side of *Full House*.

I. Loved. It.

After going through most of my life with just my mom and grandma around, slipping into the flow of Harper's big family get-togethers came surprisingly easily. Since her first invitation over Christmas, I'd spent quite a few evenings surrounded by her sisters, cousins, and extended family, the lone Matheson fish in the big Webb-Evans pond. But nobody ever made me feel like I didn't belong or like I'd crashed their party.

I'd grown up watching too many big sitcom families that made me long for just a little of that kind of raucous togetherness. Hard not to envy it, with only two other names on my family tree. Probably someone out there preferred the solitude and would have been grateful for a similar loneliness, but that'd never been me. I'd always wanted to know what life would have been like with older siblings, and now, I caught a glimpse of it through my friendships with Harper and Eliza, Wade and Jed.

Well, no. Not Jed. I definitely did *not* see him as a brother, but I loved watching how he big-brothered June to pieces. He'd taken on a similar, though noticeably less intentionally-irritating role with Harper and her sisters. I'd heard stories of him driving across town to change flat tires and helping set up back yard sheds. He'd even once subtly run Sam off when Harper wasn't sure yet she wanted to get back together with him. In short, he stepped up to help whenever and however they needed him.

I guess that's why I'd hoped he would step up to help me out, but in hindsight, my ask had been nuts. Like, full-on, squirrelly nuts. I really wish I'd thought about it longer before just going for broke and embarrassing the heck out of myself. Maybe one day, I would stop feeling like a doofus whenever I was around him.

Today was not that day.

I'd tried my best to avoid him tonight, but Jed Evans was impossible to ignore. No matter how I'd told myself not to look at him, my eyes had wills of their own, and I'd looked anyway. Maybe even admired the man for a second or two when I was certain he'd have no clue. And then, I'd gone and run smack into him, because of course I had.

But now that we'd gotten our first post-coffee date conversation out of the way—props to me for making it extra weird by mentioning the word *stalker* eighty-seven times—I figured we could go on pretty much as usual. Casual and friendly. Normal. Not stuck in bizarro world because I couldn't stop spewing at the mouth.

"Check out the pictures Sam sent today." Harper turned her phone my way, revealing a pristine waterfall. "Gorman Falls. They're on a big hike through Colorado Bend State Park. They'll be back tomorrow morning, but he's bummed to miss out on the party tonight."

Her boyfriend worked for an adventure tour outfit and was always off in some gorgeous, out-of-the-way locale. Actually, he'd become her fiancé last month. Clearly, they'd made being apart half the time work.

"Just seeing pictures of everything he does exhausts me." Hiking, climbing, rafting—his trips covered a lot of extreme sport highlights. I'd joined the group on a big hike a couple of months back, and I'd proven myself just barely up to the task. I couldn't imagine making a career out of it.

"No kidding. But he loves it, so I can't complain."

"Plus, there's always the thrill of being reunited, right?" Eliza bobbed her eyebrows at her sister in a naughty way.

Harper glared, but her cheeks flamed bright red. "That part's not so bad."

"I wouldn't be able to stand it. When Dean went on that camping trip with his brothers in the spring, I was practically crawling out of my skin by the time he got home."

He nudged her with his shoulder. "Maybe I should schedule another trip so you have a chance to miss me some more."

"Don't you dare." She poked him in the ribs, but he took her hand in his, twining their fingers together.

They were so cute. Him in his neat dress shirt and jeans, her with her blue-highlighted hair. Poster children for an opposites attract love story.

"Oh, but the part I forgot," Harper said. "Sam wants to go to Fool Hearted Memory tomorrow night after he gets back. It's six months since we went there the first time."

"You guys are celebrating half-anniversaries?" Eliza scrunched up her nose. "Sad."

"We celebrated our half-anniversary," Dean said.

She pressed a finger to his mouth as though she could cram that admission back in. "Shh."

"It's just for fun," Harper said. "So if anyone else wants to do a little dancing, you're welcome to join us. Callie, are you in? Since you're the line dancing champion around here."

"Line dancing champion?"

The voice behind me made heat coil up my back in a slow wave like all my nerve endings had come out to say hello to Jed. He moved forward, claiming his spot at my side in our little group, his eyes full of questions. Made sense, considering how little we knew each other.

"I've danced a few times." Simple and true.

"She's being ridiculously modest," Harper put in. "She's really good, knows the moves to all the songs, and she helps anybody on the dance floor who doesn't know what they're doing. She guided me like a baby my first time out."

Jed's gaze became a laser beam, his curious look making my skin tingly and warm.

"How have I never heard about your line dancing prowess?"

"We go line dancing at the honky-tonk," I said. "I didn't think you'd like to join us there. You seem like a very straight-arrow type."

He stared at me for half a second, processing his own words I'd parroted back to him. Then he threw his head back and laughed like he'd never heard anything better. Truly, *I'd* never heard anything better. His laugh was a firework bursting to life —I wanted to *ooh* and *aah* and break into applause, begging for an encore.

"Touché, darlin'."

A shiver cascaded up my spine at that short word. I knew he wasn't really calling me darling—lots of people tossed that word around—but the ripples trailed across my skin anyway.

"Well, we're in," Eliza said, halting the shivers in their progress. "Anything to dance with my man."

Dean's low-key smile was one part affection, two parts smug.

"Jed, how about you?" Harper asked. "Might be fun."

He turned to me. "I might be up for it if the line dancing champion is going."

"Oh." All the little whirls of excitement rushing through me crashed together in a full-stop. "I can't tomorrow night. I have a…"

I didn't really want to elaborate. I'd agreed to meet Greg for dinner, but nobody here needed to know a stitch of that, least of all Jed. Although, judging by the way his smile slowly faded, he probably already guessed.

"You have a what?" Eliza repeated. "A date?"

Man, she looked so eager, like I was about to tell her I had Taylor Swift tickets. I hated to disappoint her, but even if Jed weren't standing six inches away from me, I wouldn't ever crow about my plans with Greg. Also, I'd never call meeting any of the guys my gran and her friends arranged *dates. Awkward encounters with strangers I hoped never to see again* didn't have the same ring to it, though, so I guess I'd work with what I had.

I shook my head, not really in the mood to prove my lying chops tonight. "I have plans with my gran tomorrow night, I'm sorry."

A passable story, since they knew already just how deeply ingrained my granny was in my life. I kind of wished I'd come up with a better lie, since hanging out with women in their seventies didn't make me come off much stronger than admitting I was being set up on dates by women in their seventies.

"We'll miss you," Harper said. "Boot-scooting just isn't the same without you."

I forced a laugh, but Jed's laser beam eyes on me made it tough to act natural. I hated that he had any clue about what I'd really be doing tomorrow night. I'd much rather he thought I'd be spending the evening doing old lady things with my gran instead of enduring a pity date that was ninety-nine percent sure to end in disappointment on both sides.

Eliza told a story about the last time we went line dancing, but I couldn't focus on it. Grinning away at nothing, all my attention stayed stuck on the man at my side, even if I refused to actually look at him. Jed's silence was odd enough in itself—like me, he had no problem speaking up in a group—but *this* silence had a weight to it I couldn't escape, full of unasked questions and a heavy layer of judgment. Well, he could go on and judge me for my choices all he liked. A few awkward nights were nothing if it meant keeping my granny happy and on her way to Florida.

Then *I* could be happy.

Eden and Booker joined us, cutting off the tail-end of Eliza's story about a guy who'd busted out break dancing moves in the middle of the honky-tonk.

"We've got to get going," Booker said. "It's about time to get this little one to bed."

He had their two-month-old daughter tucked up against his chest, her crown of black curls beneath his chin, her pale brown fist clutched tight around his darker finger he seemed unwilling to free. I had to fight the urge to coo over the adorable scene. In my defense, seeing this big man cuddle his tiny daughter would make any woman stop and sigh for a minute. Already asleep, she worked her mouth, smacking her little lips in her dreams.

"I have something for you before you go." I rushed across the dining room to grab the box from beneath my purse where I'd left it. Returning to the group, I passed it over to Eden.

"What's this for?" She ran her fingers over the plain brown box and started undoing the orange bow.

"It's just something I made. You don't have to open it now." I didn't want to make a big deal over it—I just couldn't think of a better time to give it to them. Eden hadn't joined a girls' night since the arrival of their newborn, but popping it in the mail had felt too impersonal.

"Oh my gosh, open it now." Eliza edged behind Eden to get a better view over her shoulder. "I can't wait to see this."

"What am I missing out on?" Eden asked, lifting the lid.

"It's just a thing I made." I really should have found a better time to give it to them. Right as they were leaving a party wasn't ideal, and the crowd made it even worse.

Eden moved aside the wrapping tissue and gasped. Probably a good sign?

"You made this?"

"What is it?" Booker leaned in closer to see.

"It's a freaking masterpiece, is what it is," Eliza said.

Eden held up the embroidery, turning it around to show the others. An orange hoop framed a multi-colored honeycomb I'd stitched with *Bee* spelled out in negative space, and a fat, three-dimensional bumblebee I'd added at the top. Modern and colorful, but with a vintage nursery vibe. Or so I thought.

They'd named their daughter Brielle Beverly, but only ever called her Bee. The bright colors matched the sorts of outfits they dressed her in, and I'd thought the bee theme a natural fit. But the way everyone stared at me right now, maybe I'd really missed the mark.

I did that sometimes with gifts, especially things I'd made. What I thought of as fun and thoughtful could come across as overstepping and strange. Giving something I'd worked so hard on only to have it viewed as a sign of weirdness instead of affection? The worst. I'd cut back for a long time, but I hadn't had a friend group like this to give presents to since college. I'd thought their baby's birth warranted a present, but maybe I'd thought wrong.

An uncomfortable itch wormed through my stomach, my skin suddenly clammy as if my clothes were too tight. I really liked these women, and now I'd gone overboard and they probably thought I was doing too much and maybe—

"Callie, this is gorgeous!"

Eden stepped forward to wrap me in a hug. The rush of relief made my legs wobbly, but I managed to hug her back.

"How did you do this?" She turned the embroidery to Harper. "Look at how beautiful!"

"I told you," Eliza said. "You should really sell these, if not at the farmers' market then online or *somewhere*. They're so well done, you would rake it in."

Eden moved back to Booker's side, showing off the piece. He smiled and nodded while the others all complimented it at the same time. Meanwhile, Jed went on staring at me like he wasn't sure what he was seeing.

"The timing's all wrong, because I'm giving you a gift at June's engagement party, and I didn't want to be rude to her, but I had it ready and wasn't sure when I'd get another chance, so—" I took a breath, mentally checking the urge to keep talking. "I just like to make things."

"Well, it's perfect," Eden said. "I'm going to put it right over her crib. Thank you."

They finished saying their goodbyes a few minutes later and headed out. I figured I'd take the opportunity to leave, too—I never knew when to leave a party. Too early made me look eager to be rid of them, and too late, everyone would be eager to be rid of *me*. I didn't want to be in that particular boat.

I said my own goodbyes to Eliza and Harper and found June to let her know again how happy I was for her. Mentally saying goodbye to the rest of their family and friends, I slipped outside, letting the fresh scent of Ty's farm fill my lungs. I crunched across the gravel to my car, the only other sound out here the occasional neigh from horses in the pastures.

The little hiccups of awkwardness with Jed aside, it'd been a great night with my friends. I needed evenings like this to remind me life existed between the ages of five and seventy-five. I loved my kindergarten students, and I adored my gran and her friends. But so much of my day to day centered on one of those two extremes, I could forget a world of middle ground thrived out there.

I started the car's engine and glanced around in a totally unnecessary safety check. Something caught my eye, and I startled at the sight of a man standing on the porch, leaning both hands against the railing. For half a second, I thought maybe I'd forgotten something inside and Jed had brought it out for me, but no—purse, keys, me. All here.

He lifted one hand in a casual goodbye. He probably made the same gesture to a hundred people a day, but my chest warmed up like he'd invented it just for me. I waved back and reversed away from the house, heading home across Magnolia Ridge.

Smiling to myself, I had fresh hope Jed and I could be friends.

And maybe one day, he'd forget I ever asked him to pretend to date me.

jed

I RELISHED the sound of the billiard balls clacking together one by one as I nailed a combo shot to finish out the game. Relished Wade's groans over losing twice in a row even more.

"Tell me you did something besides play pool when you were overseas," he said, replacing his cue on the wall rack.

The Broken Hammer had a two-game limit per group on the weekends, or I would have gone on mopping the floor with him all night. He'd never been that great at pool. Darts were pretty much the same, but I only beat him at one game per outing. I tried to have a little mercy on the guy.

"I had one or two responsibilities." I snapped my cue into place and gestured to the couple waiting to play that the table was theirs.

Wade and I grabbed our drinks and looked for seats on the other side of the bar. A bit of a dive, The Broken Hammer had become our go-to bar in the same way most places in Magnolia Ridge became a favorite—we didn't have a lot of other options. We stopped in every couple of weeks to decompress over a drink or two.

Crossing the bar, I caught him checking his phone. Sometime soon, Annie would call to let him know his turn had come to take over Maisie duties, so he'd stuck with soda for the evening. I'd been nursing a beer more for the sake of something to do than any true desire to drink. I'd burned a lot of that out of me in the Army, and now with harvest, I couldn't afford the hangover. We found a free table and sat down with the half-full beer and a soft drink.

Just two brothers, ready to party.

"How's Pop handling the transfer of power?" Wade asked.

What a choice of casual convo. "Don't do that. Don't talk about work when I'm trying to enjoy myself."

"That bad?"

"Imagine I'm Luke Skywalker and Pop's Yoda sitting on my back, telling me what I should be doing."

"At least he isn't Darth Vader. Or worse, Anakin."

I groaned. "Let's not completely ruin my night by mentioning the prequels."

"Good point." Wade took a pull off his glass, making a sour face as though he'd forgotten it wasn't his usual Guinness. "Maybe he's not ready to give it all up yet."

"I never asked him to give it up. This plan to step down and hand it over—that was all him. Now, it's like I'm trying to steal his favorite toy."

He'd pulled such a one-eighty, I couldn't figure him out. After almost a year of retirement talk and preparing to hand over the reins, he'd just stopped. He dealt with customers, went over paperwork, and made plans for the orchards almost like I wasn't even there. Instead of taking on more responsibility, I'd started to feel like he didn't need me. Or didn't trust me.

Couldn't rightly blame him there. Outside of my military career, I hadn't been the best at commitment, and taking on the family farm would mean a whole lifetime of it. The practical, day-to-day operations didn't faze me, but the long-term planning? Making decisions that would affect not just this year's harvest, but ten or twenty years down the line? I didn't even know where to start.

In that light, Pop wasn't so off-base to hang around, after all.

Still, the man had practically begged me to take on the orchards and then refused to see it through. I couldn't help but have a hang-up over that kind of hesitation.

"Maybe it's an extended Yoda training," Wade offered.

"Not when he's also making decisions without my input."

A year ago, I wouldn't have even noticed. I didn't have some deep-seated need to be in charge of the farm, or an all-consuming lust for power. But when he spent months telling me he intended to step down and then made plans for new trees without a word to me, it got hard to ignore.

"So more like when Anakin marries Padmé without telling Obi-Wan."

I pointed a finger at him. "That's your last warning about that."

He chuckled. "Always good for a laugh."

Jokes aside, I couldn't figure out what Pop wanted from me. He'd encouraged me to step up, but he'd stayed in control. He wanted me to commit to running the business, but he seemed unwilling to let a single responsibility go. The one thing he couldn't have made plainer was how badly he wanted me to find a woman and settle in for the long-haul. Of all his expectations, that one proved the least realistic.

I was not a long-haul guy.

"He's only sixty-six," Wade pointed out. "That's early to retire these days."

"Maybe." The work he'd kept doing behind my back still felt like proof he didn't think I could cut it. Like maybe he'd had second thoughts and now regretted the offer in the first place. Didn't love that possibility, but I'd put off directly asking. His disappointment went down easier when I didn't actually face it.

"Hey, what's this?" Wade looked past me, deeper into the bar. "A little chick without her mother hens?"

I twisted in my seat, and my gut rolled right over, unearthing something greasy. Callie trailed a guy to the bar and hopped up on a seat next to him. She wore jeans and a loose top, those blue Converse tapping time where she propped them on the barstool's footrest. The guy was dressed nice enough, but I disliked him immediately. I knew a dirtbag when I saw one, and his body language screamed *"I'm an arrogant prick."* He leaned in close to tell her something, setting a hand on her shoulder.

I spun back around and downed the last of my beer, ignoring the churning in my gut that made me want to leap out of my seat and smack his hand away from her. So this was why she hadn't gone line dancing with Harper and the others tonight. She had a date. I'd suspected as much when she went mum about her plans, but—hey, good for her. All the best to her.

"Kind of surprised to see her without one of the girls glued to her hip." Wade watched the scene at the bar with detached interest, like listening to a bit of gossip about someone he didn't know.

Neither of us had spent all that much time with Callie. Some group interactions, a conversation here or there. But after our meeting in the coffee shop, something had shifted for me. Maybe I understood her a bit better than I had before. Maybe I sympathized a little more.

Or maybe, the voice I'd been shutting down all week said, *you like her a little more.*

"I get the feeling she doesn't have a lot of other friends." Hadn't figured out why. She always had a smile and something to say to everybody—seemed like she'd be a natural in the friend-making department. And yet, from all I'd seen, Harper and the others made up her entire friend group. Of people her age, anyway. "She mostly hangs out with her grandma."

Couldn't have a conversation for three minutes without her grandma coming up. That, or her kindergarten students. Spending all her time with either five-year-olds or seventy-five-year-olds only drove home the image of her wide-eyed innocence.

"Correct me if I'm wrong, but that is not her grandma."

I looked over my shoulder again. Maybe the smile she'd plastered on looked real to Wade, but she kept shaking her head, waving her date off every time he moved in too close. His need to get into her space made my back stiffen. The bartender came up, and from the way the two went back and forth talking over each other, easy bet the guy had tried to order her drink for her. What a tool. Callie—and the bartender, bless him—weren't having it.

The bartender served their drinks, liquor for the guy and almost assuredly a soft drink for her. Might have been a Seven and Seven, but I stood by my straight-arrow assessment. I doubted she'd go for liquor on a first date.

Unless—was this their first date? No way of knowing. Maybe it wasn't a blind date, but another attempt at securing a boyfriend. Real or fake? The thought they'd been out before rattled through me like shaking a box of rocks.

A second later, Callie pulled money out of her purse and paid for her drink, shutting down whatever the guy was saying.

I spun back around. "Date's not going so hot."

I wasn't usually the kind of guy to glory in someone else's

failure, but a spot of pleasure bloomed to life in my chest anyway.

"Looks like a tool."

I raised my empty beer glass. "I was just thinking the same thing."

Wade clinked my glass with his but leveled me with an uncharacteristically somber look. "I'll try to help out some around the orchards on my days off through harvest."

He made the same offer every summer, and turned up to lend a hand when he could. I suspected he wanted to make up for some lingering guilt for not sticking around to go into the family business. How many first-born farm kids chose a different profession from the one they'd been molded to take on? But I'd never outright asked if it bothered him. A question like that would hold too much judgment, and I didn't blame him for his choices.

"I appreciate it, but you don't have to do that." His schedule as a firefighter kept him busy enough. He'd find time to show up no matter what, but I wouldn't make him put anything on a calendar. "Don't need to take even more time away from your family, who, I assume, would like to see you now and then, too. Though I can't think why."

"You know you've got it covered over there. Whatever Pop's hangup is about stepping down, he'll sort it out."

I nodded, more in hope than actual agreement. For all I knew, Pop might hold onto the business for the next twenty years.

In the end, maybe that'd be best. I didn't know how to run a company with an eye for future plans. In the Army, I'd followed orders and done what I was told. Sure, I'd had guys I'd been in charge of, missions I'd handled, but ultimately, everything important had come from higher up. Could I really be the guy calling all the shots?

The bigger question: did I want to be him?

Wade's phone buzzed on the table. He checked it, and the weirdest expression crossed his face, like he was trying not to look thrilled. Like nothing could have made him happier than the text to come home. I didn't take it personally, because I didn't think his reaction had anything to do with who he was leaving, but who he was going home *to*.

A sudden spark of envy of all Wade had flashed to life. Someone to go home to. Someone to check up on. Little ones to tuck in, a wife to hold close at night. Things I'd never thought too hard about before suddenly glowing vivid in my mind, burning into a bright clear *want*.

But the memory of heartache and loss, of raw, unending grief, swallowed up that want. I'd realized long ago I wasn't meant for that life. Not when I knew what waited on the other side of it.

"That's me," he said, standing up. "Maisie's awake, so it's time for Daddy Duty."

Shaking off my bitter thoughts before they could take hold, I stood, too.

"You heading out?" he asked.

I turned my head and caught the jerk next to Callie lean into her personal space so he could talk straight into her ear. I would have counted it as meaningless flirting, but from her stiff posture, she didn't welcome the lean. If I had to guess, she was looking for a way to get rid of the guy.

It just so happened I had a lot of experience with that.

"I think I'll stick around a while."

Wade looked from me to where Callie sat at the bar and back again. Smiling in his Big Brother Knows Best way, he slapped me on the shoulder. "I hope you know what you're doing."

So did I.

callie

I WASN'T sure how many times I could fake a smile while simultaneously wanting to punch a guy, but tonight had to be a record. I'd dropped in on enough MMA classes with Harper to know how to do a little damage if it came down to it. The only real question, should I go for Greg's jaw or his stomach?

I should have just called it a night after dinner and gone home, but I'd let him coax me into walking the two blocks to The Broken Hammer, and now, I guess he'd figured he could coax me into whatever else he wanted, too. I'd gotten myself into this uncomfortable situation, but I sure wasn't going to do anything to make it worse.

"How have you never seen *Fight Club*? It's a classic."

Greg ran the backs of his fingers over mine where they cupped my soda glass. I didn't really think his praise of a movie about dudes beating each other to a pulp paired well with this level of flirting, but whatever. I moved my hand, looping it onto my other elbow, blocking him out.

"It's not really my taste."

He leaned closer. "What is your taste, Cassie?"

A laugh bubbled out of me, which I immediately regretted not so much because it was rude, but because he'd probably take it as encouragement. Getting my name wrong all night irritated enough, but saying it in a seductive way? Kind of hilarious.

"It's Callie, and I like actual classics, like with Katharine Hepburn and Jimmy Stewart."

"The *It's a Wonderful Life* guy? I didn't know he did anything else."

Oh, he was definitely getting punched now.

"Seriously? *Mr. Smith Goes to Washington? The Shop Around the Corner? The Philadelphia Story? Vertigo?*" I could have gone on, but Greg's blank look said not to bother.

"I'm more of an Oliver Stone, Quentin Tarantino guy."

I hated it when guys made sweeping conclusions about me when they found out I read romance novels, so I didn't want to be a judgey judgerson, but only liking violent movies wasn't a huge turn on. "They're not my favorites."

Immune to my hints, he lowered his hand to my knee. I drew in a breath, my body turning to steel as if I could erase the contact. He'd been pretty decent at the restaurant, but walking into the bar had apparently switched on his unwelcome touches setting.

"You just haven't seen the right ones. You know, my place is right around the corner. I'll introduce you to *Fight Club*."

Not wanting to make too big of a deal out of it, I brushed his hand away without acknowledging it, like a bug or a piece of lint. "It's pretty late to start a movie."

"Then we can skip the movie."

He probably thought his smile radiated charm, but I wanted to slap it off.

Just like he'd gone right on calling me Cassie despite my corrections, his hand went straight back to my leg—a smidge higher this time, to prove how thoroughly he ignored what I wanted. For Gran's sake, I behaved as politely as I could on these set-ups, but this guy had crossed my personal boundaries one too many times. I made to brush his hand away again, gearing up to call it a night and steer clear of his presumptuous plans, but a man's hand wrapped around his wrist before I got there.

Greg and I looked up to see Jed standing right behind us, eyes blazing fire. He lifted Greg's hand away from me.

"I think it's time for you to say goodnight." He didn't raise his voice or get in Greg's face, but every word carried a threat. This was no friendly suggestion, but a command.

Greg, unfortunately, didn't take commands very well. The contempt in his eyes as he looked Jed up and down made me want to roundhouse kick him straight in the teeth.

"I don't know who you are, but she wants to be with me."

Jed released his hand with the slightest shove, like tossing away a piece of trash. "You sure about that?"

Greg turned to me, but I couldn't stop staring up at Jed. I'd never seen him so deadly serious. Usually, he was all fun and games, but tonight, he held a dangerous edge. His mouth almost had a smile to it, and anyone watching would probably think we were all buddies, but the steel in his brown eyes looked lethal.

I was no damsel in distress, but he had some A-plus rescuing going on here.

Remembering I should probably say something, I dragged my eyes away from Jed to face my craptacular date. "I don't think this is going to work out, Greg."

He goggled at me for a second—had he really thought I'd choose him over Jed? Would *anyone* choose him over Jed? Greg might come in a fancier package with expensive clothes and a perfectly-styled haircut, but Jed's wrinkly T-shirt, faded jeans, and mussed-up hair did more for me than Mr. Fancypants ever could. Jed's innate confidence and appeal wasn't a suit he put on, it was just *him*. He didn't have to try, he was just...Jed.

Oh. Oh, my sweet, stupid heart. I could not have a crush on Jed Evans. Sure, he'd just done some mighty fine rescuing, but he'd also been pretty vehement when he rejected my cuckoo fake dating proposal. *Absolutely not.* Plus, he was the bacheloriest bachelor in Magnolia Ridge. It'd be like getting a crush on Leonardo DiCaprio, which—ew. Not as bad as that, but in the same ballpark of *This can't possibly go anywhere.*

I needed to use the logical part of my brain and stop ogling the man. In, like, five more minutes.

Greg stood in a huff and left. Jed waited until the last glimpse of his pressed shirt had disappeared out the door before his shoulders relaxed. It seemed impossible he thought Greg might actually fight him. More importantly, I couldn't believe he'd really been willing to do that for me.

It felt about as modern as Gran's insistence I needed a man to take care of me, but I really, *really* liked the idea of Jed going to bat for me. I would have happily watched him sock Greg in the face. Although, after all the leg-grabbing, I think I deserved first swing.

Jed finally turned to me. The dangerous light in his eyes had been replaced by concern. Worry, even. "You okay?"

Yes. Yep. Totally not imagining you beating up my handsy date.

"I'm okay. Thanks for that."

"You mind if I sit down?"

Please! the girliest of my girly thoughts cried out. But I remembered my dignity at the last second, and kept it to a casual, "Sure."

He sat on the barstool next to me, his eyes doing that laser beam of curiosity thing again. Never very far from spilling my guts on a normal day, when he looked at me that way, I wanted to talk just to fill the awkward silence. So I spilled.

"He was another set-up. A friend of a friend of an elderly friend, you could say. We had dinner, and I let him convince me to come here after, and I guess he figured he could convince me to go to his apartment, too."

Jed's gaze turned hard again, the smile that usually brightened his face nowhere to be seen. Probably best not to go into detail about how Greg had tried to order me a double Tequila Sunrise even after I'd said I didn't want any alcohol tonight.

"But obviously, I wouldn't have gone anywhere with him even if you hadn't shown up. I would have told him off at some point. Well, maybe not exactly *told him off*. I'm kind of bad at confrontation, but I would have got the message across. Eventually."

Now he looked perfectly incredulous.

"It's not that hard. I just politely say no a few times, and after a while, they get the hint and take off."

Jed blew out a breath. "They all treat you like that?"

"Well, this guy was probably the worst of the bunch. But yeah, they get pretty annoyed when I don't just fall into their beds."

That angry look came back. I liked it in my defense, but to be honest, I didn't want to see it all that much. I preferred happy, fun-loving Jed to ready-to-bloody-a-guy Jed.

"To be fair, a couple of the dates Gran arranged didn't put that kind of pressure on, but they weren't exactly dreamboats either. Even the nicest of the lot made fun of my job as a teacher, so...yeah, not the best assortment of guys."

Everything they said about how much modern dating stinks? All true. Maybe something about the anonymity of dating sites, or in this case, grandma networking. You'd think the guys would have tried harder not to be jerks when their relatives were setting them up just like mine, but so far, it hadn't worked out that way.

Would Greg have been more of a gentleman if I'd threatened to tell his grandma on him? Doubted it.

Jed sighed, dragging a hand down his face as if this night had been a hundred and fifty hours long. "All right. I'm in."

I froze, not wanting to jump to conclusions here. He'd just obliterated my bad date into dust, I wouldn't presume to ask for more.

"You're in?" My voice came out tiny and unsure.

His mouth twisted up into his usual grin. "Let's do this fake dating thing."

Relief and elation got their pom-poms out to cheer for this man. "You mean it?"

"If it will get your grandma and her friends off your back and keep you from dating guys like that, I do."

I wrapped both my hands around his forearm and—wow. Delightful. Strong and muscly, powerful and warm, I'd never held an arm quite like that one. Ten out of ten, would definitely grab again.

Remembering I'd been grabbed five minutes ago and hadn't loved it, I let him go.

"Okay, so tell me how this is supposed to work," he said, focusing all his attention on me. "Get me up to speed."

"Well…"

To be totally honest, I'd never thought through the logistics of fake dating. After the idea had come to me, it'd seemed like the solution to all my problems, and I'd been so excited, I'd immediately asked Jed to do it. I didn't know what the specifics should look like. There wasn't a Fake Dating Handbook somewhere that I knew of.

"I think we just need to be seen together around town. Pretend to go on enough dates to convince Granny we're happy so she can feel confident going off to Florida and leaving me here in your hands."

One of his eyebrows ticked up.

"Not that I'll actually be in your hands. I'll be in my own hands. It's just a figure of speech. Never mind."

"Who's going to know it's not real?"

"Just us."

That brought out another eyebrow twitch. "You won't tell Harper or June that we're just for show?"

"Oh. I hadn't thought about that. I guess I could let them in on it if that's easier on you."

Probably some slim chance existed they wouldn't judge me too hard once they knew my reasons for it. They'd known I'd been on a few bummer dates lately, but I hadn't explained it all. Something about admitting that I was going on these dates to keep a group of elderly women happy just didn't feel like a win.

"No, don't tell them."

Jed turned his body toward me, and his knee brushed mine beneath the bar top. That little spot of warmth drew all my attention, but I needed to ignore it. Twisting back slightly, he gave me space again, already several million points up on Mr. Groper.

Even if I kind of missed the touch.

"What do you say to being my plus-one to my sister's wedding next month? There's bound to be a few other events, too. Wouldn't hurt to have Pop ease up on his hints I need to settle down."

"Is he meddling, too?"

"He's made it abundantly clear he'd like me to follow in Wade's footsteps."

"And you don't want to do that?"

He watched me half a second. "I don't think that's in the cards for me."

That answer only raised more questions, but I would accept it for now. I kind of liked it better knowing this wouldn't all be for my benefit, anyway. We needed each other, in a somewhat lopsided way.

"Will it be hard for you to pretend about us in front of your family?" I asked. "Won't it make you uncomfortable?"

"Not a lot makes me uncomfortable."

I believed it. His slanted grin reinforced his casual attitude.

"Then sure, I'll be your date to June's wedding, too."

"What are the ground rules?"

"Um, you mean like PDA and stuff?"

He tilted his head down in a slow nod.

I gulped because I was smooth like that. I would *not* get caught up imagining PDA with Jed. "What do you think is best?"

He considered me for a minute, and I prayed to God he wasn't sizing up my kissing abilities. I had a feeling he'd guessed already my experience in that department was pretty slim.

"How about I let you be in charge of that whole thing?" he finally said.

"You don't want any say?"

"I trust your judgment."

Considering his initial reaction to this proposal, I wasn't sure he meant that. "So if Gran's around and I think I should touch you or hug you or just kiss you like crazy, you'd be okay with it?"

His throat worked, swallowing once before he spoke. "I'm not bothered by PDA."

Yeah, that sentence would be forever lodged in my brain.

No. I couldn't think about him that way. This would all be for show, nothing more. Even PDA, if it came to that, would all be for Gran's sake, not for the weird little dance my heart was doing over the idea. It needed to settle down.

"Okay. Then I'll captain that ship."

He smiled again, but I couldn't tell if it was because what I'd said was funny, or because *I* was funny. I would just hope for the better option.

"Oh, um, one other thing." I squirmed in my seat because this part sort of fell under the confrontation umbrella, and while not as bad as dealing with a crappy date, I wasn't excited to bring it up, either. "I'd rather you didn't see anyone else while we're doing this."

His smile disappeared, and a touch of that hardness came back into his eyes. I couldn't figure out how Greg hadn't disintegrated under that weight, because I wanted to crawl beneath the bar after just a couple of seconds of it.

"What?"

His voice held a quality I couldn't identify—not anger, not irritation, but definitely *something*—and not knowing what made me even more uncomfortable.

I couldn't look him in the eyes so I examined the woodgrain in the bar top. "It's just that we're doing this to try to convince my granny, and I'm sure you'd be discreet and whatever, but gossip in small towns, you know, and I don't think it will work very well if you were also dating someone else, so if you could just...not...do that until we're done, I would really appreciate it. Sorry."

He stared at me one beat, two. Way too dang long. Maybe he wasn't interested in pausing his social life to prop up mine. Maybe he hadn't thought I'd meant we'd be exclusive while we convinced Gran. Or maybe he wasn't an exclusive kind of guy, no matter how real the dating was.

"I know it's a lot to ask, and I'm sorry, but—"

"It's not a lot to ask, Callie. It's pretty much the lowest bar you could ask a guy to meet. Did you think I'd agree to date you and then turn around and see someone else on the side?"

"I—" I didn't know what I'd thought, honestly, I'd just needed to clarify. I hadn't meant to offend him, I just had no interest in being the other woman, even if he and I were totally pretend.

He held up a hand. "Don't answer that. I won't date anyone else but you."

"Okay. Thank you. And I, obviously, won't date anyone else either."

We stared at each other another minute, our earlier rapport gone.

"I'm sorry for asking, I just wasn't sure..."

He waved away my renewed apology. "Don't worry about it. It makes sense you'd ask. It's good to clarify."

"Okay." I didn't really feel like we'd worked through that fumble, but I'd follow his lead here.

"So what's the endgame? How will you know this scheme has worked?"

That question, at least, had an easy answer.

"All I want is for Gran to move to Florida and be happy with her friends. They're supposed to do that at the end of next month."

"Around June's wedding?"

I did some calculations. "Right around there, yeah. Then, after she's settled in, I'll figure out a time to tell her we broke up."

His mouth tipped up. "I hope you'll be kind in the aftermath."

"Nah. I'm going to dump you because you're way too old for me."

He put a hand over his chest, feigning hurt despite the huge grin on his face. "Going straight for the age. Ouch."

Personally, I didn't think the eight or so years between us amounted to all that much. Maybe if he'd acted like a crabby curmudgeon who chased youngsters off his lawn, but nothing about Jed said grumpy old man. He was the biggest flirt in town.

"Don't worry, you'll bounce back quickly. Your heart was never really in it."

His teasing smile faded a touch. I kind of wished I hadn't said that last part, even if I believed it. His apparent reluctance to dive into a serious relationship was one of the reasons I'd chosen him for my fake-dating partner. The rest of the reasons... I needed to not think about them. But after assuming he'd date other people, adding in a jab about him not caring felt like a sucker punch.

But what was the alternative? Joke that he'd never get over me? I wasn't that dumb.

"Sounds about right," he said in the end. "When do we start this acting gig?"

"Gran and her friends have a game night planned for Tuesday. Can you come by to pick me up for a date then? Just seeing us together will get the ball rolling."

Just seeing us together would get them dreaming up wedding color schemes, but I didn't need to freak him out.

He nodded. "I'll be there."

"Great. I'll text you my address."

"It's a fake date, then." He held out his hand to shake on our arrangement.

I slipped my hand into his, and everything sort of paused. We were goofing on a business deal, a perfect mime of an unemotional transaction, but this handshake brought out *all* my emotions. Embarrassment, excitement, a teensy weensy bit of desire—everyone turned up to play.

He leaned forward a touch, a devilish grin lighting his face. "Just don't fall in love with me."

"Aw." I pulled my hand from his and patted him on the arm, his bicep stupidly firm beneath my fingers. "We don't have to worry about that."

We both laughed, but pretty sure he'd been dead serious.

callie

THE DATE MIGHT HAVE BEEN fake, but the nerves? Totally real.

I'd changed clothes twice only to give up and put on my favorite yellow blouse and a pair of jeans shorts. After, I'd tried to distract myself with a new embroidery but couldn't focus. Then I'd opened up my e-reader but went back over the same page so many times, I had to shut the floral cover in defeat. The five set-ups my granny's crew had arranged had never got me twisted up like this.

I wasn't totally sure if the nerves were for having to act in front of the women making themselves at home in my dining room, or for having to act with Jed. Two halves of the same awkward coin.

His question about my comfort level with lying kept running through my head. Telling lies with my words wouldn't be that hard—I already fibbed like crazy, politely covering for every crummy set-up Gran and the others found for me. But telling lies with my behavior? Cozying up to Jed enough to make them believe it? Nerves shot around inside me like a pinball going wild. At least tonight, they wouldn't expect us to get *too* cozy. First date, and all.

I'd just deal with future dates when we got there.

Walking into the main part of the house, I found Gran and her friends gathered around the dining table. They'd stacked a bunch of board games at one end and were discussing-slash-arguing which one to lead with. I sometimes joined them for game night but didn't love how brutal they could be about them. Betting obscene amounts of retirement money on Yahtzee did that to people.

They'd developed a specific distinction: games played during the day stayed low-key. Competitive, but no stakes. They could try anything on a Tuesday afternoon with no conse-quences. On game nights, though? The house became a regular gambling parlor. Or wherever people put a ton of cash on the outcome of Phase Ten.

"My vote's on Ticket to Ride." Linda pulled a big stack of dollar bills from her purse and set it on the table in front of her. "Since last time we played worked out so well for me."

"It's a game of chance." Carmen had her own neat stack of money at the ready. In theory, they only bet singles, but inevitably, somebody would break out a ten or a twenty when they felt really lucky. Two twenties peeked out from the bottom of her stack.

"If that were true, I would win occasionally." Rita didn't sound as enthusiastic but laid out her own bills anyway.

"The cards are chance, but you need strategy to win. Which I intend to do." Gran set the game box in the center of the table, along with the shallow cut-glass dish they used to hold the antes. They made gambling over kids' games look classy.

I honestly wasn't sure how they planned to live together in Florida without driving each other into debt.

"Are you joining us tonight, Callie?" Linda asked.

"No way. I lost thirty dollars last time." Playing a dice game that consisted of passing money around the table until one person had the whole pot—what kind of a game was that?

"You don't have the cutthroat gene like your grandma," Rita said.

"All the more reason to have you play." Carmen got up to fill a plate with snacks they'd brought. Bowls of chips and pretzels littered the kitchen counters, and a fruit tray sat next to a plate of fudge. "Even things out a little."

"You mean make it easier for you to win." I laughed at her unapologetic half-shrug. Not a trace of guilt from these women.

"Someone's got to."

"You look nice tonight, Callie." Rita accepted her pieces for the game and lined them up in front of her. "Are you headed out?"

Gran's eyes hit me like a hawk searching for a field mouse to devour. Her disappointment at hearing I wouldn't be seeing Greg a second time had been hard to take, but I'd powered through knowing I had Jed up my sleeve. So to speak.

"I'm going out, yes." I figured if I just blurted out I'd magically started dating someone in the last forty-eight hours, nobody would believe me. Not that they were the most discerning—none of them had figured out any of the guys they'd set me up with were less than stellar, for one. But leaning too hard into lovesickness too fast might raise suspicions, and I needed to keep them appeased.

"Who are you going out with?" Her question sounded casual enough, but the eagerness in her eyes said it all. The dud date with Greg hadn't turned her off finding me a man. "Harper?"

"No." I dragged out the word, playing it as cool as could be.

Working them into a lather about Jed's imminent arrival would surely result in some hearty embarrassment for everyone involved, and I didn't need him bowing out of this agreement before we'd even had our first fake date. "Her cousin."

"I like that June." Linda shuffled the game cards, making a soft *snick* sound. "I'd have her redecorate my house if we were staying. Think she'd come to Sarasota to do the condo?"

"I don't know, but it's not June." Speak of the handsome devil, a truck pulled up outside. Time to rip this bandage off. "I'm having dinner with her brother, Jed."

That announcement threw the room into total silence. Linda froze, cards halfway slotted together. Carmen held a handful of pretzels poised over a bowl. Rita's fingers paused over her game pieces she'd meticulously laid out. Granny was the only one who moved, but even that seemed stuck in slo-mo. Like the creep of a glacier, her eyebrows lifted, stunned surprise giving way to a curious smile.

Her shock made sense, I guess. I hadn't been on a spontaneous, willing date since I'd come home from college. But her joy did me in, that spark of delight on a face that lately had held so much worry for me. *That* cemented my determination to sell this thing with Jed. She shouldn't be spending her days stressing about my love life and how I'd manage on my own— she should be packing her things and deciding what to wear on the beach every day of the week.

"Jed? As in, a man?"

Okay, that was a little too incredulous. "Yes, a man, Granny. And I think he's here, so all y'all need to act natural."

As if they'd read the same grandma playbook, they blinked around at each other as though my plea were mildly offensive to their delicate sensibilities. Sure. We'd just see.

The doorbell rang, and I crossed the living room before any of them could get ideas. I'd planned to just let them have a quick peek to confirm Jed's existence before high-tailing it out of there, but when I threw the door open, my brain went totally blank.

He wore a plain navy blue T-shirt and jeans with sneakers. Nothing fancy, and yet everything about him seemed different. I couldn't pinpoint it. Maybe just because he stood on my porch, where he'd never been before, waiting to take me on a date, which we'd certainly never done before. His smile sure hadn't changed, though. It sent a rush of tingles from my chest outward, zooming all the way down to my fingers and toes.

"Hi," he said, totally unfazed by the collection of eyes fixed on him.

I swallowed hard, my mouth weirdly dry. I got it now. How Jed never wanted for company. Not that I'd ever questioned it, but seeing him standing there, grinning like he'd been waiting all day to see me—I could get used to this.

"Invite the man in, honey," Gran called before I'd untied my tongue.

I lifted my eyebrows at him in silent warning. "Come on in."

He stepped into the house, and suddenly, everyone jumped to their feet, cutthroat gaming forgotten in favor of crowding around the new guy. If this had been a genuine first date, I probably would have been mortified to have them so obviously eager on my behalf, but since it was all just for show—well, no. Still pretty mortifying.

"Jed, this is my grandma, Suzie Howell."

He moved forward, hand outstretched. "Good to meet you, ma'am."

"Ooh, ma'am, I like that," Linda said behind us.

Ignoring that outburst and follow-up laughter from the others, Gran shook his hand. "Jed. I don't think I recall Callie mentioning you before."

He turned his mega-watt smile my way. "You never mentioned me? That hurts, Callie."

I shot him a look for the faux reprimand. I didn't need to be down even more points in the granny crew's eyes already.

"I told you about June's brothers." I'd definitely mentioned him a time or two, even if everything I'd told her about Jed had been a big fat lie.

She furrowed her brow at me, wheels turning. "You said both those boys were married." She looked him over, searching for evidence of a recent divorce—or worse, proof he was a cheater. Like he might have a tattoo somewhere declaring *I cannot be trusted.*

"Wade's married. I must have got it confused when I first met them."

I'd for sure told her both of them were married, only to keep her pushy hands off my back when it came to Jed. If she'd known every get together with Harper's extended family had involved a handsome, funny, very single man, she never would have stopped bringing him up.

"You confused me with my brother? Harsh."

Jed's perpetual grin said he wasn't too worried about it. By now, I was pretty well convinced the man never worried about anything.

"You do look a lot alike."

They really did. Both tall with dark hair and warm eyes, Jed had a little more laughter in his expression where Wade tended to look more skeptical. Wade was stockier, too, more muscular in an obvious way, in contrast with Jed's leanness. They sure weren't similar enough I'd ever mix the two up, though.

"But I'm more handsome, right?"

I made a so-so gesture. "In certain lighting."

His chuckle worked through me like a sparkler, but a bony

elbow to my ribs interrupted the moment. Rita stood next to me, eyebrows raised, impatiently waiting.

Right. Introductions.

"Jed, these are my gran's friends, Linda, Carmen, and Rita."

He shook hands all around, exchanging quick greetings with each woman. They cooed over him in generous approval, gray heads nodding over his every word. Rita, in particular, seemed reluctant to let him go, holding his hand in both of hers while her eyelashes batted away. Hopefully, poor Stan would never know how quickly he'd been forgotten.

"You've been holding out on us." She spoke to me, but her eyes never left Jed.

"You mean she's been holding out on me." He grinned down at her, charm shooting from his eyeballs like twinkly missiles zeroing straight in on their hearts. "I had no idea she had such lovely roommates."

Even Granny, who I privately thought of as the most sensible of the crew, tittered along with her friends. Truly, Jed had too much charisma for his own good.

"Where did you find this one, Callie?" Rita asked, still staring into his face as though unable to look away. Also, still squeezing his hand.

"We've known each other a while now." I subtly nudged her to release her grip on him since it seemed unlikely she'd opt to do it herself. "We met at Harper's family Christmas party. We didn't talk all that much then, but we've run into each other a few times. On that hike we did a couple months ago we talked a little more, and—"

Carmen patted my shoulder. "We don't need the whole history, just the abridged version will do."

"Right," I said brightly, mentally crossing out the rest of my explanation. It didn't really matter anyway, since he'd already won them over in five minutes flat.

"What is it you do, Jed?" Gran asked.

"I work on our family farm, Evans Orchards."

That earned a few more coos of approval. Their farm was pretty well known around here, and warranted at least one visit during peach season.

"You've been doing that a while, I suppose?"

"Only the last few years. Before that, I was in the Army."

They spoke as one thanking him for his service, which Jed accepted with a modest nod. He seemed to have a healthy ego about a lot of things, but his time in the Army wasn't one. I kind of respected him even more for how humbly he treated it.

"Were you ever stationed overseas?" Linda asked. One of her grandsons was currently based out of someplace in Germany.

"Yes, ma'am."

Rita leaned forward. "Ever see combat?"

His mouth shifted the tiniest bit, his smile off just a touch. I'd heard the answer to that question from June and the girls, but he sure didn't need to go into detail for the sake of my gran and her friends' idle curiosity.

"That's all the questions for now, we've got to go." Crossing to him, I put both my hands on his bicep, urging him out the door. He wasn't a bulky guy, but the man didn't budge an inch for all my pushing.

"Callie Louise," Gran said, her voice thick with a reprimand over my rudeness.

My eyes shot to his, and I witnessed up-close the realization break over his face.

I pointed a finger at him. "Forget you heard that."

"Oh, it's already locked away in my mind." A smug smile curved along his mouth like he was plotting all the ways he could use my middle name against me.

"I'm sorry, Gran, but we need to be on our way." Hearing its cue, my stomach growled into the silence, letting everyone know the nibbles I'd stolen from their snack assortment wouldn't tide me over much longer.

"I'd love to keep chatting, but I should probably take Callie to dinner." Jed smiled away at his adoring fans. "Ladies, it was a pleasure meeting y'all."

They seemed unwilling to let us go, but we finally made it out the door and into the yard. I figured we shouldn't talk about anything too close to the house for fear someone had an ear to the door, so I kept my mouth firmly shut as we walked across the grass. Jed went straight to the passenger side of his big black truck to open it for me. An older model, the inside smelled of lemony cleaner and something earthy. Mostly, though, I noticed the big jump from the ground to the passenger seat.

"Sheesh. Glad I didn't wear a skirt." The hike up would have exposed several extra inches of thigh. "This thing is a beast."

"It isn't lifted or anything." Jed's voice held way too much amusement as I gauged the least embarrassing method for climbing in. "I think you're just petite."

Making good use of the grip inside the door, I hauled myself into the seat. Wasn't the most ladylike way anybody'd ever gotten into a vehicle, but I made it. Once settled, I glared at him.

"I prefer to think of myself as fun-sized."

His smirk set off a wild fluttering in my chest.

"I'll just bet you do."

Closing the door for me, he walked around the cab and climbed in the driver's side. He watched me for a second, twirling the ignition keys on a finger. "Not bad for a first foray into this fake dating thing."

"Still think you're up for it? That was just the beginning."

The grin he flashed made me want to crawl across the center console and snuggle right up to him for the drive into town. A crazy thought...but a tempting one.

"Darlin', I hate to tell you this, but your grandma and her friends don't scare me. They're going to love me."

He started the truck, its engine rumbling to life in the night.

I sighed, recalling their dreamy-eyed stares. "Pretty much guaranteed."

Just wasn't sure now if that would make things easier, or infinitely harder.

jed

I'D NEVER BEEN a fan of awkward silences, but Callie Matheson seemed downright allergic to them. She talked the whole way into town, filling my truck with non-stop conversation.

"My gran is pretty much the Dorothy of their *Golden Girls* group: she can be stern, but she's practical to the core. She balances out her realism by being extra fanciful about my love life." She forced a laugh for emphasis. "Carmen is kind of the Sophia—she says what she wants and doesn't think too hard about whether or not people want to hear it. Linda was a teacher like me. She's extra supportive of me because of that, and I think of her a bit like Rose. Kindhearted and a little bit innocent."

Reminded me of someone else I knew, in this very truck next to me.

"And Rita, as you can guess, is the Blanche. She can be shameless so, you know—watch out. I hope your hand's recovered from all of her groping."

"I've had worse."

She laughed again, softer than before. "Sorry, I'm babbling on about my gran and her friends."

"I need the intel. Although, I feel I should tell you, I've never seen *The Golden Girls*."

She spun her head around to goggle at me. "Are you serious right now?"

"It's not on my must-watch list."

"Well, better get ready, buddy, because you're about to *live* The Golden Girls."

Her playfulness brought a big smile to my face. She seemed to sway between bright openness and an almost shy reserve I couldn't figure out. Mostly, I wanted to know how to keep the free-spirited side of her front and center.

"What are you in the mood for? Thai? Chinese? Burgers?" Magnolia Ridge was no metropolis, but we had a good variety of restaurants in town these days. Now and then, I'd drive into Georgetown if I needed something like sushi or ramen, but we wouldn't go hungry here.

"Oh, are we really going to go eat?"

The surprise in her voice confused me. "What did you think we were going to do?"

Her hands twisted in her lap, her shoulders hitching up. "I don't know. Find a parking lot somewhere and just hang out until it's time to go back?"

"Callie Louise," I chided, *tsking* away at her. "You want to go park somewhere for a couple of hours on our first date?"

Her answering gasp came with a swat at my arm. "That's not what I meant, and you were supposed to forget my middle name."

"Already told you I can't."

"More like won't."

"Exactly." I turned onto Center Street, slowing before we reached the bulk of the restaurant options. "Plus, I had a whole conversation with your stomach back at the house. We're having dinner. So? What'll it be?"

"Maybe pizza? Granny can't eat it anymore, so I don't have it all that often."

"Sounds good to me." Even if I didn't love knowing she cut everyday things like pizza out of her life to accommodate her grandmother. Seemed too much, but equally too much would be me telling her so.

I parked us a block from Slice of Delight, pulling as close as I could to the curb to make it easier for my fun-sized companion to get out. Downtown could be crowded on the weekends, but on a Tuesday night, we pretty much had our run of the place. I walked around to meet her, noting how easily she jumped out of the truck onto the sidewalk.

Did not look at her legs in the process. Much.

"Are your grandma and her friends always so welcoming to the guys you date?" I asked as we headed up the street. I'd never had the red carpet rolled out for me quite like that.

She made a sound of disgust. "They really should have toned it down a little. And no, I always meet the set-ups wherever we're going specifically to avoid that."

I nudged her with my arm. "I'm honored you let me come to your house."

She nudged me back. "Our plan wouldn't work very well if you didn't."

"Still, it shows a certain trust. An acknowledgement that I'm the inherently superior choice around here."

"That's for sure." Her laughter turned strangled. "I mean, you're better than those guys, you're not better than *everyone*."

"It's too late to take it back, you already said it."

"That's only because I'm so hungry, I can't think straight. If I weren't in this weakened state, I wouldn't have said that."

"I'm immune to your protests."

She looped a hand around my arm but immediately dropped it, a weird smile stuck on her face like she'd been caught doing something suspicious by an MP.

"Callie?" I said.

"Callie?" another voice repeated.

I looked up and did a double take—Harper and Sam stood ten feet away from us on the sidewalk. Harper looked from Callie to me and back again, the question in her eyes almost forming a word bubble over her head.

"What are you doing here?"

She didn't add *With Jed,* but everyone heard it.

I'd expected this, to be honest. Curious looks from the cousins. Protectiveness. My dating history probably didn't make me the safest bet where Callie's friends were concerned, even if they were my family. Hell, I wouldn't have encouraged her to date me, either, but we'd already jumped head-first into this thing. Not the time to second-guess when we were squarely in the deep end.

"Yeah. We're just..." Callie had become an actress who'd blanked on her lines and frankly, wasn't that great at improv. "What are you guys doing?"

Harper gestured at the shop front next to us. "Kicking a little butt at Rumble Room tonight."

That explained all the workout wear. She paused, her eyes on me impossibly heavy, like she'd set a barbell loaded with disks on my chest. Probably searching for some kind of guilty confession.

"And you two are...?"

"Headed to Slice of Delight," I put in. Even if this first date had been absolutely real, my cousin didn't need to know anything more than that, despite her telegraphing a hundred questions my way.

"You two have fun tonight." Sam took her hand and tugged

her toward the door. He grinned at me, clearly less agitated by the whole situation than Harper.

"Call me later," she said to Callie before he pulled her into the gym where they were swallowed up by a sea of muscular people ready to kickbox to their hearts' content.

Callie stood frozen on the sidewalk, that weird, fake smile strained at the edges. She'd fully powered down, broken by one small interaction with my cousin. Didn't make me overflow with confidence we'd get through two months of pretending to be happy together.

For now, I'd focus on tonight. I put a hand at the small of her back, urging her along. "Come on, let's get some food in you."

We made it inside the pizza joint and grabbed a booth, but her worried expression didn't change. She stared at the Formica tabletop, her brow furrowed, two little lines marring her forehead.

"This isn't a good sign for our first date, Callie Lou. Only women I've dated for a long time should act so horrified to be seen with me in public."

She startled, her gaze snapping to mine. Her stiffness broke apart, and she rolled her eyes, grinning at my stupid joke. Better. Anything to get rid of the anxiousness that had filled her up since she'd caught sight of Harper.

"It's not being seen with you. I know we agreed to this, to faking for your family, too, but Harper's my friend. She's going to want *details and information.*"

She whispered those last words, hinting a certain salaciousness to them. That low, naughty tone spun a heated breeze through my chest. I vacuumed up that cozy breeze, reminding myself to forget it. I'd agreed to date her out of a sense of friendship only. With a splash of protectiveness thrown in. And maybe a dash of jealousy, if we were being honest, but I wasn't about to dig any deeper.

"Being my cousin, Harper might not want all that many details."

"You know what I mean. Gran and the others will just be excited about anything I say. Harper will be like *'Oh ho, what's this about dating Jed?'* and I'll have to lie through my teeth."

"Harper talks like that?"

"She'll be excited, too," she went on, ignoring me. "Well, I think. But she'll have a lot more questions, and I am clearly not prepared to be convincing. What's our backstory here? How did we start this? What do I say?"

"First, relax." I took both her hands in mine, wrapping them up like I could squeeze her anxiety out. "Second, if she asks you point-blank, you have my permission to tell her the truth and admit you're hopelessly in love with me."

She laughed again but tugged her hands free. Served me right, I guess. But I figured keeping the tone light would be the best option all around. Too serious, and we'd risk swimming through muddy waters.

"Don't overthink it," I told her. "Just tell her we met up one night at The Broken Hammer and I asked you out. She doesn't need a play-by-play. I meant it when I said I don't think she'll have that many questions. My sister, on the other hand...well, let's just hope she's too distracted by wedding plans to ask."

If June saw a chance to get back at me for how much I'd teased her about Ty, safe bet she'd suddenly become an investigative reporter eager to get the scoop on what was going on with Callie.

She sighed, and her shoulders eased down, the pinching around her cheeks and eyes relaxing with each breath. "You're right, I'm overthinking it. I just don't have much experience with dating. I don't know how I'm supposed to act or what's normal."

A waitress came by to take our pizza order before zipping away again with our half-margherita, half-buffalo chicken request.

"I don't understand that part," I said. "You're open, fun, great-looking—seems like you'd have a line of guys outside your door eager to date you."

Didn't love the image, but I held to it. Anything beyond a lack of interest on her part didn't add up.

She ran her hands over the tabletop, making a face. "I'm bad at dating."

"I doubt that."

She leveled me a look she probably thought of as stern. Must have worked wonders on the five-year-olds she taught, but it couldn't intimidate me.

"Dating is all about concealing who you really are, curating yourself to show only your best features in the hopes you get that next date. Can't go too deep or too dark, or you'll scare the person off. I'm not the best at that. *Relationships* are about going all in and sharing who you really are with someone, showing them all your best and worst bits. That's more what I'm cut out for, but I've learned people don't like it when you dive into the deeper stuff first."

A weight pressed against my ribs, although I couldn't say exactly why. Maybe the thought of Callie editing herself to make some guy feel more comfortable. Or maybe because the people I'd allowed to see the deeper parts of me didn't extend beyond my immediate family. Sometimes not even then.

"What about you?" she asked.

I smiled wide. "I'm good at dating."

She watched me a full minute, apparently waiting for me to

spill my guts. Examining me. Quite possibly judging me. All of her staring made me weirdly itchy. "What?"

"I just told you my whole dating versus relationships philosophy, and you won't tell me anything about you?"

"I don't have a dating philosophy."

Like her stern look, her glare proved more adorable than frightening. "Then tell me something I should know about my fake boyfriend. At least give me some pet peeves to work with."

"You should probably ix-nay on the ake-fay if you're trying to sell this thing."

She looked around the pizza place, but nobody was close enough to have heard her.

"You're right. You're my boyfriend."

She emphasized the word with a resolute nod paired with a sassy little wink. This woman would be the death of me, I swear.

I leaned back, trying to come up with something to give her.

"Pet peeves, okay. I can't stand when someone says 'Don't take this personally' and then says something personally offensive. I don't like calendar apps or alarm clocks. People who say 'It's my way or the highway.' Chewing sounds turn my stomach. I'd rather be with a crowd of strangers than alone in the silence any day."

That last one...might have been more than just a pet peeve. Wasn't quite the moment for cracking my heart open to figure out what hid inside, though.

"But didn't you have to get up early and have people tell you to do things their way in the Army?"

"Yep. That's why I don't do it anymore." Still woke up before dawn most days, but I didn't have anyone blaring into my ear that I had to, and that made all the difference.

"Fair."

"Your turn for pet peeves." Now I could watch and wait while *she* squirmed under my gaze.

"I don't have to go, I already said that other stuff."

"But I need to know about my girlfriend."

All this tossing *boyfriend* and *girlfriend* around worked a strange tingling through my chest, like a muscle overcome by pins and needles as it woke up. Wasn't entirely sure I liked the feeling.

"Well... I don't like when people forget plans. Or talk during movies. Or when I'm in a big store and two people stop with their carts in the middle of the aisle to have a chat. When I go to the hardware store and men ask me why my husband isn't handling all that for me. When people act like they know what's best for me."

I could guess where her mind had gone there. This whole scenario had come out of her grandma thinking she knew what would be best for her. Coming from a place of love didn't make it any easier to take. I could relate, what with Pop's gentle nudges in whatever direction he saw fit.

"Oh, and trucks that are way too big for normal-sized humans to get into."

"Feels oddly specific, Callie Lou."

She grinned wide, and I had to stop for a second just to appreciate the sight. How had I never realized she had a dimple? Just the one, which seemed more remarkable than if she'd had a matching set. Surely, I'd noticed it—I'd just never thought about it before. But here it was, one perfect indentation in her full right cheek.

Kind of liked that smug smile on her.

"What sort of projects have you been doing that they're giving you a hard time about at the hardware store?"

"I did a drip system for Gran's flower beds this spring. They didn't trust I was buying the right parts." She rolled her eyes as if to say *Men.* "I put up some wainscoting in the living room, and they wanted to be sure I had someone who could install it for me. Like nail guns are so hard to figure out."

Callie with a nail gun sounded weirdly hot. Best scrub that thought from my brain.

"Drip systems and wainscoting, huh? You must be a pro at home repair."

"It's just Gran and me, so it's either that, or pay loads of money for someone else to do it."

"Sounds like you're putting a lot of love into your home." That's what June always called it. My sister's job as an interior designer had her sorting out half the houses in town, finding ways to update and upgrade everything from a new wall color to a new addition. Nothing made her happier than finding the exact right way to make someone's house more of a home.

Callie's smile faded a touch. "Yeah. It's a good house."

"You don't sound so sure."

"No, it is a good house, it's just..." She drew in a breath as if searching for the right words among a field of landmines. "It's not my forever home, you know?"

"I can relate." For a dozen years, I'd traveled from base to base, never settling in to make any place a true home. Certainly never put love into a place like she'd done. Since I'd been back in Magnolia Ridge, I'd coasted with a rental and liked it fine, but it had temporary written all over it.

Kind of like me.

"But hey, my pop's been pestering me to help him with some updates to his house. Lucky me, my new girlfriend's ready and willing to do all that for him now."

She leaned both elbows on the table. "Aw. Do you want to get up close and personal with my nail gun?"

"Can't tell if that's flirting or a threat."

Her grin shone out again. "Can't it be both?"

I laughed, loving this night already. I'd expected a whole lot more awkwardness, but we'd fallen into a friendly groove of faux-flirtation that suited me just fine. Being Callie's pretend-boyfriend would be easier than I'd thought.

As long as everyone stayed clear on the pretend part.

callie

BEING out with Jed wasn't anything like those dates Gran had set up. No pressure, no judgment, just a fun night eating pizza and talking with my new friend. Boyfriend. *Fake* boyfriend.

Also? I'd forgotten pizza was seriously the food of the gods. I ate my entire half-pizza and a slice of Jed's buffalo chicken. By the time he drove me home, I was stuffed and just a tiny bit bloated, but I didn't regret a single bite.

"I've been meaning to ask you something."

The seriousness in his voice made my heart leap up in my throat as though I had a guilty secret he'd found out. Didn't make sense, considering all my current secrets directly involved him.

"How come you never invited me to give a presentation to your class about farming?" He turned, and the dash light revealed a giant grin, illuminating it like a spotlight.

"Oh. I didn't have time in my schedule last spring, but I just might ask you next year. I think they'd really love it."

"I do wow a crowd."

I laughed over his silliness. "I think you'll get along great with a room full of five-year-olds."

"Sounds a little shady, but I'll take that as a compliment."

"It is. Not everybody can handle the pressure."

He chuckled to himself. "I'm surprised Wade didn't flop."

"It's usually easier when it's a parent. Dylan's enthusiasm to have his dad there spread to the rest of the kids. Plus, it's hard to beat a firefighter."

He lifted a finger at me. "That's a challenge, Callie Lou. Kids love farmers. I'll blow my brother straight out of the water."

"Then I'd better pencil you in on the calendar and prepare myself to be wowed."

He glanced at me while we slowly drove through town. "You miss it during the summer, or are you glad for the break?"

"Both, really. The end of the school year is always hard. Exciting to be done, but emotional to see my students go. I miss them like crazy for the first few weeks, but right about now, I'm getting ready to fall in love with my next class, wondering what they'll be like, what the mix of kids will be. Everybody says it, but it really is such a fun age."

He had the air conditioning up, and I stretched my arms in front of me, trying to ease a smidge of the humidity from my skin even though the effect wouldn't last.

"The kindergarten rooms are getting painted and re-carpeted right now, so everything's a mess. I'll have a lot to do to put it back together in a week or two. I can't wait to go see how it looks, but it's always weird to be in an empty classroom. I like it in the craziness with the kids, when it's a little bit wild. When there's some life to it. But when there's nobody in it, it's not my favorite. It's too silent."

"I'd think silence wouldn't really be a problem with you around."

I dropped my hands into my lap, embarrassment churning

through my stomach at a hundred and fifty miles an hour. *"Do you have something to say, or do you just like to hear yourself talk?"* How much had I prattled on tonight? How often had I taken over without realizing it? Jed had obviously noticed my tendency to run my mouth. Impossible not to, really.

"I'm sorry." I tried to laugh, but the sound I made wouldn't have fooled anyone. "I was babbling."

"Callie—"

"It's okay. I know I talk a lot."

Would not tell him just how many times it'd been brought to my attention. My father, my gran and her friends, my ex-boyfriend, girlfriends, well-meaning coworkers—everybody noticed. Even my sweet, innocent students had occasionally mentioned it. *Miss Callie is chatty.* From the mouths of babes, right?

"That was a dick thing for me to say. I shouldn't have said it even as a joke, and I hate that I made you feel bad. I apologize."

His easy-going attitude had been replaced by concern, and I didn't love the change. This kind of sincerity from a guy who usually found the humor in everything only made the whole thing that much more embarrassing. I should have just laughed it off and moved on.

"You don't have to do that. I'm working on it, but sometimes, I forget."

He reached across the console and covered my clasped hands with his strong one. "You don't have to work on anything. That was rude of me, and I'm sorry I said it. Can you forgive me?"

The last guy who'd apologized to me had been a student saying sorry for calling me Mommy, so Jed's apology struck me as kind of a big deal. I appreciated it, even if I wasn't sure I deserved it. I *did* talk a lot. I couldn't count the times I'd been told it veered over into annoying. He was well within his rights to think the same thing.

"You didn't have to apologize, but I forgive you."

"Thank you."

His hand over mine squeezed once, his warmth seeping through me like a physical confirmation of his apology. Like he needed to know I was okay. Embarrassing...and extremely comforting. He let go to put his hand back on the wheel, but mine went right on tingling the whole rest of the drive to my house.

When he pulled up, all of that good sensation disappeared.

"Cars are still here." He sounded like he'd just heard the long-awaited punchline to a well-worn joke.

I should have expected it, but hadn't thought through this possibility. I hadn't thought through very much of this fake dating scenario, now that it came to it. "They're waiting for us to get back."

"I'd better walk you to the porch, then."

He got out of the truck, and before I could do it myself, he'd opened my door. Jumping out of this thing had been a whole lot easier with the curb in town giving me a shorter drop. Add it to my list of disadvantages to being fun-sized, right below reaching things off the top shelf at the grocery store—getting out of monster trucks with grace.

Holding out a hand, Jed grinned like he'd heard all the thoughts in my head. Keeping every last sassy remark to myself, I slipped my hand into his and hopped down to the street. Like a lady. I would just ignore the little chuckle in the back of his throat that said this whole production amused him more than he thought proper to say.

We walked up the path through the yard, his hand firmly holding mine. Which honestly, I liked more than *I* thought proper to say.

"Now, these ladies would never make good stalkers." He *tutted* under his breath. "No stealth at all."

I looked up, and my mouth dropped right open. All four women stood in our front window, poised just right to peer through the blinds at us. They'd turned out the light in the front room so they probably thought they'd become invisible, but the dining room light illuminated them from behind. They might as well have had their noses pressed to the glass and passed bowls of popcorn between them.

How nice would it be for the earth to swallow me up whole right about now. Would have been a good reprieve from the mortification they seemed determined to shower on me.

"They're not always this bad. They're just excited about you."

"I'm flattered."

"Don't be. That'll only encourage them."

We reached the door, where Granny and her friends would see us perfectly under the porch light. I put my back to them and faced him, figuring that of the two of us, he could probably handle their close scrutiny best. Hopefully, enduring embarrassment had fallen under some kind of Army training protocol. As expected, he pretended not to see them.

"I had a good time, thank you for taking me out," I said a little too loudly. I wasn't sure what they'd be able to hear through the window but figured better safe than sorry.

A smile worked its way across his mouth. I watched it bend and pull at his lips until I realized I was staring, and snapped my gaze back to his eyes.

"It was my pleasure, darlin'."

His low voice rippled up my back, making my heart pound a frantic beat in my chest. No part of my body had received the memo that everything he said and did was for the benefit of the four peeping Tammys behind us. My skin tingled, my stomach swooped, and my palms got all sweaty, even though none of this was really meant for them.

"Should you kiss me goodnight?" I whispered. His eyebrows ticked up at my question. *Way to be forward, Callie.* "I mean, would you, if you were out with a woman you liked?"

He scrutinized me a minute, his eyes roving over my face like he was pondering the question. Apparently thinking hard, he took his time. "I don't know. I might be too nervous."

I laughed out loud, spoiling our quiet exchange. Jed was *not* a man to get nervous about anything. Confidence radiated from him like a supernova—he definitely didn't get nervous over a goodnight kiss.

"If I really liked her," he said softly, "and wanted to see her again, I'd just feel lucky she went out with me at all. I'd probably give her a hug on the first date."

He leaned down what seemed an impossible distance—just how tall was he?—to wrap his arms around me. I'd expected him to let go again right away, considering our enthralled audience, but he held me close, his cheek warm against mine. His hands spanned my back, the weight of them drawing me in, anchoring me to him.

It'd been too long since I'd hugged someone so fully. My heart seemed to feed off the embrace, growing warmer and softer with every second that ticked by. I sighed against him like this one perfect hug had healed over a long-forgotten wound.

As if realizing he'd done his job and then some, he released me. I stepped back, my pulse thundering in my ears as I came back to reality. The bright light fell stark on his face, making him even more brutally handsome. He had no right to be this gorgeous and this good of a hugger. He could have one or the other. Greedy to take both, really.

"Goodnight, Callie."

His voice sounded rough, but no way would I convince

myself he'd been as affected by that hug as I'd been. I knew for a fact Jed Evans wasn't starved for affection like me.

"Night."

He lifted a hand, turned, and hopped off the porch. In a few long strides, he reached his truck, gave me another farewell, and drove off into the night.

The taillights on his truck might as well have been warning beacons flashing their alarm. That fluttery, cozy feeling going on in my chest needed to knock it right the heck off if we were ever going to get through the next two months without this fake relationship blowing up in my face.

callie

I NEEDED A COUPLE MORE HANDS.

Lounging on my couch, I stitched away at a new embroidery project while *Rear Window* played on the TV, my laptop open to a realtor website. I could stitch and watch a movie okay—especially when I already had the movie memorized—but adding scrolling the internet to the mix proved impossible. Maybe I could use my toes to scroll on the track pad? Probably a bad idea.

Between stitches and pivotal movie moments, I browsed houses, most of which I'd already seen. With a lot of free time over the summer, I'd spent most of it on this very website. But new listings would drop later in the week to spice things up and add to my unrealistic wish lists.

I knew more or less what my house might sell for, so ogling homes with fancy pools and walk-in pantries? Probably not the best idea. But browse I did, dreaming of some magical, imaginary day when I'd live in a house where my closet would be big enough to have an actual window. For the most part, though, I kept my searches within budget. All I asked for was a modest house with good bones and zero bad memories.

Gran joined me in the living room, and I shut the laptop with a snap. I didn't need her knowing anything about my secret searches yet. Deep down, I knew she'd understand my need to get out from under this house, but I couldn't tell her before she was ready to leave. What kind of a person would kick out their grandma?

She aimed an all-too-satisfied smile my way as she sank onto the opposite end of the couch. "Hear anything from Jed yet?"

I snorted. For all her more traditional sensibilities, she sure expected Jed to get straight to the point without delay.

"We just went on our first date last night."

As soon as I'd walked in the door, she and the others had grilled me with questions.

I'd only panicked a little since, miraculously, nobody had asked for details on anything I'd needed to make up. Where did we go? What did we have for dinner? Why hadn't I told them about that gorgeous hunk of a man?

Rita's words, not mine.

"I'm surprised he didn't ask you out for the weekend already."

She'd said as much last night, too, but Jed and I hadn't thought to arrange our next date yet. Seemed normal to me, but Gran sure hadn't taken it that way.

"He has a lot of work, and it's kind of a weird schedule over there. It might be tricky for him to plan that far in advance."

We hadn't talked much about his job, but it sounded like they harvested twelve hours a day, and if he wasn't in the orchards, he'd be helping out in their farm store. He didn't have the same kind of days off I did at the moment.

Waving a hand at me as though my protests were nothing, she went on. "If a man wants to, he will. Remember that."

"I'll stitch it and put it up on my wall." I was only sort of kidding. I'd taken to stitching phrases lately, some silly, some serious, and that one would go pretty well with my collection. I might even attribute it to her to make it extra special.

"I'm just saying, if that man likes you, he'll find a way to see you, busy schedule or not."

Way to put the pressure on, Gran.

"Well, until he fills up the rest of my summer with non-stop dates, I've still got time to help you pack."

Stomping around on thin ice, here, but I had to try.

That hand came up again. "Oh, you're busy."

I waved at the television. "I'm watching Hitchcock movies, I'm not all that busy."

"You've got your classroom to get ready and your curriculum to do."

"True, but not for a while yet. I can pack up your dishes or help you with your clothes, whatever you need."

I would have done all her packing without complaint if she'd just confirm her plans either way. Well, preferably only one way—that she intended to go to Florida with her friends. But she'd been playing it coy with me these last couple of weeks, saying nothing outright, her finger hovering over a button she refused to press.

"Don't you worry about it, little Cal."

So reassuring.

My phone buzzed on the couch next to me. Gran's eyes lit up in cartoonish hope. I glanced at the screen, and nerves flared to life in my stomach. "It's Harper."

She hefted herself off the couch. "I'm sure you two have a lot to talk about."

Yeah, we did. She probably had a specific reason in mind for the call, starting with the letter J.

Granny disappeared down the hall as I answered. "Hey, Harper."

"Hi, Callie."

Her moment of hesitation proved the call wasn't all that casual.

"How was Rumble Room last night?" Maybe I could distract her with questions of my own.

"Great, I'm getting better at the front kick-back kick combo."

"Oh, was it the cardio class last night?"

"Yeah, I think I like the workout better than the full MMA course because that way I—*hey*. Nice try. I think you know why I'm calling."

She probably would not like to know how much she sounded like Eliza just now. The youngest of the sisters could be very *in your face* with her questions and comments. I didn't really see Harper as one to snoop, but she obviously wasn't unaffected by curiosity.

"You want to tell me about Fool Hearted Memory last weekend?"

"Callie. Come on. Were you on a date with Jed last night? Or was it more of a...friend thing?"

She didn't sound as if that option were very likely. Fingers crossed Jed's *She won't want details* claim turned out to be accurate. "It was a date."

"Was it your first date? How long have you been seeing each other? Why didn't you tell me he asked you out? Or did you ask him out?"

Those nerves in my stomach multiplied and had babies, wriggling around and erasing my thoughts. What was our story again? I couldn't remember a thing. I should have written this down.

Harper groaned. "I'm sorry, I shouldn't pry. You don't have to tell me anything."

"It's okay, it's just new. There's not too much to tell yet."

"I didn't see it coming. Not in a bad way," she hurried to add. "Just unexpected, that's all."

"It's unexpected for me, too." Totally true. Before my wild *Let's fake date* idea, I never would have seen myself with Jed, either. Although, now that I thought about it, I couldn't figure out exactly why. I'd liked him well enough—he'd just seemed... out of reach.

"He's a good guy," I said more to myself than her. "When we're all together, if anyone's left out or on their own, he loops them back in. When we went on that big hike, he took up last spot to make sure nobody fell behind. When people talk, he gives them his full attention. He steps up when other guys wouldn't."

"Oh, wow," she said in a hushed voice. "You do like him."

My heart banged around in my chest, thundering its confirmation. Her soft tone told me my emphatic defense of him had been fully convincing. A-plus girlfriend material there, and totally unscripted. Which only made my heart flop around more.

"There's a lot to like."

"There is. And you're right, he is a good guy. There's a lot more to Jed than most people see, you know? He's had trouble getting on his feet since he's been home from the Army, but I think you could be good for him. I like this. For both of you."

Her encouragement soared through me, giving my awkward heart wings. But only because it would have been pretty terrible if my friends didn't support my relationship. No other reason.

"But if he breaks your heart, I'll help you egg his truck."

I laughed, grateful she had my back if worst came to worst.

No. My soaring heart came back to earth with a thud. Not *if*. When.

My relationship with Jed would be over in two months. I couldn't let myself get caught up in what ifs when I knew exactly what lay in store for us: a couple of months of fake dating followed by a very real break up.

jed

I DIDN'T CLOCK my assailants until too late.

Their whispering should have been my first clue something was up. Usually, they spoke just below the *rattling your eardrums* range. The giggling was pretty typical, although if I'd been paying more attention, I might have noticed the slightly sinister tone to it. Evil little imps plotting their offensive.

But I'd sat there like a dope, unaware of the sneak attack until I had two kids dog pile on me, tiny fists pummeling away. Dylan slammed into my shoulder trying to knock me out of the chair, but Beau got me where it hurt—my full stomach.

Little kids could be the worst.

Recovering quickly, I retaliated against my nephews, roaring and tickling both at once. They fell into my lap, laughter overtaking their drive to lay me out. For now, anyway. They'd get their second, or third, or tenth wind here in another few minutes and try to take me down again. At four and six years old, they didn't seem to need much rest.

"We got you, Uncle Jed." Dylan shouted straight into my ear to be sure I wouldn't miss it.

"Got you." Beau, his big brother's echo, grinned up at me, traces of our taco dinner still on his mouth.

"Jed, don't rile them up this late in the day," Wade called in mock defeat from across our pop's living room. "Makes it harder to get them to bed."

"I'm innocent in this one." Although, to be fair, I did instigate a good number of our wrestle-fests.

"Jed? Innocent?" June joined us and settled onto a couch. "I don't buy it."

"That ship sailed a long time ago." Ty took his place at her side.

Wasn't sure I'd seen them more than three feet apart since their engagement.

A few seconds later, the rest of the clan filed in and found seats. Pop and Marilyn had us over every couple of weeks, alternating with her two grown daughters and their families. Our newly blended clan'd had dinner together twice, but the house really wasn't big enough for the full Brady Bunch experience.

"I'd defend myself, but I know how to pick my battles." I hadn't had much innocence about me in years.

Pop eased into his recliner, working one shoulder in circles and rubbing at his muscles. Speaking of picking battles.

I couldn't say how long Pop spent in the orchards each day, but I always showed up early and still found him either out in the trees or doing walk-throughs at the roadside store. Today, I'd found him up a ladder picking fruit, right where I didn't want him to be. He wasn't infirm, but he sure did a lot of manual labor for a man who claimed he wanted to retire.

"Let me handle the harvesting, Pop. No sense you being out in the trees at seven in the morning." We employed a couple of people, but we'd generally accounted for all of us pitching in to get through the season. As Pop stepped back, I figured we'd have to adjust. If he ever stepped back, that was.

He went on digging his fingers into his flesh as though a couple minutes of massage could undo years of repetitive stress on his shoulders. "That's what happens when you only live steps from your job. You could have the same set-up if you wanted it."

The hope in that man's voice made my heart hurt.

On the opposite end of the orchards from Pop's house lay a secluded parcel of land he and mom had set aside for the next generation to take over. Wade and June had gone off and done their thing, but I'd found my way back to the farm. Here I was, the next generation, and that land still waited. And now, Pop was waiting on me.

Some days, it was like I had the weight of the whole two acres sitting across my back, urging me to act. I'd never thought empty land could be the source of so much pressure.

"It's pretty out there, but I'm not ready to think about house plans and sewer lines just yet."

Building a house on that land meant forever, and I wasn't sure yet I knew the definition of the word. I wanted to keep working on the farm, but living on it signaled an all-new commitment I didn't know if I could keep.

"You'll get there."

Felt like unfounded optimism to me.

The boys slipped off my lap and flopped on their bellies to play with die cast cars. Maisie crawled across the floor to them, blowing raspberries at an impressive volume. Wait—no. Wrong end making that sound.

Wade and Annie exchanged a look. He tilted his head toward the baby, she lifted an eyebrow in return.

"All right, I'm on it." He scooped Maisie up and tucked her beneath his arm. Seemed a dangerous position to be in, but he'd made his choices. Grabbing the diaper bag he'd left by the door, he disappeared upstairs.

Annie scooted closer to June on the couch. "How's the whirlwind wedding planning?"

My cue to tune out.

They talked for a while, throwing out words like *rustic*, *vintage*, and *lace*, but it all washed over me like a bee buzzing in my ear. Or maybe that was just the tinnitus. I'd pitch in when they needed physical help, but nobody would turn to me for opinions on wedding decor or dress styles. Lord willing.

"Just tell me when you want to clear out your barn," I said to Ty. Figured he wouldn't be much needed in their conversation, either.

"I think closer to the wedding. I'll nail something down with Booker and text you."

"Text me about it, too, won't you, Ty?" Marilyn said. "I'd still like to invite my daughter's friend to help out."

Her eyes cut to me. A sigh worked through my ribcage, emptying my lungs from the top down. At least she'd be easy to read if we ever played poker together.

"She's a real nice woman," Pop put in, no longer dancing around their goal. "She'd be worth meeting."

June glanced from me to him, and understanding dawned. "Oh, Pop, I don't think my wedding's the time to try to find Jed's true love. I want things to stay casual and low-stress."

I appreciated that she had my back. "Kind of wish you'd said that sooner. I already got a date."

It'd been a joke, a light-hearted way to let that cat out of the bag, but all five of them stared at me, mouths open. Might as well have declared I'd won the lottery. Or had leprosy.

"Who?" June asked.

Good to know Harper had kept our run-in to herself.

"I asked Callie." The longer they stared, the more agitated I got. I'd never so much as introduced a woman to the family, let alone thought to invite one to a wedding. The blowback from this fake dating experiment might wind up worse than I'd originally imagined.

"Callie?" Pop blinked like he'd stepped into bright sunlight. "Harper's friend?"

"That's her."

Wade tromped down the stairs and set his daughter next to the boys. Walking into the middle of the room, he finally noticed the shocked looks on everyone's faces. I didn't think asking a woman to a wedding warranted quite this much surprise, frankly.

"What's going on? What'd I miss?"

"Jed asked Callie to be his date to June's wedding." Annie didn't *sound* like this was such an impossible scenario, but the way she glanced at Wade told a different story.

Spousal telepathy. I didn't like it.

He whipped his head around to me.

I considered myself an easy-going guy—maybe too much, sometimes—but all this amazement worked an antsy sort of irritation through me that reverberated all the way down to my bones. "It's not so unbelievable. She's a nice girl."

"That's kind of the unbelievable part."

I hadn't thrown a punch at my brother since we were kids, but I had the sudden urge to take him outside and see what happened.

Pop shushed Wade. "Don't pay him any mind. I didn't know you were seeing Callie or we wouldn't have been trying to introduce you to someone else."

"It hasn't been all that long."

"I guess a lot more happened that night at the Hammer than you told me."

Wade sounded a touch disappointed, as though we ever talked about my relationships. Or lack of them. I'd never had all that much to report, but maybe I should have this time just to keep up appearances.

June looked between the two of us, a furrow deep between her eyebrows. "What happened at the Hammer?"

"Sounds like Jed rescued Callie from her jerk date."

Now that set them off, everyone asking questions at the same time. Except for Ty, God love him.

Sitting there, I tried to remember everything I'd told Callie about handling my family. Mostly, I'd reassured her they wouldn't turn into the Spanish Inquisition, but now, I regretted that optimism.

"Look, it's simple. We've spent some time together. I helped her fend off a not-great guy, and we started talking. That's all."

"But you invited her to my wedding already?" June said.

Okay, not all that simple. Maybe I shouldn't have led with that bit of information. "Yes, I invited her."

"You don't usually plan that far in advance, do you?"

Didn't really see the wisdom in trying to plan beyond the here and now, but admitting as much wouldn't put me ahead in this conversation. Not with a whole crowd of planners who had their eyes glued on forever.

I lifted a shoulder. "Didn't seem like something I should leave until the last minute."

"So you're seeing each other?" Wade's eyebrows raised up to his hairline.

Aside from the kids playing on the floor, everyone in the room froze, gazes stuck on me. Their silence gave the question too much weight, like my answer held unforeseen power.

"Yeah." Not eloquent, but it did the job.

They went from staring at me open-mouthed like a bunch of fishes, to brimming with pride. Seemed too much for a brand-new relationship, even if nobody knew it was doomed to end in a couple of months. Too much...but I still basked in the moment. It wouldn't last, so might as well enjoy their happiness on my behalf.

Pop grinned biggest of all, joy and relief and *hope* shining through. That smile cut me like a knife between my ribs, knowing what he hoped for Callie and me didn't have a chance.

"Bring her around to dinner one of these weeks," he said, Marilyn nodding away at his side.

"I'll see what I can do."

"So how long has all of this been going on?" Annie asked.

I paused, working out the timeline. Wasn't sure if knowing just how new things were would make their response better or worse.

Behind me, Maisie burst into wailing tears. Annie hopped off the couch and hauled her up, patting her back and making soothing sounds.

"We should probably call it a night." She nodded to Wade, who got up to gather their kids' things, along with the kids. "She's getting to that stage where nothing's going to make her happy now."

"We could try letting her bite Jed." Wade slung the diaper bag back across his shoulder. "That always cheers her right up."

I covered the wound, defending myself from another Maisie attack. "My shoulder's still bruised."

"Poor guy. I bet your Army buddies would love to hear about your injury."

"We're going to head out, too." June signaled Ty, and suddenly, everyone had got to their feet, ready to break up the party.

I took last place for the goodbye processional, but Pop pulled me aside on the porch. The others drove off into the night while I waited for whatever hammer was surely about to fall. He didn't look upset, but I knew better than to think he'd have nothing to say.

"I'm happy for you, son."

His delight served up a side of guilt that sank through my stomach. I didn't deserve the pride that shone from his eyes, even if his joy had a whole lot more to do with Callie than it did me. I'd agreed to all this for mostly selfless reasons, but it still came with a two-month expiration date. We weren't gearing up to ride off into the sunset together—we were just idling in the driveway for a bit.

"We've only been on one date, Pop. It's a little early to celebrate."

"I know. But that you'd ask her to the wedding at all says plenty." The pride dimmed a touch, swapped out for a stern look of warning I hadn't seen much since I'd turned eighteen. "I want you to be careful with her."

I'd told myself the same thing when I'd agreed to her scheme, but the warning from Pop carried a heavier weight.

"She seems like the type of girl who might get her hopes up. She could get real hurt if you're not serious, too."

Called out so openly, I couldn't come up with a defense. I'd dated around, but I hadn't left a trail of broken hearts. The women I'd seen had known I hadn't been looking for anything serious, and neither had they. But Pop didn't know any of that, and frankly, wouldn't have been much relieved to hear it. Thinking I'd just carelessly use Callie and set her aside said more about his opinion of me than I cared to know.

I tried for a grin. "How come nobody's worried about her breaking my heart?"

Pop laid a hand on my shoulder, his eyes serious as all get-out. "I'm worried about that, too, to be honest, but I don't know her well enough to give her a talking-to."

Her *nobody's going to lose their heart in this situation* remark rattled around in my brain. I wasn't looking for forever, and she had no intention of falling for me. The lack of risk should have been a relief, but tonight, it tugged at my chest like a muscle spasming out of place.

"I promise, I won't break Callie's heart."

Pop nodded once, gave my shoulder a squeeze, and released me. "Glad to hear it."

A wave of guilt crested, ready to swallow me up. I wouldn't break her heart, but when everything ended between us, it just might break my pop's.

callie

IT WOULDN'T HAVE FIT with Gran's 1950s sentiments very well, but I'd texted Jed to arrange our next date. I'd sort of hoped he might get in touch with me first, just so I wouldn't feel like I was being a pain, but after a few days of waiting—and Gran's incessant check-ins—I'd taken the leap.

Callie: What should we do for our next date?
Jed: You're captaining that ship, matey
Callie: I thought I was captaining the SS PDA
Jed: You're in charge of the whole fleet
Callie: Wouldn't that make me Admiral?
Jed: Whoa there, you're flying up the ranks
Callie: Maybe the farmers' market on Saturday? Seems like a good low-key second date
Jed: Aye aye
Callie: You're a goof. How about eleven?
Jed: See you then, Cap'n Callie

He showed up at my door Saturday morning right on time. Also on time? Gran conveniently having something urgent to do in the living room. But since every minute of this arrangement had been planned out for her sake, I wouldn't complain she'd come out to witness a little more of it.

Until she did more than just witness.

When Jed rang the bell, she managed to be closest to the door, mostly by standing around until he'd reached the porch. She welcomed him in, and he greeted her with perfect politeness. But when he turned to find me and his face lit up with a grin, all the air whooshed from my lungs.

He wore a T-shirt and jeans, his damp hair almost black, sticking up in places like he'd just run his fingers through it. Dark stubble accentuated his jawline, and his caramel-brown eyes sparkled with mischief. My stomach dove, and my cheeks warmed as though I'd never looked at a man before.

Although, let's be honest—no other man looked quite like Jed.

"Callie Lou," he said, grinning away at me.

"Jed, hi." I'd suddenly become as shy as a fifteen-year-old girl, and just as speechless. I loved the way he said his nickname for me, teasing and tender both at once.

"I expected to see you again before now."

"Gran." I goggled at her boldness.

He went right on smiling, unfazed by her prodding. "I should have been by sooner. We've been working around the clock with harvest, and I didn't want to give Callie less than my best."

She side-eyed him as though debating whether or not to accept his very sweet explanation. "Well. I suppose I can understand that. I like a strong work ethic."

"Not many slackers in the farming community."

"Is that what you plan to do for the rest of your life?"

I had to fight a rude eye-roll. Only Gran would ask a man for his fifty-year plan.

"The farm's got my name on it. Can't very well give it to someone else."

He seemed cheerful enough, but he didn't say it *was* his plan, or even what he wanted. Did he have doubts? Hopes for something else? Did he even expect to stick around Magnolia Ridge? I filed my questions away for another time.

"Where are you off to today?"

As though she didn't already know.

"Callie's taking me to the farmers' market. She said it's a must-see, and I've never gone."

"Your farm doesn't have a booth there?"

"No, ma'am, we sell out every day at our farm store. Never saw the need to add the market in town."

That seemed worthy of more than the barest hint of pride in his voice. As much of a showboat as Jed could be sometimes, he didn't have an inflated ego over the important things. What he did for his family, his farm, his country—those things he wore with a humility that, in turn, made me want to shout about him for all the town to hear.

"Linda and I are running to the market in a bit, too, we just might see you there."

Seriously? I would not react to that unwelcome piece of news, but it'd been my fault for revealing our plans to her in advance. I might as well have given her a map of our route through the market.

"Come say hi if you do." Jed turned those gorgeous eyes back to me and held out a hand. "Are you ready?"

For anything.

Ugh, no. I couldn't let my thoughts go there. Shaking it off, I slipped my hand into his and said a quick goodbye to my nosy granny.

"I didn't even ask if you had time for this today," I said

quietly as we crossed the yard. "I should have taken your schedule into consideration."

"Nah, I needed the break. I've been looking forward to this all week."

I swear I could feel his smile all the way down to the tips of my toes.

"Plus, it gave me an excuse for my weekly shower."

My laugh came out more snort than anything else. His eyes practically turned into sunbeams over that indelicate sound.

"There's a new goal for our dates. Get you to make that sound again."

When we reached his truck, he opened the door for me. Right. Time to hit another highlight to add to the snort-laugh—hitching myself up into the seat. I'd worn my cutoff jeans overalls and a tee for browsing the market, but I still didn't love this maneuver.

"You know, modern trucks come with running boards." Or so I figured. I'd never paid all that much attention, but that convenient step up apparently hadn't come standard on his older model.

"Where's the fun in that?" Jed laced his fingers together, turning his palms up, and bent low. "Do you want a boost?"

I shoved his shoulder but didn't move him an inch.

"I could lift you in."

"Like a toddler? No, thanks." Five-foot-two wasn't all *that* short. Just in relation to this ginormous truck.

"I was thinking more like a girlfriend." The light in his eyes turned warm—still teasing, but something else glowed there, too.

I'd become a little baby deer caught in the beams of his heated look, my insides tumbling as I stared at him. A bad idea to get lost there, but I indulged a minute, anyway. Hypnotists should visit Jed for lessons.

Remembering what usually happened to baby deer who got caught up staring at bright, mesmerizing lights, I pulled myself together. Glancing past him to the house, I suspected Granny watched this whole procedure from an air-conditioned perch somewhere inside. During the day, her spying could go undetected.

On one hand, she'd probably get a big thrill out of him lifting me into the truck. On the other hand, *I'd* get an even bigger thrill out of it, and I needed to keep whatever shred of sensibility I still had.

"You lift a lot of girlfriends into your truck?" *Stupid brain. Do not ask.*

"Sure. It's part of the thoughtful boyfriend package."

He stepped closer, caging me in between him and the seat behind me. He didn't get into my space, but close enough for me to realize his pale brown eyes held flecks of green. Hazel, then. Why that was important, I couldn't say, but it seemed like I should write it down somewhere for safekeeping.

"Or you can hoist yourself in while I take notes on your methods. I'm good with either one."

His saucy grin broke me out of my embarrassing trance.

"Just for that, I spitefully refuse your offer." Turning from him, I clambered onto the seat, pretending I couldn't hear him chuckling behind me.

"Spitefully, huh? I see how it's going to be." Still laughing, he closed my door and walked around to his side. He climbed in and turned to me, his eyes dancing. "You're keeping me on my toes, Callie Lou. I like it."

So did I. So, so much.

* * *

We walked the market aisles, browsing booths and ogling five hundred things we didn't need. I visited the Saturday market pretty regularly, so I had several vendors in mind to show Jed in the spirit of giving him the full experience. We didn't buy anything, but looked at everything from handmade jewelry to custom yarn wall hangings to laser-cut metal signs.

Bumping together as we wove through the crowd, our arms and hands tangled. Jed took it a step further and laced his fingers with mine, continuing on without acknowledging that small touch as though we did it every day.

I'd thought it might be weird to do this so publicly, but he pretty much made it impossible to feel awkward. I couldn't get too anxious about whoever might be watching us when he was so obviously relaxed at my side. His carefree attitude proved a nice antidote to my undercurrent of social worries.

"Eliza's booth is down that way," I said, pointing to where his cousin sold her handmade soaps. "Should we head that direction?"

"She'll waylay us all afternoon with her questions. Save it for another time?"

"Probably a good idea." Eliza wouldn't have any problem asking questions point-blank, and I still wasn't convinced I'd be able to put on a good enough show for his family. I'd sold Harper on us easily enough, but she hadn't asked me anything —I'd just...word-vomited my appreciation for Jed.

Avoiding pointed questions was probably the smarter move.

"What do you think of this?" He veered toward a booth hung with delicately knitted scarves and shawls.

"These are beautiful." I ran a hand over them, careful not to snag the perfect stitches. "I've never really got the hang of knitting."

Tugging a bright yellow shawl from its loop, he held it up in front of me at different angles. "I think this one suits you. It's sunshiney, just like you."

He looped the soft yarn around my shoulders, but shook his head when the ends hit halfway down my thighs. "We might need to take it in."

Twisting his hands, he shortened the slack on the shawl, pulling me to him. I took an awkward step forward to crash against his chest. My hands went to his stomach, bracing myself even though his tight hold on the shawl meant I wouldn't fall.

Only...the way he grinned down at me, I couldn't be sure of that.

"Whoops," he said softly, not sounding like he regretted it at all.

Without thinking, my fingers flexed against his stomach, his warm muscles firm beneath his T-shirt. And oh man, those muscles. Their gentle ripple beneath my fingertips made my own stomach twist and dip.

"I like it even better like this."

His voice had gone so sinfully low, I felt it in my bones like a bass beat. I swallowed hard, willing myself to keep it together, but my eyes dropped to his mouth anyway. Full lips curved at the edges into a smirk at my obvious staring. I licked my lips, because I was definitely *not* keeping it together.

He leaned closer, his face gliding past my mouth, past my cheek. The air stopped up in my lungs, my body frozen with anticipation. His breath on my ear rocked a shiver through me. Was he—was he going to kiss me like this, here in the middle of the farmers' market? I really didn't care about the crowds at that point, I just wanted him to do it. Wanted to feel that press of his lips against the shell of my ear.

Now, please.

"Your grandma and her friend are watching us."

My poor brain struggled with that whispered sentence for five full seconds before it made sense. Understanding broke over me like I'd jumped into an ice-cold lake. *Oh.* This had all been for show. Part of the thoughtful boyfriend package. I'd asked him to play make-believe with me, and now, I'd got it in full.

Really, I should be grateful Jed was so convincing.

I would absolutely forget how totally I'd been convinced. My cheeks had never felt so uncomfortably hot. But hey, in for a penny, right? Gran and Linda were probably still watching.

I ran my hands from his stomach up to his hard chest, and if that journey would forever be etched in my brain, so be it. He drew back a little, looking down at me with a question in his eyes. I ticked my shoulders up because I had no more clue what I was doing than he did. My entire plan apparently consisted of caressing his chest.

Not a bad plan, but not a very thorough one, either.

"It's a lovely shawl, isn't it?"

The vendor's chilly voice broke us apart. Jed released me and replaced the shawl where he'd found it. Meanwhile, I pretended my internal temperature hadn't just dropped a million degrees from the crush of disappointed hopes.

"You have really beautiful work," I told her. "Really impressive. And this yarn is so soft."

"Thank you." She sounded like she knew already she wouldn't be making that sale, despite all our romantic nonsense with her product.

"I crochet a little bit, but I can't knit at all. Even then, I always get the ending stitches wrong, and whatever I'm making gets smaller and smaller until it disappears." I laughed, but she didn't seem to find my story all that funny. Maybe she didn't crochet. "I'm bad at counting out the stitches in every row, and that's never a good sign your work's going to turn out right. I'm a teacher, so you'd think I could sort out the numbers, but nope."

She watched me like I had a screw loose.

"Sorry, I'm babbling. Have a good day, I hope you make a lot of sales!"

I grabbed Jed's hand, bolting away from the booth and hopefully far from wherever Gran and Linda were. Marching us between shoppers, I broke out into a sweat not entirely due to the sweltering summer sun. I hated acting like a fool, and I'd just done exactly that in front of Jed. Again. Ugh.

"Are you hungry?" We'd reached a cluster of food trucks where fifty different smells assaulted our senses. Spicy, sweet, tangy—a little bit of everything filled the air. "Tacos? Corn-dogs? Chili?"

"Mmm, chili." He rubbed his stomach. "What could be better than a hot bowl of chili on a hundred-degree day?"

He tugged at my hand, letting me in on his joke. The brittle embarrassment inside me softened some, and I exhaled a laugh.

"Ice cream?" I said.

"Now you're talking."

He bought us scoops of specialty hand-crafted ice cream while I chewed on a thumbnail when he wasn't looking. I was still worked up over letting myself get...well, so worked up, and I didn't want to know if he'd realized it. Probably hadn't. We'd agreed to pretend to date, so I needed to act the part. But if he *had* realized, the rest of our fake relationship could turn all sorts of awkward. If I didn't want to lose all my goals here, I needed to get a grip.

We walked away from the market while we ate our cones, and the crowd thinned down to more typical Saturday after-noon sidewalk traffic. Jed nodded toward an open bench.

"Do you want to sit for a while?"

I slumped down, my bare thighs grateful the wrought-iron

bench had been in the shade all morning. Finally relaxing a little, my heart rate and my thoughts settled back down to normal levels. Savoring the sweet-salty crunch of the cool candy bar confection I'd chosen, I made a sound in the back of my throat.

He turned to me, eyebrows raised.

"I'm sorry, it's just really good ice cream." Maybe not so good I needed to moan over it, but it'd been a wild morning.

"I didn't complain. I encourage your yummy sounds."

I rolled my eyes, nudging him with my elbow. "Shush."

He took a bite of his cone, licking his lips afterward in a truly scandalous way. I'd never stared quite so intently at someone's mouth before. My insides heated, and my heart rate spiked all over again. His eyes darted to me, his lips lifting into a little smirk.

Just great. Jed's attractiveness already sat at unhealthily high levels, but if he was going to add a little extra *zhuzh* to it just for fun, we'd have widespread carnage. Women for fifty miles around would swoon without knowing why.

"How's your strawberry buttermilk?" I needed a distraction. Ice cream flavors probably wasn't the best option, but anything would help.

"Perfect combo of sweet and tart."

"I can never decide if I want fruit or chocolate. Fruit flavors are light and bright, you know? And I can eat a lot before I regret it. But chocolate is just so decadent and rich, it's hard to resist. Even if later, I'll feel like I ate a whole tub of it." I started crunching on my cone. "Sorry," I said around the bite. "I'm babbling about ice cream."

"Can I ask you a question?"

The softness in his voice made me sit up straighter. Oh boy. Here it comes. He'd noticed the wanton longing in my eyes during the shawl debacle and wanted to talk it out. Remind me of our arrangement, and my promise not to fall for him. Something that carried the words *absolutely not* with it.

"Okay."

"Why do you do that? Why do you always say you're babbling?"

Oh. The tautness inside me eased up. Much better than asking about the way I'd lightly groped him earlier. "I was talking a lot."

"I didn't complain."

"I know, but it's an annoying habit. People don't like it."

"What people?"

I pointed vaguely at the market crowds. "People."

"They didn't complain, either."

Sighing, I crumpled up my cone's paper wrapper. I didn't know exactly where to start here, but figured I'd go with the glaring choice.

"My college boyfriend wasn't the greatest, okay? It took me a long time to realize it, since I'd never dated in high school."

"I have a hard time believing that."

"Believe it." I lifted a shoulder. "I wasn't a pariah or anything, but nobody asked me out. So when Andrew did my second year in college, it was exciting and new. I let a lot of stuff slide because I thought it was normal."

He shifted toward me, giving me his full attention. "What kind of stuff?"

"Well...his compliments always came with criticism. Like, 'You look so good in that dress, have you ever thought about losing some weight?'. Or 'You're smarter than I thought' when I did something really obvious."

Jed's mouth thinned, and a line formed between his eyebrows where they pulled together.

"I realize now he probably thought if he pointed out my flaws, I wouldn't think I could leave him. Who else would want me, right? I guess there's a name for that dating tactic and everything. But I didn't know that then, I just knew he left me confused and scrambling to make him happy."

Strange to look back and think a twenty-year-old guy could have had such a hold on me. I'd internalized his half-insults, his jabs about my chosen major or classes, his jokes at my expense that I'd tried to laugh over even though they hurt. He hadn't been worth a minute of my time, and I'd dated him almost two semesters.

"His biggest thing was that I talked too much. Sometimes, he'd yawn really wide in the middle of a story, or just cut me off entirely. Or he'd listen, and then instead of responding to what I'd told him, he'd say I must really like hearing my own voice." I scratched at the fraying hem of my shorts. "He'd tell me I was embarrassing myself."

Never mind how often he'd intentionally embarrassed me in front of his friends.

"Anyway," I said, pulling myself back into the present. "I'm long past everything with him, but that part kind of stuck. I mean, I do talk a lot. He wasn't exactly wrong. You said so, too."

"Callie."

Jed's tender voice curled around my heart like a bear hug. He slid closer on the bench and took my hand in his. His strength and warmth worked together to chase away the bad memories of Andrew. I didn't revisit them a lot, but when they came up, they could hit hard.

"You can talk as much as you please, about whatever you please. Always. Not just with me, but *especially* with me." He squeezed my hand, tucking it carefully inside his. The small gesture made me feel protected and cared for instead of ridiculous and dumb. "I meant what I said as a joke, truly, but I'll never say anything like that to you again."

"Thank you."

"That guy sounds like a real ass. How'd you get rid of him?"

I couldn't help the tiny smile that peeked out. "I had a little help. I'd been seeing a campus therapist, mostly because of my grief about losing my mom. But he'd pulled my confidence down to zero that year, and she'd noticed. When we finally talked about him, she gently pointed out how his comments had never been designed to help me improve myself, the way he always claimed. And I started to realize how badly he'd affected me. I wasn't sure how to break up with him, though—I mentioned before I hate conflict. I'm the kind of person who'll eat the wrong meal the waitress brought rather than complain."

I tried to laugh, but he didn't seem to find that amusing.

"Anyway, at the end of that year, I declared early childhood education as my major. I was already taking the classes, but I made it official. He said he wasn't sure he could date somebody with such low ambitions, and I saw my chance. I said if that was how he felt, we should stop dating, for his sake."

"Oh, how the turn tables."

I smiled wider. "Nice *Office* reference. Yeah, he tried to backtrack, but I held him to it, said I didn't want my low ambitions to negatively affect him, so the best thing would be if he just never spoke to me again."

"You badass."

"It didn't go as easily as all that, but once he realized I was really done, he moved on. My therapist and I had some new things to talk about for a while, but college got better after that."

"'Low ambitions'." Jed shook his head, eyes stormy. "Any idea where I can find good old Andrew these days?"

Understanding his veiled threat, I laughed. Then I all-out giggled. Maybe not the best response, but I couldn't hold it in. Leaning against him, I felt lighter than I had in a long time. I hadn't told anyone else about Andrew, thinking the story could only make me look like a dummy for putting up with a guy who'd insulted me for so long. But Jed hadn't judged me a bit. He'd listened, comforted, and lightly threatened my ex.

My heart swelled fit to burst, glad to have a man like Jed by my side. For however long I had him. It wouldn't be very long, I knew that. But maybe it would be enough.

"He's not worth it," I said, laying my head on his shoulder.

He pressed a kiss to the top of my head. "Nope. But you are."

callie

I FOLLOWED the directions Harper had given me to Jed's family farm, squinting so I wouldn't miss the sign she'd mentioned even though my GPS gave me constant progress updates. A little whirl of nervous excitement skimmed around in my stomach, but that made sense since I was on my way to ambush a guy at his house with baked goods.

Actually, not his house—his dad's. By all rights, I was about to ambush Jed at his work, which wasn't any better than turning up to his house uninvited. But I hadn't been able to get this idea out of my head, so I'd followed through, figuring I could deal with the fallout later.

According to the GPS, that fallout would come in approximately one thousand feet.

I turned onto the property and found a short drive leading to a pretty farmhouse. Peach trees in neat rows came right up to the yard, and a big storage barn sat a little farther in the distance. I'd passed the Evans Orchards farm store on my way here, thinking the personal visit more casual.

My gut didn't feel all that casual when I parked in front of the farmhouse, churning away like it could turn my nerves into butter.

Callie: Are you close to your dad's house? I brought you a treat

A truck sat in the shade of an ash tree, but not Jed's. I didn't even know for sure he'd be out here today, I'd just assumed. The longer I sat in front of his dad's house peering out at the orchards like I was waiting for a glimpse of a Sasquatch between the trees, the more ridiculous I felt.

Jed: My head is spinning with ideas. Be there in five

Right as I exhaled my relief, Jed's father walked out onto his front porch. Kind of a relief-terror one-two punch.

He hunched down until he could see me where I still sat in my car like a creep. This was his house, after all—of course he'd want to know who had turned up and then didn't bother knocking at the door. When recognition dawned, a huge smile popped onto his face, reassuring me my sudden presence out here wasn't totally unwelcome.

Finally kicking my brain into gear, I climbed out of my car.

"Well, Callie, it's good to see you again."

His apparent delight at my visit wrapped me up like a warm, cozy blanket. I'd only ever known him from a bit of a distance so far, but he sounded as though he'd been waiting all morning for me to arrive.

"Hi, Mr. Evans. I just stopped by to bring something to Jed. I texted him, and he's on his way here."

"What'd you bring for him?"

I wasn't sure I'd ever seen him smile so wide, like this conversation already made his whole week.

I opened up the back door of my car and grabbed the glass dish where I'd nestled it in a bed of fluffy towels behind the driver's seat. It would have spoiled the visit pretty quick to find a couple of pounds of cobbler all over the floor.

Nudging the door closed again, I held the casserole dish up as evidence. "Just a little treat."

"You know the way to a man's heart. Come in, no sense in you waiting out here in the heat. And please, call me Clint."

He opened his front door and beckoned me inside. Chill air conditioning cooled the sticky sweat that had pooled at my lower back while I'd sat in the car, and I said a silent prayer of thanks to whoever had invented that wonderful machine.

"Why don't you set it here on the table." He knocked his knuckles against the dining room table, peering at the dish I put down. "It smells delicious."

I lifted the lid to show off the still-warm cobbler, and berry-scented steam wafted up in a little cloud. "Seemed like a good day to bake."

"That's awfully sweet of you."

Hopefully, Jed would be equally as pleased with my gift, because his dad positively glowed.

"Well, I have the time."

The long summer breaks took some getting used to. I worked dang hard during the school year, but summer idleness could set me a little adrift. Owning up to my free time—especially to someone who worked so hard all summer—I felt a bit like the grasshopper talking to the ant. Like I played all day while they got so much done.

"How's your break treating you?" he asked.

"Oh. It's been...good."

His sharp eyes seemed to soften over my hesitation. "That's not a ringing endorsement. Something troubling you?"

"Well..." I wasn't quite sure how to answer, but Clint had

such a warm, benevolent way about him, I didn't want to blow off his question. "My grandma is supposed to move next month. A big retirement kind of move. It's hard to imagine not having her around, but she's sort of put it on hold. I don't know how to encourage her without feeling like I'm forcing her."

I hadn't expected her to start packing again the minute I started dating Jed, but so far, she'd put off all my offers to help. She hadn't even mentioned the move again, which only made me antsier to get her in gear.

"Growing pains are bittersweet," he said. "We want to move on, but we don't want to leave anyone behind. We can get caught swimming upstream, afraid to let go because we can't see what's around the bend."

He tilted his head down and narrowed his eyes at me with such a meaningful look, I saw where Jed had got ninety percent of his DNA. Clint's eyes were blue, but they were remarkably similar to my fake boyfriend's.

"But just between you and me, nobody else can let go for you."

"I know. I just want her to go be happy with her friends." I'd said it so many times, it felt like a mantra, *Go be happy, Go be happy.* "She's given me so much, it's time for her to relax and not worry about me."

He laughed, scraping a hand down his silver stubble. "I'll tell you right now, that'll never happen. We always worry about the ones we love. She'll be just as worried about you wherever she moves to as she is here, I guarantee it. I never worried about my kids less when they were in Austin or Georgetown or Afghanistan."

The thought of Jed in Afghanistan shuddered through me. I thanked the good Lord he'd come home safe.

"I'm just a farmer, I'm not an expert on these things," Clint said. "But I think it's normal to have mixed feelings about good things. That includes you, too."

I wasn't sure how he'd seen my uncertainty, since I didn't like to see it myself. "I think I've been feeling like if I'm not completely happy about her move, I'm being selfish."

I wanted her to move, make no mistake. But that didn't mean I never wandered through the house missing her in advance as I thought how different it would be with her gone, what it would be like when she was no longer a room away. But Clint was right—I could feel all those jumbled emotions and still know her move would be the best for both of us.

"I don't know you that well, Callie, but I've yet to see a selfish act from you."

I grinned. "I'm saving up all my bad traits for when you know me a lot better."

He chuckled over my little joke. "I'll be waiting."

Jed walked in the front door and—okay, wow. Everyday, rumpled Jed proved pretty delicious, but head-to-toe dirty, T-shirt clinging to him from sweat, mildly dangerous-looking Jed? Devastating.

My breath checked out as he stomped his work boots on the mat outside before crossing the room to us. He grinned, his white teeth shining on his dusty face, and my poor heart did cartwheels. Girls who swooned over men in suits could have them—give me this dirty farmer any day.

"Callie Lou," he said in that cozy way that made my insides turn to goo. "What brings you here today?"

"I..." Couldn't really remember, what with my eyes devouring him and begging for more. What, Callie? What brought you to his dad's house, giving you this front-row view of his glorious form? *Find words, brain.*

His grin tilted to the side, and I loved the sight, but that smirk snapped me out of my dumbfounded staring. I cleared my throat like a normal person and gestured at the casserole dish behind me. "I made a cobbler. So I brought it here. For you. To eat."

I should have been more specific when I asked my brain for words. From the way he watched me, my fumbling response amused him to pieces.

Shaking off the nonsense, I tried again.

"I mean, I was baking this morning, and I wanted to bring one of the cobblers to you. This one's blackberry, I hope you like those. I also made a peach one, but I figured bringing a peach cobbler to a peach farmer would be too meta, so I saved it for me."

"I love blackberries, thank you. I can't wait to dig into this." He eyed the cobbler appreciatively, but then his gaze snapped back to me. "Wait, where'd you get the peaches for your cobbler? Are you cheating on me with a competitor's peaches?"

He shook his head in pretend disappointment, and his teasing made my stomach flip. Turned out I liked dirty farmers and jokesters. Learned something about myself every day.

"I stopped by your market here yesterday and got a couple of pounds. I'm no traitor."

I'd waited in line thirty minutes, but it'd been worth it. I'd already eaten two and could safely say the next time someone asked me what was one food I could eat for the rest of my life, I'd have my answer.

"Darlin', you ever want peaches, you come straight to me. I'll pick you a whole bushel of the most delicious fruit you ever tasted."

The mischievous look in his eyes proved impossible to resist. I needed to give him a little of his sass back. "A bushel sounds like too much. Maybe I'll just take a peck."

"Oh, you want a peck?" He tipped his head down, his sly

grin hinting at naughtiness. "I'll give you all the pecks you can handle."

Chuckling snapped us out of our weirdo flirting over forms of fruit measurement. Right. Because his dad still stood here, watching us like he'd just found his new favorite TV show.

Jed and I relaxed some. We didn't move apart, but we no longer leaned into each other's spaces so obviously. As if that would erase the last few minutes of sauciness from Clint's mind.

"Well, I don't want to keep you, I know you're busy out there." I gestured vaguely and turned toward the door.

"You're leaving already?"

His surprise stopped me in my tracks. I'd meant to minimize the time I took him away from his work, not prolong it. "I don't want to waste your time."

"I don't see that ever happening."

"Why don't you show Callie the property?" Clint said.

"Show me the farm?"

I probably sounded pathetically eager. I wasn't sure I'd ever had a tour of a farm before but suddenly I had a desperate urge to see this one. Especially if one particular farmer were my tour guide.

"He can show you that on the way, too. I think you'll like the property." He turned to Jed, nodding like it'd all been decided. "Take a blanket out there and enjoy some time in the shade for a bit. I'll cover things here."

Jed's mouth twisted. He so rarely wore anything other than a bright smile, this disappointed look didn't quite fit him right.

"Don't work too hard."

Clint made a small sound of disgust. "I've been working this farm since before you were born. I think I'll do all right."

Jed shot him a stern look but seemed to accept his defeat. Gesturing for me to follow, he crossed the room and opened the door. As soon as I walked through, he called back to his dad.

"I hope I can trust you with my cobbler."

Clint held his hands up, sidestepping away from the table and the precious dessert.

Outside, Jed looked me over, his eyes warming but not lingering in any one place. "My truck's over at the store, we'll have to take an ATV out to the property. Might get a little dirty. Are you sure you want to?"

"I'm not fancy. My T-shirt and shorts can handle it."

"Okay. ATV's in the shed out there." He gestured to the storage barn I'd seen, and started walking. "Hope Pop didn't give you a hard time while you waited for me."

"Not at all. I like him. Being around your pop...it's nice. I never really had that. Not that I remember much of, anyway."

He turned to me, his pace slowing. "What happened with your dad? If that's okay to ask."

I kicked a rock and tracked its progress as it skipped in the grass that grew wild between the farmhouse and the storage barn. "He left my mom when I was nine. Things weren't great before that, but one day, he just...took off."

I skimmed my hand in the air, gesturing into the distance.

"You haven't heard from him again in all that time?"

We reached the barn he'd indicated. Just inside the door sat a red all-terrain vehicle with a soft, sherpa-like material covering the large seat. I gripped the handle just to give me something to do, the rubber warmed by the sun.

"Nope. I mean, Mom did, enough for them to get divorced. Child support came through, so he didn't go total deadbeat. But he never got in touch with me. I used to check the mailbox like it'd become my religion, hoping for a letter, a postcard. Anything."

Seeing that mailbox empty day after day for years on end

had kept those wounds open, fresh slices on a cut that didn't want to heal. I didn't like thinking about those early years too much, when I'd still believed he might come home to us.

"Eventually, I learned better than to hope to hear from him."

I'd considered looking him up online—try to find out where he was, if he'd married again, if I had half-siblings out there somewhere. I'd never checked, though. His total indifference to me had solidified mine for him. Wherever he'd gone over the years, my address had always stayed the same.

"Oh, darlin'."

Jed's tender expression made a lump leap up into my throat. I didn't feel much when I talked about my dad anymore, but his sweet concern had me on the verge of tears. Like he really cared for me, and hurt simply because *I'd* been hurt.

"I'd offer to hug you," he said, "but I'm covered in dirt."

Nice try, farmer. I wanted that hug.

"I'm not fancy."

He stepped closer and wrapped me up in his arms, nestling me to him. One hand moved up and down my back in slow, soothing strokes, and I could have purred like a cat. He smelled of dirt, the sweet scent of peaches, and, yes, a teensy note of sweat, but I didn't care a bit. Actually, I kind of liked how he smelled, which seemed the strangest of all. Looking good dirty? Made sense in a primal way. Smelling good dirty? Hello, weirdo.

After a minute, he released me, keeping a light hold on my biceps. "I'm sorry he wasn't there for you."

"It's okay." I loved his sweetness, but absolutely did not want him thinking of me as this sad, damaged girl. Yes, my dad had left us. Yes, I'd dated a loser in college. But neither of those things said a whole lot about *me*. "I'm sorry I got sidetracked when I was trying to say that I like your dad. He seems like a really good father."

Jed let go of my arms, seemingly content I wasn't about to fall into a million pieces. "He is. A mite pushy now and then, and it'd be nice if he sorted out this whole retirement situation, but yeah. He's a good father. I probably don't tell him enough."

He looked off into the distance as if he could see his dad back at the house. Frowning a touch, he seemed almost sad, but when he turned back to me, his eyes lit with mischief again. That tiny look sent my senses into overdrive.

"Are you ready to go for a ride?"

jed

CALLIE HOPPED straight onto the ATV as soon as I suggested it, her hands on the grips testing them out. "I've never ridden one before. Are they very hard to drive?"

"Nope. Just climb aboard and go." I moved into the shade of the barn and shuffled a few things around until I found a blanket. A little dusty, but good enough for sitting on. Had to admit, Pop's idea of settling in for a bit with Callie was a good one. Wouldn't expect to spend too long out there in this heat, but it'd be alright in the shade. "You'll do great."

"Me?" Her warm brown eyes turned into sunbursts. "You'll let me drive it?"

"Sure." I set the folded blanket on the seat and climbed on behind her. A bit of a squeeze—the utility ATV wasn't built for two—but I couldn't say I minded. "Riding ATVs is most fun for the driver."

She looked over the buttons and dials like she was trying to memorize them. "What do I do?"

I wrapped around her from behind to give a quick lesson on the controls. Wasn't much to know for a two-mile trip on a flat, dry dirt road. Sitting this close to her, though, I had an urge to drag out the tutoring as long as possible. She smelled like oranges, fresh and delicious, and I had to stop myself from breathing her in like a creep.

Other than some hand-holding and a couple of hugs, we hadn't touched much yet in our fake dating foray. But this...her back against my chest, my arms caging her in...this could get interesting.

She turned a touch, her face a breath away from mine. Close enough to nuzzle against her cheek. Close enough to taste those lips. She froze as if she'd heard all those thoughts, and my senses came back to me.

Reining myself in, I shifted back on the ATV, figuring she had all the info she needed. "Turn the key and fire her up."

The engine purred to life, and Callie laughed in response. She twisted around to see me. "Are you seriously going to let me drive this on my own?"

Her wide grin showed exactly how she felt about the prospect. No way would I want to stop her now.

Leaning back, I curled my fingers around the storage rack. "I'll just be relaxing back here if you need me."

She turned forward again, took hold of the hand grips, and released the parking brake like I'd showed her. Her thumb went to the throttle lever, and I braced myself, having a good hunch what would come next.

She pressed down, the engine revved, and she released the throttle again, lurching us forward about three feet.

"Oh, crap!" Laughing, she rolled out her shoulders, hyping herself up to try again. "Okay, I'll get it."

"I know you will, darlin'. Just give it a soft, steady touch."

She shook her head, turning so I could see her profile. "Don't make it sound so sexy."

I leaned closer to speak in her ear. "You want to caress the throttle using firm but gentle pressure—"

She hitched her elbow back, giving my stomach a light tap. "Hey, hey, this ATV ride is strictly G-rated."

I gave her space again, shifting farther back on the seat. "I never agreed to that."

Swiveling my way, she grinned. "Maybe PG-13."

Didn't have much time to consider the benefits of that adjustment before she'd hit the throttle again. This time, she kept it low and steady, letting us pick up speed. Relatively speaking. Eight miles an hour wouldn't break the sound barrier, but it got us moving through the trees well enough.

"It's so pretty out here!" she shouted back to me.

I guess it was. I'd never really looked at the orchards as scenery. A place of work, yes, a place I'd needed to escape as a teen, absolutely. Now, I saw a checklist of tasks—pruning, spraying, harvesting—more than the trees themselves.

But it *was* pretty, cruising through the rows of green, with the rich brown earth underneath. Bright blue sky and wisps of cotton candy clouds spread thin overhead. Smelled good, too, the air filled with the sweet scent of peaches warming in the sun. I spent most of every day out here, but I hadn't ever viewed it quite like this.

Callie laughed every time we jostled over a bump in the path like we were on a rollercoaster at an amusement park. I directed her to take a couple of turns until finally, the rows of peach trees were replaced by soapberries and red oaks. Driving beneath the branches of a sycamore, we reached an open area covered in long grass and a few stray scrub brushes.

She slowed the machine to a crawl. "Are we here?"

"We're here. You can park us anywhere."

Cranking the handlebars to bring us back around to some shade, she got the ATV situated beneath a tree and shut it down. We climbed off, and she wandered around in the grass that came up past her ankles. I let her explore while I shook the dust off the blanket and spread it out. Would have been nice to have a picnic lunch ready, too. Next time.

I joined her in the grass, where she spun a circle with her arms wide, one flowy skirt short of breaking into a *Sound of Music* chorus.

"It's beautiful out here." She stopped her spinning and faced me, lifting both hands up to her forehead to shade her eyes from the sun. "What's it for?"

I beckoned her back into the shade before we got sunburned for our troubles. We sat on the blanket facing the grassy, open acres, the ATV engine *tick-tick-ticking* as it cooled down. She pulled her ankles up to sit crisscross—I stretched my legs out long and leaned back on my hands.

"Mom and Pop set the space aside when they planted this end of the orchards. It was meant to be for Wade, so when he took over the farm there'd be room for him to build a house. Pass the land and the business on to the next generation."

She turned to me, her eyes soft. "But he's not taking over the farm, is he?"

"Nope. He found his calling in firefighting. Then I went off to the Army, and June moved on to Austin. She's back, and pretty well sorted out now, too."

"What about you? Are you sorted out?"

Her gentle question snaked through me, only because I didn't have an answer.

"I'm working on the farm, anyway. As soon as I came home again, Pop let me know I could have this land to build on whenever I wanted it."

A generous gift, considering what two acres of land could go for around here.

Callie stared straight ahead, a smile tugging the corner of her mouth. "I can see it. A modern farmhouse with a wraparound porch. Or a craftsman bungalow with a big back porch for a bed swing. Maybe a cozy little ranch."

"With a porch?"

"Obviously."

I made a sound of agreement and laid back, resting my head on my laced fingers, elbows to the sides. Sparrows whistled in the trees, and I closed my eyes, trying not to imagine Callie's vision for the property. Her enthusiasm snuck in anyway.

"Why haven't you built a house out here yet?" she asked.

"I guess I'm just waiting for the right time."

An excuse, but I didn't have a better answer. I had the money—I'd never been a big spender, and I'd come out of my stint in the Army with a decent nest egg. But the house and the land and the job all rolled together in one neat package, and I didn't know yet if I was ready to sign on that line.

The blanket rustled, and I cracked an eye open to see she'd laid out next to me, propped up on her side.

"I can't wait to move into a new house. Start from scratch, where every room has endless possibilities, and I can turn it into anything I want."

"You and June must get along great." I closed my eyes again, letting the heat of the day relax my muscles. Probably not a good idea to get used to siestas during harvest, but I had a few minutes to spare.

"I haven't asked her that much about decorating yet. I don't want her to think I'm weird."

I rolled to face her and laid my head on my bicep. "She wouldn't think you're weird, she'd be glad to talk to someone as enthusiastic about houses as she is."

She ran a hand over the plaid blanket between us. "Maybe."

"What would you do if you had a house to decorate from the bare bones?"

Sunlight dappled over Callie's bright smile. "I'd go bold.

Color everywhere, rich jewel tones on the walls and furniture. Big patterns. Maybe some really striking wallpaper in a powder room or something. Not anything too busy or hectic, but definitely no beige or gray."

I closed my eyes again. "I like that for you."

Bright, bold colors suited her.

"What's your house like?" she asked.

"All beige and gray."

She laughed. "I don't believe you. You're not a beige kind of guy."

My eyes popped open. "No? I've been told I'm quite drab."

"You're such a liar. Nobody sees you and thinks drab."

I could say the same about her. Still couldn't understand how she'd flown this far under the radar in town, even if the selfish side of me was glad of it. From her dark brown eyes that noticed everything to her soft, full lips, every part of her appealed on a visceral level. The deeper parts—her endless optimism, her infectious enthusiasm, her genuine love of life— well, let's just say, a guy could fall pretty hard for Callie Matheson.

"It's unfair, really," she said. "You're so good-looking, it's just gross."

I blew out a laugh. "You sure know how to give a compliment."

"It's true, though. Your hair looks good no matter how messy it is. Your eyebrows are stupidly thick."

She ran a finger over one eyebrow, and I struggled not to lean into that small touch.

"Your eyelashes are the whole reason mascara was invented. Your jawline is romance-novel perfect." She lightly pinched my chin, punctuating her rundown of my features. "Your only aesthetic flaw is maybe your eyes are a little too close together."

That earned another laugh. "My eyes are too close together?"

"I only said maybe."

Her gaze went up to my hair, and her fingers followed, pulling through the strands in light strokes that made my stomach flip. Laying on the blanket with a few inches of nothing between us, all her casual touching could get real dangerous real quick.

"Even these gray hairs look good."

This woman could never seem to decide if she wanted to boost my ego or crush it like a bug. I'd found a few gray hairs scattered over my temples, the first dash of salt into my pepper. Hadn't thought anyone else had noticed yet.

"A nicer girlfriend wouldn't have pointed them out."

She ran her fingers through my hair again, her eyes trailing their path. "I like them."

When she pulled her hand away to place it back on the blanket between us, I felt like I'd lost something I wanted back.

"Even scars would probably look good on you, but you don't have a single one."

She had no idea.

"I have scars." I'd meant to treat it like a joke, but old pain laced through my voice against my will. Her face twisted, eyebrows pinching together. We both knew I meant the kind of scars you couldn't see.

"I'm sorry, that was so thoughtless, I shouldn't have—"

I put my hand over hers and held it tight. "Don't apologize. You didn't say anything wrong."

"I'm sorry," she said again. "For...whatever happened."

She didn't ask for more, but the question hung silent in the air. She'd been so open with me from day one, didn't seem right to shut her out, no matter how little I wanted to talk about this.

I slipped her hand in mine closer to my chest, like it'd give me courage.

"I lost a good friend. We were fighting together. He went down, and I didn't. To this day, I couldn't tell you why."

We weren't supposed to ask *Why me?*—a futile question that never solved anything. Didn't stop me from asking myself a hundred times a day the first weeks after. Years, maybe. Even now, if I thought about it too long, the grief could suck me down to that dark place where I asked myself why I still lived but he'd died. Why I got more days and his had come to an end.

If I could have saved him. That was the real question that kept me up at night.

"He was engaged. Had all these plans for his future, the family they wanted, what he'd do when he got out of the Army. And then...it was all gone."

I'd never been good at thinking ahead, but then and there, I truly saw the futility of it. Everybody who died had had plans, once. Plans didn't promise anything.

"Jed." Her soft whisper squeezed between my ribs to pierce my heart. I'd never thought it had a bullseye, but she'd found it. She twisted our hands to hold mine more firmly. "I'm so sorry."

I ticked my head to the side as if I could shake all her apologies away. "Comes with the territory."

Couldn't very well participate in combat without witnessing the results. Wasn't always death, but casualties were part of the deal. I'd seen my fair share of suffering on both sides. Nothing I'd ever want to burden her with. Even what I'd said already felt like too much.

What was I doing? Alone with Callie out here, and I'd opted to bring up my losses. Not the smoothest of moves.

"I have physical scars, too, but I don't think about those much. But I'll show them to you sometime if you ask real nice." I waggled my eyebrows at her, trying to move past the somber mood I'd brought down on us like I'd pulled a storm cloud into a clear blue sky.

She fixed me with her stern little look, fighting laughter. "I'll keep that in mind." The laughter didn't last, and her expression turned more sober. "I'm sorry about your friend."

I took a long, slow breath, her soft condolences wrapping around my heart. "I am, too."

"I'd hug you, but we're kind of in an awkward position for it."

Not awkward. Hugging Callie lying down like this? I could think of a hundred other descriptions for that, not one involving awkwardness. Perfection sat right at the top. I'd tuck her right up to me, nestle her in close, and hold on tight.

And then? Nothing but danger ahead.

"We should probably go back, anyway." Sighing, I curled upright, then stood. "I've slacked off long enough. Pop'll probably send out a search party after us in a few more minutes."

Fat chance. More likely, he'd encourage us to stay out here as long as possible.

She sat up, too, and I reached a hand down to help her up. As soon as she got to her feet, she stepped closer to slip her arms around me. I returned her embrace, tucking my chin down to touch the top of her head, mentally fortifying the walls around those thoughts I never liked to stray into for very long. I wasn't one for veering into the morose, but certain memories handed me an express ticket.

Somehow, this hug went a long way to easing that. Didn't understand it, but I wouldn't question it, either.

When she pulled back, I suspected she wasn't quite ready to let the subject go. I appreciated her concern, but I'd delved into that sadness enough for one day. Any more, and I wouldn't be able to get to sleep tonight. I'd been on a streak of good nights lately and wanted to keep it that way.

"Ready to drive us back?" I asked before she could voice the question forming in that sweet, curious brain of hers.

She hesitated, but seemed to understand what I needed. "Sure."

"Maybe you'll try popping a wheelie this time."

She laughed and rolled her eyes at me. "I'm going to catch air over every bump in the road."

"Now you're talking."

"I might even hit ten miles an hour."

"You daredevil."

Her big, exaggerated wink made something in my chest tighten. I'd known getting involved with her would be a bad idea, but this—confiding in her and then laughing with her, sharing an ache and then soothing it—proved I'd underestimated the threat.

jed

I WASN'T surprised when I rolled up to Callie's house for our next date, to find the driveway already full of cars. She'd said her grandma and friends had weekly round-robin dinners and conveniently planned to be here tonight. Still, hadn't expected the little shiver of nerves that wove through me.

I wanted to impress these women. It'd never slipped my notice that I usually impressed women, just not for any reasons that really mattered. But these women knew Callie better than anyone, and they wanted only the best for her. And now, in spite of my initial arguments to the contrary, I wanted them to believe *I* could be the best for her.

Even if I knew it couldn't last, I wanted to believe it, too.

As I rang the doorbell, anticipation buzzed up my arm like the thing'd been electrified. The granny crew would likely watch our every interaction so they could pick us apart as soon as we left, but that'd been the point. Give them a better chance to see us together and maybe set her grandma's mind at ease. I just needed to rock the whole boyfriend schtick.

Truth be told, being Callie's boyfriend got easier by the day.

The door flew open, revealing Rita in a hot pink blouse cut

lower than I'd really expect to see on a woman in her seventies. No age-shaming here, but the cut seemed excessive for a friendly dinner party.

"Well, Jed, how wonderful to see you." She batted her eyelashes and presented her hand, more like she wanted me to kiss it than shake it, but I took it in mine. "Don't you look handsome tonight?"

"Thank you, ma'am. You're looking lovely yourself."

"Oh." She fluttered that hand in front of her chest. "Aren't you the sweetest?"

"All right, Rita, you've had your fun." Callie appeared out of nowhere, slipping her arm around my waist and gluing herself to my side. "Let the man be."

If this was her staking a claim, I encouraged it. Not that she had any worries where Rita was concerned, but I liked the possessiveness.

She tilted her chin up to face me. "Hey."

"Well, hey, Callie Lou." I snaked an arm around her, locking her in tight. "Are you ready to go?"

Her mouth dropped open to answer, but a voice from the next room cut her off.

"Why don't y'all come in and say hello for a minute?" Her grandma Suzie stood in the dining room, beckoning us closer. And—was that a knife in her hand? "Unless you've got a schedule to keep."

Glancing down at Callie, we exchanged a silent back and forth. Seeing her smile, I nodded to Suzie. "No schedule tonight."

Also, probably best not to argue with the woman holding a knife.

"Come see what we're making. It's going to be delicious."

We followed Rita into the kitchen. The rest of their group made full use of the small space, whether chopping ingredients or stirring something simmering on the stove. Every last one beamed at me, making it known I was more than welcome.

At least I'd never want for approval in this house.

"It smells incredible in here." The scent of ginger and beef wafted around in the air, along with subtler notes I couldn't identify. "What are you fixing?"

"We're making pho." Suzie put her knife to work slicing what looked like beef sirloin.

"Authentic pho," Carmen clarified as she chopped up a bundle of basil.

I couldn't imagine I'd have known the difference between real and fake pho, but from everything the ladies were chopping and seasoning, they took the task seriously. "Sure looks like you're doing it right."

Linda pulled stock bones from the steaming pot on the stove with a pair of tongs. "It always tastes better with real stock."

Carmen made a face. "Everything tastes better with real stock. Pre-made is for college students who don't know any better."

The others laughed at their friend's scorn. Didn't feel like the right time to admit I'd never made stock from scratch in my life.

"Well, this smells as good as the place I get pho in Georgetown," I said. "It's one of my favorite places to eat when I visit my brother."

"Since you like it so much, why don't you join us tonight?" Linda pulled a bag of bean sprouts from the fridge. "There's plenty to go around."

"They don't want to have dinner with us," Rita said before Callie or I could answer. "You want to be alone, don't you?"

"Well—" Callie only got the one word out before her grandma interrupted her.

"You could eat in Callie's rooms, if you wanted. You don't have to sit with us all night."

"Eating soup isn't something you can do really well on a couch," Callie said.

"Another time." Suzie's determined nod told me she'd only accept a limited number of rejections.

"How about next week?" Rita put in. "Jed can join us for game night."

"You just want someone else to walk away the biggest loser of the night," Linda said, rinsing the sprouts in the sink.

"I don't think that's her motivation," Carmen muttered.

Callie frowned, and I kind of loved it. Was she seriously jealous over a woman twice my age? I set a hand on her back, pulling her closer, and that frown eased. Might have even looked a touch smug.

Smug away, darlin'.

"You should join us for game night next week, Jed." Suzie paused her slicing. "We'd love to spend a little more time with you. We can play low stakes, if you like."

"What sort of games?" I asked Callie.

"Anything," she said. "Card games, kids' games, board games. They'll bet on it all."

"How much money are we talking?"

Her mouth tipped up into a smirk. "How much do you have?"

"Sounds treacherous. What's your favorite game?"

"I don't mind any of the games, really, as long as I'm not losing all my money. I've tried to get them to play some of the more complex board games out there, but they're not really into it. There's this one world-building game I want to play, where you're a woodland creature trying to establish a new town so you have to gather resources and abilities—"

"And that's why we don't play those types of games. It takes even longer for her to describe it than it does to play it."

Carmen's tart reply shriveled up Callie's enthusiasm. She snapped her mouth shut, pasting on an awkward smile probably calculated to look like the dismissal hadn't bothered her. I knew better now.

My hand at her back drew her a touch closer. "I'd like to hear more about that game."

This time, the smile she aimed my way was genuine. "I haven't actually played it yet, it just sounded fun to me. Even if it is kind of long. What could be cuter than building a little town full of chipmunks and rabbits?"

"You know, Harper's kind of the game nut in our family. She'd probably love to get involved in something like that."

"I'll have to ask her sometime."

"Well, I doubt we'll play any world-building games." Suzie pursed her lips as if the idea were absurd. "But the offer stands. We'd love to have you."

"Then I'll be there."

Callie's grin shot through me like a soda can shaken up and fizzing over. She had the kind of smile I could build my whole day around, especially when that dimple peeked out to drive me mad.

"Why don't you show Jed your rooms?"

Callie closed her eyes as though praying for patience. "Granny."

"What? They're not a secret, are they?"

She flashed me a look of silent apology. Didn't see the need, since the second Suzie had suggested it, I'd wanted to see where Callie lived. The parts of the house I'd been in more likely matched her granny's tastes, not hers. I wanted to see some of the bright and colorful Callie shine through.

Leaning in, I bobbed my eyebrows. "I won't say no to seeing your rooms."

She shook her head at me but grabbed my hand and pulled me from the kitchen. On the far side of the living room, a short hallway led off to spaces I hadn't been in yet.

Tugging me into the next room, she hitched a shoulder. "There's not that much to see, really."

I stopped, several arguments springing to mind. The other rooms mostly subscribed to her disliked beige and gray color scheme, but in here, she'd given the house life. Turquoise walls with white wainscoting made the space look both sophisticated and playful. An orange TV console held dozens of DVDs. The off-white couch had been livened up with multi-colored pillows, and a bright rug tied it all together.

At least, that sounded like something I'd heard my sister say.

"You should definitely talk about houses with June."

She hitched a shoulder. "My style is too much for Gran, so I haven't messed with the rest of the house. But back here, I've kind of done my own thing."

"I like it."

"Yeah?"

"Hell, yeah. It's fun." Better than my bland walls any day. I wouldn't even know where to start to liven up my place. June would have gladly told me, but I didn't think my landlord would appreciate it if I put my own stamp on a place I had to renew every year. "Exactly how I pictured the Callie Lou wing."

"Ooh, I like that. It used to be a den and office, but when I moved back in after college, I took it over to have a little more space. I couldn't sleep in my old bedroom again, not after my mom passed away here. She wanted to be home, not in a hospital or hospice center, and I understood that, I guess. But it's hard to be in the bedrooms and not think about those days. I don't even go in the room where she died anymore."

I slipped my hand into hers, twining our fingers together. "I'm sorry. That's got to be rough."

No wonder she wanted to sell this place. I wouldn't have wanted to face the place someone I cared about had died, either. Just the thought of the hospital where my mom had died or the desert where I'd lost Zach made my skin crawl.

"Yeah. But that's why I took over this end of the house. My new bedroom doesn't have a closet, but I make it work."

A door stood ajar on the far side of the room, tempting me. "Can I take a peek?"

Probably too bold and a bad idea all the way around, but I wanted to see it.

"Sure. It's just a bedroom."

She led us over, pushed the door open, and waved me inside.

"Just a bedroom?" Should have known by now Callie would undersell it.

Her bedroom seemed a microcosm of everything she'd described to me out in the orchards. Bright color, bold patterns, absolutely nothing gray or beige in here. The bed had been laid out with blankets and pillows in florals, stripes, and geometric markings that should have looked terrible together, but their colors worked somehow. Two metal clothes racks stood against one wall, next to a vintage dresser that had been painted moss green.

Most striking of all, the walls boasted twenty or thirty colorful embroidery hoops like the one she'd given Eden and Booker. Color blocks, garden scenes, carefully stitched lettering —I couldn't even take in everything she had on the walls. The familiarity here stole the air from my lungs.

"Did you make all these?" I said once I'd caught my breath again.

"Yeah. They've been my obsession lately. It's sort of meditative to just stitch, you know? I guess you probably don't know. But I like it, so I keep making them, even if I don't know what to do with them. Eliza keeps saying I should open a booth at the farmers' market and sell them."

"I bet you'd make a killing, too." I moved closer to look at the ones nearest us. She'd made a stylized little cabin in one, surrounded by wildflowers like something out of a children's book. Next to it hung a...well, a flaming trash bin. She'd stitched *'I'm not a hot mess, I'm a spicy disaster'* around it. "Yeah, these would definitely sell out."

I moved around the room, soaking up this glimpse into her private life, this secret, vibrant world nobody saw. A stack of brightly-colored books sat on her nightstand, most of them with the word 'love' in the title. A few pieces of children's artwork mingled with the embroideries on the wall, undoubtedly gifts from her students. A picture of her as a teenager and a woman who must have been her mother sat on the dresser. A white lacy bit of something peeked out of the top drawer, waving hello.

Do not look.

I spun away, swallowing hard. Time to leave before I got attached to this cozy room and the woman who'd created it.

Way too late for that.

"What do you think?" Her eyes seemed to ask more questions than just the one.

"I think June could learn a thing or two from you." I took her hand again. "Ready to go?"

She nodded, but I got the feeling I'd answered the wrong question. We walked back through her part of the house to the main rooms and fielded goodbyes from her grandma and the rest. Cutting out before they could entice us to stay for pho—that admittedly smelled pretty darn good—we made it outside.

The humid evening air did nothing to ease the tightness in my chest, like I'd held a breath too long. Ignoring it, I kept a tight grip on Callie's hand, knocking it against my leg as we crossed the yard to my truck. I opened the passenger door for her, and she'd just started to hike her leg up when she noticed what I'd done.

"*Oh.*"

That soft little sound of surprise made my stomach tighten. I wanted to hear it again. And again. At least a hundred more times.

She spun around, tilting her face up to look at me. "You installed a running board?"

"Figured you shouldn't have to struggle to get in and out of my truck."

Her wide smile made that solitary dimple pop. "That's the sweetest thing ever."

Seemed like a pretty basic concession for her comfort, but I'd accept the compliment. "Take it for a test run."

She put a foot on the step and boosted herself up, towering over me. "Now this, I like."

Turning to me, she rested her hands on my shoulders, her face hovering inches above mine. "This is how it should always be."

I put my hands on her waist without thinking. "You like having power, huh?"

"Nah. I like having power over *you*."

Little by little, her smile disappeared, the playful moment turning into something entirely too weighty. Her eyes dropped to my mouth, and my stomach dipped, twisting with longing. She tilted her head a sliver in invitation, and good Lord, did I want to accept. I should have kissed her already, pulled her into my arms and held her there good and tight.

I needed to get ahold of myself. I'd agreed to this relationship to get her out from under her grandma's thumb and away from the jerks she'd been dating—a temporary solution to a temporary problem. Kissing her just might create a permanent problem, and I wasn't made for those.

Taking my hands off her waist, I shifted away from her. "Better climb on in. Dinner awaits."

The confusion in her eyes made my heart stutter, and I knew I'd hurt her again. But in another second, she'd packed it away, flashing a smile that touched her lips but not her eyes. "Right. Well. I like the step."

She tucked herself into the cab and buckled in, staring straight ahead. I closed the door on her and walked around the bed of the truck, five seconds from punching myself. She might not know it, but that woman already had way too much power over me.

callie

WHAT'S the word for when you almost kissed your fake boyfriend but then he dodged you at the last second, leaving you feeling like the world's biggest moron? Had to be a term for it. Whatever it was, I wore that tonight like a freaking gold star.

Really, this was a good thing. I'd needed the reminder about the whole *fake* aspect. I hadn't forgotten, but I'd definitely let it get fuzzy in my mind. Spending an afternoon laid out on a blanket listening to a man share the tenderest parts of his heart would do that to anybody.

But no, this was good. Better to remind myself now, before I could go and do something really dumb like fall for Jed Evans. Wouldn't that be terrible?

So. Very. Terrible.

We sat in a booth at Homegrown, waiting for our burgers and fries, our conversation dried up and weird after that almost-kiss.

"I'll pay for dinner tonight."

I'd thought he might meet my announcement with a grin or a thank you, but a line formed between his eyebrows. "I've got it."

"You've paid for everything we've done so far, it's only fair."

He didn't seem to have a lot of interest in the fairness of it. "That's not really how dating works with me."

I raised an eyebrow at him. "So you're very attached to gender roles in dating?"

Now his grin did make an appearance. "I'm very attached to taking care of the woman I'm out with."

I grinned back, but it faded away as the thoughts I'd been blocking out for weeks now crashed into my brain like the Kool-Aid Man. He dated around, I'd always known that. What were the women like? Just how short-lived were his relationships? Were we talking a few weeks or one date only?

I didn't care. I did not. None of that had anything to do with what we were doing here. We were doing this to get Gran to Florida and me into a new house, not to soothe my insecurities. I needed to focus on this fake date with my fake boyfriend and ignore all those very real concerns.

"You take care of a lot of women."

That's not how ignoring things works, Callie.

His grin froze, and that line reappeared on his forehead.

"I'm sorry, that came out wrong. It's just that you seem to have had a healthy share of romantic interests."

He stared at me two whole seconds, making sweat prickle over my back before he burst into laughter.

"I'm writing that down. You have a way with words, Callie Lou."

"Never mind." I should have kept my big mouth shut. Why was I bringing this up now? Couldn't have had anything to do with the little rejection earlier, could it? What was so wrong with me that he had no interest? On second thought, I really didn't want to know.

Looking around the diner, I pretended deep fascination in the decor in here. Yeah, because I was so great at pretending.

"Right now, I only have the one romantic interest."

His soft voice didn't soothe. We'd gotten tangled up in this because I'd asked, and let's not forget, he'd said no at first. Maybe he'd even been mildly horrified by the suggestion. And if I'd started to think that maybe there could be something real between us...well, that was all on me.

"Why did you join the Army?"

His mouth thinned like he saw my question for the distraction it was. But what else would I say here? *I know I said I'd never fall for you, but I'm kind of probably definitely developing a crush on you and it's making our fake dating arrangement super inconvenient, my bad?*

To quote Jed, *Absolutely Not.*

"I'm just curious. You're not exactly the usual military type. You're a lot more...Jed."

He shook his head at me. "It's like you see my healthy ego and think, 'I can take that down a peg'."

"Pretty sure your ego will survive."

"Oh, guaranteed." He watched me a beat, a silent stare-down in the middle of the diner. "It's not the best story. Your opinion of me will only drop lower. Is that still possible, or has it reached rock bottom?"

Ha. If only he knew.

"Come on, I want to know. If it's not private or something."

Our waiter came by to drop off our platters of food. Home-grown's portions were absurd, our massive burgers and mountains of golden fries enough to feed at least three more people, but we dug in. And, fine. Their burgers might be impossible to eat without getting ketchup all over your face, but they were worth every messy bite.

"The story?" I prompted when I wasn't funneling fries into my maw like a duck eating bread.

He wiped a napkin across his mouth. "Senior year of high

school's coming to an end, I've got nothing planned. No college, no trade, not even really set on staying home to help Mom and Pop around the farm. Just…nothing. So my history teacher asks us our career goals, mostly because she wanted to rain on everyone's parade and point out our unrealistic expectations. For some reason, I pipe up with 'I'm joining the Army.'

"The teacher laughed straight in my face. Said that requires discipline, respect for authority, and that I wouldn't make it two weeks in Basic. Obviously, I had no choice but to enlist and prove her wrong."

I laughed, trying to imagine making a major career decision purely out of spite. I could understand the impulse, just not seeing it through. "Obviously."

"Pop was so proud, though. Hadn't been expecting that, but he took it as a sign I was finally growing up a little. Learning a little self-control. And I did…eventually. Basic was tough, not gonna lie, but after that, I liked the hands-on work. Practical results, working on a team, the challenge of it all. I took pride in what I did. Whatever that teacher thought, it suited me well."

"What was your rank?"

"Staff Sergeant."

I couldn't help giving him a hard time. "So I should call you Staff Sergeant Evans when I really want you to do something for me?"

He leaned forward, his eyes lit with pure fire. "Oh, darlin', that's not how that works. Only call me Staff Sergeant if you're planning on following every order *I* give *you*."

Heat unspooled in my belly, all my empty promises to not catch feelings for Jed burning to a crisp. Wasn't sure what kinds of orders he might give me, but I had no doubt I'd like them all.

This was so wrong. Sitting in a family restaurant, making veiled sexy talk over Army rank. I was definitely going to Hell.

"Why'd you leave?"

"When my mom passed away, I realized I didn't want to be away from my family so much anymore. So I came home."

"Do you miss it?"

Relaxing back into the booth, he seemed to consider. "It's more that I got used to it. It was easy, after a while, doing what I was told, completing tasks. I don't want to go back, but I don't always feel like I'm out, either. I moved around every couple of years, sometimes halfway across the world. I've been back in Magnolia Ridge three years, and I feel like I'm supposed to get my change of station orders any day now."

"Do you like that kind of constant variety?" I couldn't help thinking I'd circled back to the *romantic interests* conversation.

He watched me a long time, like maybe he'd had the same thought.

"I used to. These days, I guess it doesn't have the same appeal."

jed

I DROVE Callie back to her place wondering why I hadn't thought to add something else to our evening. A movie, drinks —even going inside to try the pho sounded better than calling it a night when we reached her door. But I told myself we weren't doing this for me—much—and I'd intended to follow her lead, letting her ask for what she wanted.

I had a feeling once I started asking for what I wanted with Callie, I'd never stop.

"Gran's dead serious about game night—about the invite, and the games themselves. They weren't joking around about betting, so definitely only bring as much cash as you're willing to lose. They'll sniff out anything you don't ante up and pressure you to bet it, anyway, fair warning."

"One question: Will they accept nickels?"

She waved a dismissive hand. "Sorry, cash bills only. But there's always way too much food, so be prepared to eat."

"Should I bring something? I remember you saying your gran was adamant you shouldn't show up to places empty handed."

"Please. I'm sure they'd make an exception for you. You'll be the guest of honor."

"Don't need to risk it, though. Uh, speaking of being the guest of honor." *Super smooth there, Jed.* "My pop wants to invite you to family dinner next weekend. He said Saturday, if you're free. Honestly, if you're not free, he'll just move the date to whatever works for you."

Pretty sure at this point, Callie could show up any night of the week without me and he'd welcome her in with open arms.

"He's so sweet. I can go Saturday."

"Perfect."

I pulled in front of her house and walked around the truck to get her door. She climbed out using the running board, and I didn't think I'd ever been quite so happy over anything quite so simple in my life. One small step for Callie, one giant leap for Jed's dumb heart.

She turned toward the house but stopped, grabbing my arm to halt me, too. "They're doing it again."

"Who's doing what?"

Ticking her head toward the house, she indicated with wide eyes. "Gran and her friends."

I started to turn, but she held my shoulder. "Don't look. They're all lined up in the window, it's humiliating. Let's just... let's pretend we're having a flirty conversation."

She flipped her hair back and fake-laughed like she was auditioning for a bit part in a bad movie.

I lifted an eyebrow. "That's you flirting?"

"Okay, Mr. Relationship Expert, do you want to show me how it's done?"

"Sure." I leaned against the side of the truck, my head angled down, my eyes intent on her. Tucking her hair behind her ear, I slowly skimmed my fingers over her skin and through the strands until she shivered. "The key is keeping it casual."

What a liar. The excitement rocketing around in my chest didn't feel anything close to casual.

Her mouth curled as she moved closer, resting one hand on the center of my chest, the other at my waist. Her fingers moved in small circles, trailing heat like they were made of flame.

"Like this?" she asked, her low voice so seductive, I had to stop myself from crushing her to me like a cave man.

I deeply regretted starting this game.

"I think you've got it."

She looked behind me, her mouth twisting. "They're still there."

"Isn't that the point? To prove we're together?"

Her eyes snapped to mine. "I think you should kiss me."

My stomach performed a perfect loop-the-loop, rising and falling in a scared little circle. "What?"

I'd apparently reached the stage where I feigned confusion when a woman asked me to kiss her. Couldn't pretend I wasn't intrigued when my hands on her waist itched to explore, and my eyes had already strayed to her soft, full mouth. As much as I wanted to act on the urge, following through would be a terrible idea.

Because then, I'd want all the follow-through, too.

"They're all staring." She spoke through a smile that looked about as natural as her faux-flirting. "We should kiss."

My mouth went dry, my attention fixed on her lips as she spoke. How would they feel moving against mine? What would they taste like? Would I have the strength to stop kissing them once I started?

"It's only our second date." The flimsiest excuse I'd ever used. Actually, had I ever refused a kiss before? Couldn't remember. My mind had been erased and refilled with thought after thought of Callie's mouth on mine.

Her eyebrows tugged together. "You expect me to believe you don't kiss until the third date?"

She had me there.

"If I really liked a woman and wanted to see her again—"

She ignored my spiel, her hand sliding up my chest to the back of my neck, pulling me closer. I didn't resist. Stretching up on tip-toes, she leaned against me in her quest to reach my mouth.

"You said I could captain this ship, so I'm captaining."

Well. She did outrank me.

Her mouth finally met mine, and I reacted on instinct. My hands stroked over her hips and back, my body firing up with need undercut with something sweeter. Her full lips teased in the best way, sending currents of electricity through my veins. I let her keep control of the kiss, never asking for more but willing to follow wherever she'd lead.

The kiss might have lasted ten seconds or ten minutes—I only knew it didn't last nearly long enough.

When she finally broke away, I had to fight the urge to return my mouth to hers where it belonged. She looked up at me, eyes hazy but pleased, her body soft against mine. This woman was everything sweet and joyful and good, a gift I wanted to go on opening every day. But in another minute, her satisfied expression transformed, her mouth twisting as she drew away.

I let her slip from my arms, every last nerve ending shouting at me to scoop her back up and go for another kiss.

"That, uh…" Running her fingers over her pink mouth, she swallowed, her eyes just missing me. "That was…"

The kind of kiss that made a man question if he'd ever truly kissed a woman before, because nothing had ever felt quite like that. The kind of kiss that felt like crossing a line in the sand, a

Before and *After*. Like affection for this ray of sunshine had stirred awake my long-dormant heart.

So, just your run-of-the-mill life-altering kiss.

"Flirty?" I offered instead.

Laughing off her awkwardness, she rolled her eyes at me. "Something like that. Sorry if I manhandled you."

"You didn't do anything I didn't want you to do."

The skeptical little line between her eyebrows said she didn't quite believe me. "Okay. Good. Well...goodnight, Jed."

"Night, Callie Lou."

She flashed one last smile before darting across the yard, onto the porch, and through her front door. I climbed back into my truck, frowning as I started up the engine. I touched my own lips, knowing that kiss would live on repeat in my mind for the foreseeable future.

The messy, complicated bits I'd been afraid of when Callie first proposed this fake dating arrangement had finally showed up to wreck everything. Mostly me.

callie

OF ALL THE games they could have picked tonight, I never expected Pit. Even more unexpected? How badly my gran and the others played in order to let Jed win.

I'd figured their cut-throat game play would only notch higher with him in the mix, but they went out of their way to slide cards to him like every woman had made it her personal mission to ensure he took the pot of money each round. He was like their mafia don, and they'd become perennial losers, eager to suck up to him by falling on their own bad hands.

When he won his fifth hand—and I'd lost my fifth dollar—I'd had enough of that.

"You're going down, my friend." I squinted at him, hoping I looked more menacing than confused.

Jed fanned out the singles he'd won in front of his face. "My big wad of cash says otherwise."

Our chairs sat snugged together on one side of the dining table, our arms knocking against each other every time we moved. All the little touches kept our kiss front and center in my mind. Not that I'd stopped thinking about it for one minute of the last several days. But I'd done it to convince Gran and the others we were really a couple, that was all.

Okay, that, and I'd wanted to kiss him for a while. Impossible not to, what with all his easygoing charm and sweet confidences. I'd known it was a bad idea to get a real crush on my fake boyfriend, and here I sat anyway. But that might be a good thing, right? My genuine interest in Jed could only help sell this phony relationship.

Or so I'd been telling myself.

Unfortunately, I couldn't tell if he'd been as affected by the kiss as I had. He'd waltzed into the house tonight wearing his usual smile, scooped me up into a hug, and whispered hellos into my ear. I would have taken it as a positive sign except for the troubling little fact we'd been on full display again for the grandmas. His affectionate greeting might have been more for them than for me. Hadn't he said he had no problem with lying or PDA?

I didn't exactly love the confusion his affection carried with it, but I'd gotten myself into this—nothing to do now but roll with it.

"Looks like it's time for me to beat your butt," I said, trying hard not to think about said butt. His jeans had addled my brain.

He just smirked. "That's big talk, considering I'm currently the undefeated champion."

"Because they're helping you win."

His mouth dropped open in mock protest. "Callie Lou, you take that back."

The others muttered similar complaints, but I was no dummy. They'd never had a problem cleaning out *my* wallet on game night.

"Now, kids," Gran said, smiling to herself as she shuffled the deck. "Let's all be good sports about it."

She dealt the cards, and the next round began, a chaotic mess of everyone shouting numbers and passing cards at the same time. No surprise, whenever I tried to trade cards with someone, they moved their hand away, offering theirs to Jed if they could. I leaned across him to try to make a trade before he could reach it, but he got there first.

"No fair, your arms are ten feet long."

He chuckled. "That's what you get for being fun-sized."

Pushing my chair back, I stood and angled myself in front of him to block his next trade. Linda *tsked*, unhappy with the change, but I didn't care. They'd been edging me out of trades all night. Jed and I elbowed each other out of the way, tussling over cards as we struggled for dominance. I shrieked with laughter, knowing I looked a right fool, but I needed some vindication here.

We'd both come down to one card, passing frantically with each of the grannies only to pass it right to the next when it wasn't the one we wanted. Any second now, one of us would win the game, and I couldn't get this close and still come up empty. Rita made to slip him a single card, but I took it instead, crowing when I saw I finally had a complete hand. I slapped my palm on the bell in the middle of the table, declaring myself the winner.

"Well," Carmen said, laying her cards down. "That's one way to win."

"Y'all drove me to this."

Rita smirked as she gave me a once-over. "I think you drove yourself."

I looked down, and my brain caught up to the fact that in my eagerness to cut off Jed's access to the cards, I'd wormed my way onto his lap. One of his hands held his useless cards, the other rested on my hip, my butt squarely parked on his thigh. He hadn't complained, and by the way his chest at my back kept shaking, pretty sure he was laughing over it. Still...maybe just a teensy bit more forward than I'd intended to be.

"I think it's time for a break, girls, what do you say?" Gran corralled the others with a significant look, and in another second, they'd gathered in the kitchen, leaving us somewhat on our own.

"Sorry." I twisted around to see Jed's face better. "I might have gotten a little carried away."

"No apologies necessary. I like it when you get carried away."

His gaze felt way too heavy, and I started to think I might not have been the only one reliving our kiss the other night. Sitting in his lap like this, our faces inches apart, it wouldn't take much to get carried away again right now.

Well. Except for the little problem of the four elderly women in the next room who watched our every move. They might as well have whipped out binoculars and started taking notes, for all their eager glances our way.

"I thought you said *they* were competitive."

His mouth tipped up, and my eyes traced his lips. I wanted to kiss off that smirk. That'd teach him. Maybe Gran and the others still needed some convincing.

"I lost five rounds with grace. That was my limit."

He lightly squeezed my side. "I'll keep that in mind next time I'm on a winning streak."

"Which will be in about five minutes at the rate they're going."

"They're just trying to make me feel welcome. Honestly, I'm surprised my comfort isn't a higher priority for my girlfriend."

I frowned at him but couldn't maintain it very well when he grinned up at me like this. "Comfort and ego aren't the same thing."

"I've been thinking you don't prioritize my ego the way you should."

This man's eyes positively sparkled.

"I feel like that would be a full-time job."

His fingers twitched on my waist. "There are generous perks."

I think my whole body sighed. I'd been dreaming up all sorts of fringe benefits since our just-for-show, totally not-real kiss.

"How generous?" My voice had gone low like some kind of vixen, partially so the grans wouldn't overhear me being so brazen, but mostly because he made me *feel* like a vixen. Like I was desirable and fascinating and he couldn't get enough of me. Maybe it was all part of the Thoughtful Boyfriend Package, but I wanted to soak up this exhilarating feeling as long as it lasted.

Jed's gaze turned so heated, everything in his vicinity should have gone up in flames.

"First—"

"Are you two going to get something to eat, or are you going to fool around all night?"

Ugh, these women. They shoved me in a man's direction, then interrupted us when we were getting to the good part. I tried to telegraph ten different apologies with my eyes, but Jed didn't seem all that bothered by Linda's interruption.

He stared straight at me. "We're opting to fool around all night."

Laughing, I stood from his lap, missing my cozy spot the second I left it. "I don't think that's on the table. Let's get some food."

"What? She just said it was an option."

I tugged on his hand, coaxing him up to follow me to the kitchen. The excited shivers still coursing through my body needed to cool it, but they firmly ignored my shushing. I tried to look reasonably collected as I inspected the food, like I wasn't still riding the high of our flirtation.

Food might distract me, but I doubted it. The usual assortment of semi-healthy items littered the counters, along with the cream cheese brownies I'd made this morning and the chips and guacamole Jed had brought.

"Where did you get this guacamole?" Carmen asked, spooning some onto a plate. "It's delicious."

"Thank you, I made it."

His matter-of-fact reply brought out approving nods and wide-eyed glances my way, all of them saying *Look at this keeper*. I didn't need their hints. Believe me, I was looking.

"You didn't have to bring anything," Gran said, ever the hostess. "But we appreciate it all the same."

"I heard it's best not to show up empty-handed."

He grinned down at me and shot a little wink that rippled over my skin, the big flirt.

"I'm surprised you had the time." Rita divvied up my pan of brownies. "You must be pretty busy with harvest. Everyone I know has paid a visit to Evans Orchards this season."

"That's what I like to hear. It's busy, but I don't mind. You get used to the rhythm of the seasons. Once September hits, we'll slow back down again, so I don't have long to complain even if I thought to."

"We're so glad you're able to find some time to see our Callie."

Gran's approval practically oozed out her eyeballs, but I kind of loved how enamored she was of him.

His eyes hit mine again. "It's no hardship to make time to be with Callie."

Affection surged through me for this man. I tried to squash it back down, considering, but I knew I'd never win that battle.

He was a good guy and easy to like on a normal day, but when he aimed all his charm my way? Might as well raise the white flag now.

"I understand you ladies aren't sticking around town much longer." He started to fill a plate with a little bit of everything laid out on the counter. "When do you move to Florida?"

"Just a few weeks now," Carmen said. "The trucks are reserved, and our condo's waiting for us."

"And then, the beach!" Rita chimed in, raising a tortilla chip in triumph.

"Sounds like a good change for y'all," he said.

"It would be if we'd all make up our minds." Carmen side-eyed Gran with her usual subtle shade.

"I've got a lot I'll be leaving behind." Gran sent a sweet, soft look my way. "My grandbaby, and maybe soon, great-grandbabies."

I almost breathed a mouthful of guacamole straight into my lungs. I prayed we wouldn't round out the night with a little Heimlich maneuver. Seriously, Gran? Why'd she have to go and say something like that in front of my—well, in front of Jed? Even if we'd been one hundred percent genuine, I never would have brought up *babies* with him at this stage, and especially not with this rapt audience.

I wasn't even sure he wanted to get married, much less have babies some day. Hadn't he said settling down wasn't in the cards? Then again, I'd seen him with his niece at June's engagement party. She'd had him wrapped tight around her little finger, and he'd eaten up their time together. Yeah...I could see it. Playful and fun-loving, he'd encourage his kids into all kinds of silly mischief, and shower them with his endless affection. He'd be the same for his wife, supportive and steady, and always ready to mix things up with laughter when things got routine.

Now that I'd thought about it, pretty sure I'd go right on thinking it, dreaming of Jed as a husband and father. As if I weren't torn up enough over imaginary scenarios already.

Good job, Granny.

He patted me on the center of my back, part comfort, part trying to dislodge whatever I still coughed on.

"I think you're making Callie nervous with all the great-grandbaby talk," he said to her.

At least he could stay cool under pressure. Must have been that military training. Meanwhile, I still had tears streaming from my eyes and avocado in my throat.

She waved a hand, as moved by my embarrassment as she ever was. "She knows what I mean. Way off in the future."

Right. But just a minute ago, she'd hoped it would be *soon.* Jed hadn't run from the house screaming, but I didn't find a lot of consolation in any part of this scenario.

"Callie will visit us in Florida, won't you?" Rita said, nodding my way.

I cleared my throat to be sure I could speak. "Of course. It will give me a place to go every summer vacation."

Just like that, everything inside me seemed to shift, like I'd been jolted out of a dream. Obviously, I'd known things would change when she moved, but like I'd told Clint Evans the other day, I managed to overlook that troublesome fact most of the time. But every now and then, it'd hit me just how much my life would alter after she'd gone.

She'd been with me all my life, my most important—and only—family for the last eight years. Soon, it'd be just me. I wanted that, but it'd also rip my heart out when she drove away.

I glanced at her, but she didn't look wistful or sad. Frankly, she was probably still dreaming up great-grandbabies.

"Speaking of summer vacation," Linda said around a bite of

guacamole, "have you had a chance to see how your classroom looks yet?"

I took a deep breath and brought my thoughts back into the moment. "Not yet."

"It's about time they changed out that carpet. It was brand new my first year teaching there in the eighties."

"That old carpet had seen some things." Half the pattern was just undetermined stains—and in a kindergarten classroom, we were all better off not knowing. "I'll go in Thursday to put all the furniture back."

"Sounds like a lot of work," Gran said. "You need any help?"

"Oh, no, don't worry about it. It's just a lot of moving desks around, I can handle it."

"Ahem." Jed nudged me. "I'm good at moving desks around."

I hadn't asked him because I'd already asked so much of him. I didn't want to put his work in jeopardy because of this scenario I'd concocted.

"I figured you'd be busy with your own work."

"I'm never too busy for you, Callie Lou."

I grinned a big dumb smile because oh, I loved hearing him talk like that. I knew it was strictly for the benefit of the women around us, but still. Swoon city.

"Are you sure? It's probably a big old mess."

His rakish grin sent my insides tumbling. "I'm not afraid of mess."

Good thing. Because my tangled up heart felt like it had the potential to turn into a whole lot of mess if I didn't rein it in right quick.

I just wasn't sure I had the ability anymore.

NINETEEN

THURSDAY MORNING, I unlocked my classroom door, pushed it open, and flicked on the overhead lights. I groaned as the full scope of the project came into view. Kind of wanted to flip the lights off again. I couldn't guess just how long this would take to set to rights. Behind me, Jed made a sound of surprise.

I turned to him. "You want to rethink volunteering for this?"

"Not a chance. Just wasn't expecting...this, that's all."

Neither was I. Apparently, the crews had emptied the room before they painted and re-carpeted, and then put everything back as quickly as possible. No sense of a plan here, just desks, chairs, and storage cabinets pushed at random into the room. A junk yard would have looked more thought out.

"We can handle it." I gave him a stout nod, already getting into my extra-optimistic teacher mode. "To create order, you have to create a little chaos. And I'm a pro at chaos."

I winked at him, and got a satisfied little thrill when it made him laugh.

Apart from the furniture mess, I liked the changes. The new navy blue carpet dotted with rainbow stripes was soft underfoot—not plush, but not tired and gritty like the old carpet had been. I much preferred the light blue walls to the previous gray, and loved how the colors livened up the room. Soon, my students would love it, too.

"This is going to be good. We just need to deal with that." I waved at the big pile of furniture as if it wouldn't be an all-day ordeal.

"Tell me what to do, Captain. I'm at your service."

My stomach dipped at that tempting offer. What would I do with Jed at my service? Nothing to do with my classroom, that's for sure. Before I could get lost cataloguing enticing options, I shoved my thoughts in the direction of the task at hand.

We moved cabinets and arranged desks, trying to minimize moving things multiple times, but the way everything had been left jumbled together, we didn't have a lot of choice. I thanked my lucky stars Jed had offered to help out, since the process would have taken three times as long if I'd been working on my own. He picked up desks like they weighed nothing while I struggled with mine in one-foot bursts across the room.

As usual, I talked while we worked. Mostly, I shared my excitement for the next school year and what it might hold. I wouldn't receive a class roster until a couple of days before summer ended, but it didn't really matter. It'd be a good class.

"I can't wait for Meet The Teacher night. The kids will absolutely light up when they walk around this classroom for the first time. Okay, not every kid—there's always one or two who are really shy or don't like school yet. But I love seeing that look of wonder when they explore the room and start imagining how the year will go."

"Just like you're doing now." He grinned at me, arranging desks into clusters of three or four.

"I can't help it, it's exciting. It's the same when I buy

supplies. I love stocking up on markers, pencils, and construction paper."

"You have to buy your own supplies?"

I put empty storage bins in one of the cabinets, trying to get it more or less the way I'd had it last year. "Every student gets a list of supplies to bring for class, but it's a lot of stuff. Not every family can afford all of that. So I usually buy a bunch of things to have on hand if we need it."

"Does that work out to be a lot?"

I shrugged. "It's better than kids not having what they need."

We teamed up to put my desk where I liked it, each of us taking an end. A corner set-up worked best in this room and proved the least distracting for the class, but of course, the desk had been left on the opposite end of the room.

"I don't imagine you sit behind this desk very much, do you?" he said when we got it in place. "I bet you're out here with the kids, on the floor mixing it up with them. You probably get into the crayons and paints, too."

My mouth dropped open to defend myself until I saw the way he watched me. His usual playfulness lit his eyes, but affection warmed them, too. Anybody else, and I might have thought they were making fun of me, pointing out how I got down on my knees to help kids with their crayon drawings daily. More than one of my set-up dates had made light of what I did, insinuating my job made me nothing more than a babysitter.

But Jed had never been like that, and shame swirled around in my stomach that I'd forgotten it even for a second.

"I don't sit at my desk much during class time, no."

"I like that. I've got a feeling you make learning fun for them."

"That's the goal."

He stepped closer to me. "Only one thing I would change to make it their best year ever."

My eyebrows lifted. "You're going to give me teaching tips?"

"It's a pretty important one, but I'll share it with you." He looked around as if searching for listening ears. "As long as you keep it to yourself."

"What's that?"

His grin tipped up. "Meet the Farmer day."

I snort-laughed. This man. "I'll be sure not to skip it this year."

He stepped even closer. "But you have to ask the right one. Can't be just any farmer. Has to be a special one."

I tilted my head back, smiling up at him like a fool. "I know a pretty special one."

"Yeah?"

Good gracious, his smiles were like fireworks going off, pops and fizzes hitting me straight in the heart. "He's a peach farmer."

He'd reached me now, staring down at me while we flirted and teased. "Those are the best sort."

"I think so, too." My hands went to his waist of their own accord, little magnets drawn to the steel of his abs.

He dipped his head toward me. "Only trouble is, you've got to ask real nice."

"I'll ask him real nice," I said slowly, my fingers sliding across his T-shirt.

"How will you ask him?" His deep voice positively melted my insides.

"I'll say, 'Clint Evans, could you pretty please—'"

Jed scooped me into a big bear hug, growling out his pretend frustration into my neck while I cackled, my feet dangling in the air. His breath on my collarbone sent shivers rippling down my back, and I held his shoulders tighter.

"You fight dirty, Callie Lou."

So did he. Holding me this way, my face hovered over his. Kind of seriously loved the way he grinned up at me, like I was the best thing he'd ever seen. Wouldn't take anything at all to close that distance and kiss him to pieces.

He must have had the same thought. His gaze dropped to my mouth, and I licked my lips on autopilot, wondering if he'd share captain duties and kiss me, or if I was still the leader when it came to all that.

The moment dragged on, but he didn't make a move. Didn't put me down, either, but he didn't lean up for the kiss. Fine, I could take control of the situation. I'd done it once before, right? Tilting my head to go for it, I'd almost reached his mouth when my classroom door burst open.

"We heard something and—oh."

Jed and I turned to see two of my fellow teachers standing in the doorway, mouths open and eyes wide as they stared at us. He set me back on my feet, and I took half a second to reset my foggy brain, my pounding heart rebelling at the interruption.

"Jed, this is Amy and Lisa, they're the other kindergarten teachers here. This is my boyfriend, Jed Evans."

Funny how the words came so naturally, they didn't feel like a lie at all.

Twenty and thirty years older than I was respectively, Amy and Lisa had offered endless hints and tips to help me get through my first couple of years of teaching. I had nothing but gratitude for them…just would have been more grateful if they'd stayed in their rooms today.

He crossed over to them and shook their hands. Meanwhile, they goggled at him like their favorite country music singer had just stepped off stage to greet his adoring fans. I got it—the man was head-to-toe gorgeous. Plus, I'd never mentioned having a significant other or even a date. A little bit of gawking was probably warranted.

"It's nice to meet you," Amy said, slipping a pink container of pepper spray into her purse. "We were talking in the next room and thought we heard screaming, but I guess it was laughter."

"Didn't mean to startle you," Jed said.

"We might have been a little too cautious in rushing right over here."

"No such thing."

"Don't you just love the changes?" Lisa looked around the classroom, a mirror image of hers next door. "We've been angling for new carpet for ten years."

"And that old paint," Amy chimed in. "Booger gray is what my husband called it. Much prefer the new shade."

"I'm a little bit in love with my new room," I said.

"Yes, well, there's a lot to love in here." Lisa raked her eyes over Jed before casting a significant look at me. You could have fried an egg on my cheeks, they'd grown so hot. "We won't keep you, just wanted to check on the noise."

"We'll know better next time. Good to meet you, Jed."

They slipped out into the hall, and the door closed behind them.

"Sorry about that." They hadn't been as bad as Gran and her friends, but I wasn't sure anyone could be.

"Don't be, I'm glad they're looking after you. She was a quick draw on that pepper spray."

Of course he'd noticed.

"It can be a little creepy working in the school after hours. Being alone in the quiet, that's when the ghosts come out." I hooked my fingers into a claw like a cartoon witch. Would not add how much being alone in the big echoing school could freak me out.

He nodded, but that sparkle in his eyes had dimmed. "That they do."

Yeah, nothing like joking around about spooky things to kill a mood.

"Do you need to get back to the farm?" The interruption had reminded me of the time. We'd gotten much more done than I ever would have managed alone, but I couldn't take up his whole day.

He shook his head. "I can spare a little more time. What's next?"

"If we set up the library, that will take care of the biggest jobs."

"Then let's get that library done."

I couldn't help the disappointment swirling through me that we weren't going to pick up right where we'd left off with that near-kiss. But whatever sparks I'd seen in his gaze a few minutes ago, they were gone now. Then again, maybe I'd only seen the reflection of all the flames in my own eyes.

jed

IT'D TAKEN ALL my self-control not to kiss Callie senseless in the middle of her kindergarten classroom. If it hadn't been for the other teachers interrupting us, I wasn't sure my tenuous hold on that control wouldn't have snapped. Felt like that said something specific about me, just didn't want to think too hard about what.

I'd told her she could be in charge of the PDA, but when I held her, everything inside me wanted to steer that ship. Of course, I'd probably steer us straight to deep waters, so I wasn't really the best one to put in charge. I knew that. Didn't make it any easier to fight.

I moved the three short particleboard book cases to where she'd indicated, and we filled the shelves with brightly colored bins of books. She brought over a few beanbags and laid them out to make a cozy little reading spot for the kids. Her colorful style and personality fit perfectly with her room, and I could just imagine her in here teaching. Her obvious affection for students she didn't even know yet tugged at my chest. Who had this kind of love for people she hadn't met?

"How'd you get into teaching? Unless...wait. Did someone

say you'd make a terrible teacher so you set out to prove them wrong?"

She laughed as she slipped books onto shelves. "Nothing like that. My mom was a kindergarten teacher."

The air in the room seemed to shift. She didn't do anything outwardly, but I could feel it was a sensitive subject for her, just like talking about my mom was for me. She hadn't shared much about her mom yet, but I wanted to know whatever she'd tell me. On any subject.

"Do you want to talk about her?"

Her soft smile wore a sadness around the edges. "You know me so well."

I didn't know her nearly as well as I wanted to. Wasn't sure I'd ever reach a spot where I thought I'd had enough of Callie Louise Matheson. That urge to know everything about her worried me, even though so far, I hadn't done much to fight it.

She sank into one of the beanbag chairs, and I did the same. Wasn't the most comfortable spot for a six-three guy, but I wouldn't complain.

"She was everybody's favorite, you know? She just had this life to her, this zest. She could make everything fun. And she loved children. I think she would have had a dozen babies if she could have. She put everything she had into teaching, and her students loved her. I knew I wanted to do the same thing even before she died, but I like having that connection to her now."

Her joy in sharing about her mom held sorrow, too, no attempt to hide how much she still hurt. Of course she did. I understood—the same sorrow ran through me, coloring every-thing like ink on a wet page. That kind of loss didn't go away simply because a few years had gone by. We had to keep going because the world kept on turning, but the pain could still cut us just as deep today if we let it.

"She sounds like a great teacher and an amazing mom. I

was thirty when I lost mine, and it gutted me. I can't imagine going through that as a teenager."

Seeing her grief now sliced my heart to ribbons—I couldn't think how it'd been for her when it had been fresh.

Callie nodded, no longer looking at me. "She died of cancer, just like yours. She was diagnosed when I was fifteen, and had one remission where we thought we were out of the woods. It didn't last long." Her mouth twisted, her shaky breaths making me guess tears weren't far behind. "Watching the person you love most in the world slowly wither up and die was just…"

I shifted closer, the *swish swish* of the beanbag chair accentuating every move, but I needed to take her hand. My fingers closed around hers, and that small smile returned to her face. Not entirely happy, but not nearly so sad. I would take it.

"I spent all my time with her like I could bottle it up and save it for later. We watched all her favorite old movies, I read books to her…I didn't want to do anything else but be with her. My friends couldn't understand, and after a while, they stopped trying to get me to hang out. By the time she passed away, I'd become that weird girl with the dying mom. Some girls tried to keep in touch, but they didn't want sad me, or grieving me, or confused about finding sparks of happiness when I still had a broken heart me. They just wanted fun, happy Callie, and not the rest."

I understood that, too. After Zach's death, I'd had friends who'd expected me to just turn my smile back on and be the life of the party. People who'd rather I pretended the hurt didn't exist than sit with me in it.

Hand holding wasn't nearly enough. I got up and sat next to her on her small, awkward cushion and wrapped my arms around her. She came right to me, sighing against my chest, letting me comfort her however I could.

"What happened with your mom?"

I could have avoided her gentle question. Could have moved on or brushed it aside. I never talked about this with anyone but my family...and yet, I couldn't *not* talk about it with Callie.

"By the time they found her cancer, it was already too late. I'd been deployed overseas, and I couldn't get leave until after. I wasn't here for her." I hated to admit I'd failed her that way. I'd been virtually unreachable while she slipped out of this world. "All I could think about was how many years I'd been gone, how much time I could have had with her if I'd just stuck around. I'd thought I had years and years to spend with her, and suddenly, there was nothing left."

Her arms tightened around me, her hands offering gentle caresses in consolation. The guilt had chewed me up hard, regret over strings of choices that had led me to be on the other side of the world when my mother died. I hadn't re-upped after, and I'd come home, but it was all too little, too late.

"But I had my pop. My brother and sister. Aunts and uncles and cousins. I can see why you and your grandma are so close."

They must have been close anyway after her dad walked out, but losing her mom? They'd been through fire together.

"We had to lean on each other."

"Are you sure you want to let her go to Florida?"

Her head moved in an emphatic nod against my chest. "Totally. She wants this, even if she's being silly about leaving me behind. I know she wants to be with her friends, and I want her to be happy."

This sweet woman's huge heart would just give and give all her love away endlessly. I admired it. And sort of feared it. Because me? I'd just take and take.

"You ever think about going with her?"

"And ruin their Golden Girls lifestyle? Never. I'm good here. I love my job, my new friends. Magnolia Ridge is my home."

A tension inside me I hadn't recognized before eased, as if

I'd needed that reassurance she wouldn't move away to Florida one day, too.

"Anyway, what would I do without my boyfriend?"

"I expect you'd replace me pretty easily."

Should have been a joke, but the pang in my heart knew better. I'd pretty well avoided thinking about how I'd have to give her up when all this came to an end, but that image barreled in now, stark and miserable. One way or another, we'd have to wrap this up. Either she'd remember all those reasons I wasn't a good long-term bet, or *I'd* remember exactly why I wasn't meant for forever.

Even if, lately, she made me wish I could be.

"Nah," she said, rubbing her cheek against my chest. "You're the only Jed there is. You're irreplaceable."

As much as I liked the sentiment, I needed to keep our endgame in mind. As soon as her grandma moved on to Florida, Callie would be free to do what she wanted. We were just temporary.

I'd never minded temporary before. I'd bounced from woman to woman, each so-called relationship shorter than the last, and I'd never been fazed.

This time around, when everything ended, I couldn't be sure I'd recover.

NERVES WOUND THROUGH MY INSIDES, tying tiny little knots around my organs so every time I moved, I couldn't tell if I was in pain or about to be sick. I paced around the kitchen, trying to decide if a snack would settle my stomach or upend everything.

This afternoon was not the big deal my brain was making it out to be. Just dinner with Jed's family. Just his entire family all at once, sitting down to a meal together. With me. Totally normal and fine.

I'd met them all a time or two, not like we were strangers. I'd watched their big family dynamic at a few gatherings now, so I had some idea how things would go. Still...watching from the sidelines wouldn't be quite the same as sitting down at the table tonight as Jed's girlfriend.

My stomach squeezed again.

"Oh, Callie, you look so pretty." Granny walked into the kitchen, interrupting my fourth perusal of every last item in the cupboards. "That dress is a nice touch."

She'd encouraged me to venture outside my usual shorts-shirt combo pack tonight. It'd seemed appropriate, but now, I couldn't be sure. I'd chosen a green sleeveless sundress that would hopefully look nice without baking me in the heat, and I'd paired it with my navy Converse to keep it from looking too fancy. I hoped.

"I'm glad things are going so well with you and Jed."

I tried not to laugh, I really did. She'd said some variation of the same thing several times in the last few days, but I wouldn't stop her gloating. Especially since I'd found a couple more boxes packed up and sealed. I'd take all the gloating she wanted to dish out if it came with move progress.

"He's a really good guy. I like him a lot."

Vague but enthusiastic seemed the best tack, for Gran and me. I'd always known he was charming, and his good looks were never in question. But his sweet heart had taken me by surprise, turning my own all squishy and soft in response. If I wasn't careful—actually, who was I kidding? I'd already jumped head-first into a serious crush on Jed Evans, and all indications pointed to more of the same ahead. Too late to worry about the *No Diving* signs now.

"I can tell you do, sweetheart. He's exactly the kind of man I'd hoped you'd find. A good one, ready and willing to step up and take care of you."

I smiled, refusing to let my real response to that show on my face. The refrain that I needed to be looked after and taken care of just added to the nausea I had going on. Almost twenty-five years old, and she still saw me as the fifteen-year-old girl I'd been when Mom got cancer and she moved in with us. I'd needed Gran desperately through those years, but I was a whole grown woman now, and I didn't need Jed to take care of me.

Need and want were very different things.

"Maybe Jed's the one who needs me to take care of him, did you ever think of that?"

Her smile hit a little too close to patronizing. "That man doesn't need a thing."

Neither do I. But arguing over it had never gotten me anywhere.

"Actually," she said, "I've been thinking about something Jed might need."

I did not like where this was going already. "What do you mean?"

"Does he ever make sausage?"

"Does he ever...what?"

She rolled her eyes, patting a box on the counter. "Make sausage. I found this meat grinder under the cupboards. I know you never use it, but I hate to just get rid of such a good old grinder. Does he have a mixer set up?"

Gran took pieces out of the box, displaying various sizes of blades and attachments. I couldn't remember ever seeing that thing, much less anyone using it.

"I've never asked him about meat grinding." This whole conversation was ten kinds of wrong.

"Well, does he have a lot of fancy appliances? He might not want a hand-crank option if he's got a nicer one."

"I don't have a clue what's in his kitchen."

The metal pieces rattling together formed an exclamation point on everything I'd just said wrong. She stared at me, surprise spelled out in her low eyebrows and thinned mouth.

"You've never seen where he lives?"

Way to stay on top of things. I scrambled to come up with a fake kitchen, but making up lies about his house seemed ridiculous when I'd already given myself away. "I haven't been over there, no."

"Callie Louise. It's been weeks."

"I can't believe you're encouraging me to go to a guy's place, Granny." Maybe a joke would play off my mistake?

"You know what I mean. You learn a lot about a person by seeing where they live. He could be a slob, he could have cockroaches, he could have a wife."

"He doesn't have a wife. I thought you liked Jed."

"I do, but I think it's a little worrying he hasn't at least brought you by his place."

Was it? I didn't really know what the appropriate timeline for visiting a man's apartment was. Probably a lot quicker when the dating—and everything that went with it—was entirely real.

Jed's knock on the door busted up our conversation, thank the Lord.

"I'll let him in." Gran rushed to the door as though she hadn't just hinted he might be hiding a wife in his apartment like Mr. Rochester. Either that, or a million cockroaches.

She threw the door open, and my breath caught. Sure, he was the most attractive man for miles around, but that wasn't what left me so breathless. The way his eyes sought me out and how wide he smiled when he saw me made my heart flutter, that look that said he'd never been happier to see anybody. Maybe it was naive and short-sighted, but the idea that *I* could be the reason he smiled like that set my whole chest on fire.

He nodded to my Gran. "Evening, ma'am." His eyes returned to me, sparkling brighter than before. "Callie Lou."

Yeah, his nickname for me put the cherry on top. He said it in that soft, rolling drawl of his that sent shivers tingling through me every time. Pretty sure he knew it. Only explanation for why he said it so much.

"Jed." Did I grin like a fool? Yes. Did I care? Not a bit.

"What do you have there?" Gran asked.

In all my ogling his gorgeous smile and general too-muchness, I hadn't even noticed he held a big box in his arms.

"It's for Callie."

She waved him inside, and he crossed the room to bring the box to the dining table.

"For me?" I trailed behind, wondering what on earth he might have brought me. Fingers crossed it wasn't a hand-crank meat grinder.

Gran joined us at the table, looking from us to the box, that sneaky grin on her face.

"Not so much for you, I guess," he said. "For your students."

He opened the top, and I peered past him. Tears instantly slid their way through my ducts, ready for me to bawl my eyes out. I clapped a hand to my mouth as if I could keep all my emotions inside, even though they were sure to break free. Somewhere in my brain, I registered Gran say, "Aren't you a sweetheart?"

He'd crammed the box full of cartons of crayons, colored pencils, paint sets, and markers. Glue sticks, children's scissors, erasers, and even a few bundles of construction paper were tucked inside, too. He'd given me enough school supplies to cover anything students didn't have for the whole year.

"I can't believe you did this," I squeaked out between the fingers covering my mouth.

"I thought about buying you flowers with my game night winnings." His eyes shone down at me. "Figured this would be better."

I threw my arms around his middle. Instead of a stream of tears, laughter bubbled out against his chest, like his generosity had made me giddy. No way what he took home that night covered even half of those supplies. "It's perfect."

You're perfect.

His hands traced over my back to my shoulders, holding me to him. "I heard the way to a teacher's heart is through her supply closet."

I laughed even harder. "I'm going to have to stitch that."

"Yes, immortalize me in thread."

I held onto him another minute, my laughter dying out until calm took over. Contentment. Nowhere else could be better than Jed's arms. Warm and cozy like the way he said my nickname, I could have stayed there forever.

However...Gran's shuffling presence nearby prevented me from testing that theory. I released him, slipping away when I wanted nothing more than to lock my arms back around him.

"You really are the sweetest man." She sounded like he'd done a whole lot more than buy a couple hundred dollars of supplies, but I couldn't blame her. Nobody had ever done anything like this for me or my class before.

He hitched a shoulder. This seemed to be one of the times his humility won out over his cheeky ego.

"I have my moments." He turned to me. "You look gorgeous, by the way. I got sidetracked, or I would have said it before."

"Thank you. The dress isn't too much?"

"It's the exact right amount of much. I love it. Are you all set?"

I grabbed the two containers of cookies I'd prepped. "I'm all set."

He nodded at them. "What'd you choose?"

"Chocolate chip caramel. They seem to be a pretty big hit with most of your family. One bin's for them, and I made another batch for you."

His slow grin felt like a caress over my skin, all luxurious and tingly.

"You're spoiling me, Callie Lou."

"I'm probably the best girlfriend you ever had."

"Ain't that the truth."

"Those cookies don't handle the heat well," Gran said, interrupting our sparkly stare down. "Better refrigerate yours, or they'll turn into a mess."

"Ask her how she knows. She once took a batch of these to a book club meeting, but she ran a whole bunch of errands first. By the time book club started, they were just caramel-chocolate goo. That wasn't fun to clean up. Sorry, I'm—"

I met Jed's eyes and swallowed back the rest. His gentle smile reminded me I didn't need to apologize. After years of saying sorry, it'd probably be a while before I could completely let that old habit go, but it was enough to know he didn't think I had to.

"Jed, do you by any chance make sausage?" Gran asked.

His eyes went wide, and I must have looked pretty much the same. Okay, so we were really going to have the sausage conversation.

"I've never tried. Why do you ask?"

She explained about the meat grinder she'd rediscovered in the bowels of the kitchen. "I don't see myself having a need for it in Florida, but I thought you might like to take it."

"That's kind of you. I think I will." He turned to me. "Think there's such a thing as peach sausage?"

"You don't have to take that." Even though now, I kind of wanted to know what peach sausage would taste like.

"Why don't you run it by your house now? Then you can put those cookies in the fridge and not risk ruining them." Gran's sweet as pie smile didn't hide one bit of her deviousness.

"Oh my gosh, let's go." I steered Jed out of the kitchen before she could put the pressure on for anything else.

He scooped up the box of metal parts on the way. "Thanks again, Suzie."

"You kids have fun," she called after us.

Outside, I shook my head at her brazenness.

"Why do I feel like I missed something?" Jed asked.

I released a baby bear growl of frustration. "I accidentally let it slip that I've never seen your apartment. Gran thought that was kind of odd, thus all the pressure for you to take me there. And the meat grinder thing is just strange."

He stopped next to his truck. "You want to see my place?"

"Well...I mean, I don't have to, if it's weird for you."

"It's not weird for me. I can take you there right now, it's on the way to my pop's."

"I don't want to make us late to your family dinner."

He opened the passenger side of his truck and put the box behind the seats. Then, he took the containers of cookies from me and set them in the back, too. "It's not tea with the Queen, we can show up when we want."

"Okay. But I think it's tea with the King now."

"Doesn't have the same ring to it."

Ten minutes later, he parked in front of a duplex. From the outside, it looked homey and comfortable, but he gave me a sheepish look as though he expected criticism.

"It's just a rental," he said, unlocking the door. "Nothing fancy."

"I have no expectations."

He pushed the door open, and I crept inside, feeling as though I were peeking in when he wasn't home even though he stood right next to me. The front room's big picture window made it bright, and the comfy couch lent a welcoming air. I wandered around the room, trying not to look like a snoop even though I was.

Other than a couple of baseball caps and a stack of books about horticulture, he didn't have much of *him* in the room. Reminded me a bit of my college dorm room the day I moved in, like it was still waiting for its occupant. And he'd been here three years?

"It's...nice."

His grin held a hint of vulnerability. "That bad?"

"It's just kind of..." *Not yours* was what I wanted to say, but what did I know? Maybe every man's house looked like this. Doubted it, but maybe. He'd said he hadn't quite felt like he'd settled in here yet, but this drove it home.

"Beige," he finished for me.

The painting over the couch was the only spark of real life in the whole room. A smoky sunset sky sank low over forest scenery, part realistic landscape, part abstract dreamscape. The blue and purple sky offset the inky greens perfectly. "I like this."

"Yeah?"

"It's so vibrant. I love the layers of color and depth." From all the obvious brushstrokes, pretty sure he hadn't picked this up in a local big box store. "This wouldn't be out of place in my room."

"I thought that, too."

In the lower right corner, something I'd taken to be part of the scenery clarified into the painter's initials. JAE.

I whipped my head around to him. "What's your middle name?"

"Alexander."

My mouth dropped open. "You painted this?"

His smile twitched. "Depends on how much you like it."

"I love it."

"Then I painted it."

"Seriously?" Usually, I picked up on his teasing pretty well, but just now, I couldn't be sure. I'd never pictured him as an artist, and my brain struggled to adapt to the idea.

"I'm a man of many talents."

Somebody had cranked up the heat in the room. I kept telling myself not to think about Jed's talents, but here he was, giving me an opening and...yeah. He was probably the *most* talented.

"Where, uh," I said, swallowing because my neck was

suddenly hotter than the asphalt outside. "Where do you paint?"

He crooked a finger, and I followed him to a short hallway that led to two rooms. Ushering me into one, déjà vu hit me so hard, I sucked in a breath. Half a dozen paintings lined the room, each depicting a different colorful landscape. Some held simple cabins or more complicated greenery, but most I'd call fairly basic. And yet, they were the prettiest paintings I'd ever seen.

"This reminds me of my room." I couldn't even believe how alike they were.

"I had the same thought."

His soft voice made me turn to face him, but that proved too much. I couldn't name exactly what his eyes held, but whatever it was, it overwhelmed. Fighting that weird sense of *too much*, I made a quick circuit of the room, examining the beautiful paintings and expressing my admiration over each one. Like he often did when something really mattered to him, he accepted my praise with humility, smiling and nodding without a trace of crowing.

One corner held an easel over a drop cloth. The canvas there held bright swaths of greens and blues, like the sky over pastures but less defined.

"Is this for June and Ty?"

"It's for their wedding. How could you tell?"

"It just looks like them." Like he'd captured them in color somehow. "When did you start painting?"

Leaning against the door frame, he hitched his shoulders. "Just the last year. It's something to distract me when I can't sleep."

He sounded casual enough, but I suspected something deeper there.

"You have a hard time sleeping sometimes?"

His mouth twisted like he struggled over the answer. "If by sometimes, you mean a lot, then yes."

"Do you have PTSD?" I asked gently.

His lips pulled into a soft smile. "Not quite. But not all my memories are good ones, and since I've been home, they can crowd me. I can outrun it during the day when I'm busy, but at night, when there's nothing to keep me occupied, I sometimes fixate on the negative. I don't like that feeling, so—"

He gestured at the paintings surrounding us. I couldn't imagine how many sleepless nights this room represented. My heart hurt thinking of him that way. He so often wore such a light-hearted demeanor, hard to believe it didn't go all the way down.

"I know what you mean," I said. "Thoughts can run away with me when I'm alone at night, too."

"That's why I try to never be alone at night."

He'd probably meant to be cheeky, but the reminder sank like rocks in my gut. Jed wasn't the kind of guy to be alone much. I'd always known it, but tonight, that knowledge stung. When this was all over, when Gran made it to Florida and Jed was free to do whatever he wanted...how long before he would totally move on?

Maybe the bigger question—how long before I would? I was starting to suspect it'd be a long, long time before I got over Jed Evans.

"Yeah. Um, it's probably time for us to go."

I moved to pass him out the door, but he stopped me with a gentle hand on my arm. "I'm sorry. That was a terrible thing to say."

"No, don't worry about it." Good Lord, I hoped I sounded casual and not like my stupid little heart had turned to dust. "It's none of my business what you do when you're...alone."

That answer made his eyebrows tug together, the deep line

between them proving his displeasure. For a second, he ran his thumb over my arm but seemed to realize what he was doing, and pulled that hand over his forehead instead as though he could iron the lines out.

"It is, though. You're my—I need you to understand. After I came home, I started getting really bad insomnia. When I did sleep, I had nightmares. I learned pretty quick that being around people worked as a good distraction. I spent time with my family, friends...but also women I didn't date very long. I'm not proud to tell you that, Callie." The tortured look in his eyes confirmed it. "It wasn't all because of the insomnia, but enough of it was. Some nights, I couldn't sleep at all on my own. I was like a little kid seeking out someone else for comfort. I stayed over at Pop's sometimes. Other times..."

"You don't have to tell me this." I wished my voice hadn't gone so whispery, but I couldn't seem to make it louder.

"I feel like I do. Pop said I was trying to fill the emptiness in here." He touched his chest, his eyes stuck on me. "Maybe he was right. I took this up to try to lose myself in something else."

"Does it work?"

His little smile didn't look all that happy. "It helps. Some nights, I paint straight through until morning. And clearly, I'm not all that good at it."

"I think they're beautiful. But..." I wasn't sure the kindest way to put this. "Have you thought about trying therapy for the insomnia and the bad memories?"

I'd been a big fan of therapy since my teens, but not everybody sought that path.

"There's a counselor in Georgetown who has experience with veterans. I just haven't called him yet." He touched my fingers like he was seeking reassurance in that small gesture, a meek, questioning touch. "Have I made you rethink this whole thing?"

He had no idea that every time he opened up, it only made me like him more.

"I understand better than you think. I'm planning to sell my house to try to escape my bad memories. And I mean, I started doing needlework to get my mind off my mom. We're not all that different." I'd never tried dating around to take my mind off the grief, but I could see how it might work, in a backwards kind of way. Distractions were just that.

I didn't judge him for the decisions he'd made, whatever his reasons. A tiny thread of jealousy over the women he'd dated pricked like a burr in my heart, but I didn't think worse of him. Nothing had changed for me.

"I'm sorry for every single one of your losses, Callie. If I could…"

He reached up to cup my jaw, stroking his thumb across my cheek. Emotions I couldn't follow flashed in his eyes like they tore him in four different directions. He dropped his hand, shaking his head, and I could tell he'd discounted whatever he'd thought to say.

"You deserve the best life," he said.

Both of us knew nobody got to choose the hand they were dealt. Sometimes, with the big stuff, what we deserved didn't factor in. But I understood wanting the best for someone.

"So do you."

jed

THE SECOND I pulled up to my pop's house, June appeared on the porch. I'd expected a scolding for being late, considering Ty had been the principal chef behind tonight's dinner, but turned out she wasn't waiting on me.

June grabbed Callie's hand as soon as I helped her out of the truck.

"I'm so glad you're here, come on inside," she said, spiriting her away from me.

"Don't mind me, your blood relation left out in the cold."

She looked at me over her shoulder, not a bit contrite. "It's ninety degrees out, I think you'll live."

Callie looked over her shoulder, too, a touch more worry in her features. "Would you bring in the cookies?"

Okay, so she'd only been worried about the dessert. I deserved that.

I gave her a nod right before they disappeared into my pop's house. Had to laugh a little. But my heart warmed, too, seeing how well my sister got along with Callie. If a hint of dread coiled underneath that warmth, waiting for everything to fall apart, well...I'd deal with that when it struck.

Not that I'd been good at waiting. I'd thrown my past in Callie's face like I'd needed her to remember every last one of my faults. Maybe I'd needed us both to remember. Because this thing we were playing at couldn't be real for a guy like me. Even if she made me want to believe in fairy tales, I'd been around the block a few too many times to think a happily ever after still waited in my future.

Inside, the house had reached peak pre-dinner chaos. Ty and Marilyn were putting the finishing touches on the meal while Annie and Pop shuttled plates to the table. Wade outfitted his two youngest kids with bibs, and Dylan jumped around like he had ants in his pants. June had an arm around Callie, talking low about something I couldn't hear and probably would rather not know.

"Callie brought cookies." I held the container aloft like a hunting trophy, to much applause.

"I'm tempted to skip right to dessert," Pop said.

Ty eyed him. "I'm going to overlook that."

Pop laughed and clapped him on the back. "Now, son, you know I don't mean any harm."

"Ty worked hard on this ginger chicken," June put in. "At least eat *some* dinner before you dig into the cookies."

She tried to scold, but her satisfied smile said she liked hearing Pop call Ty *son*. He'd always been that way with Annie, considering himself her second father, not just in law. As far as he was concerned, family was family, didn't matter how they came into the fold. He'd be that way with Callie, too.

The image came into my mind unbidden but perfectly clear. Callie, sitting at this table for family dinners far into the future. Christmases and birthdays and cookouts, her hand laced in mine, right by my side where she belonged.

I shook my head like a dog trying to clear water from its

ears, but the idea had stuck. I knew futures weren't guaranteed, but I sure wanted that one.

Unfortunately, I wasn't the only one dreaming of sitting by Callie. Dylan crammed his little body next to her, way more comfortable hanging out with his former teacher than I would have been at that age. Then again, my kindergarten teacher had been about a hundred years old and smelled like cough drops. Callie was endlessly soft and smelled of sweet orange flowers.

Pull it together, Evans.

Dinner progressed almost normally. Almost, because my family kept glancing from Callie to me like they'd just spotted the cutest specimens in the zoo. Pop and Marilyn especially, whose gloating grins made them look like Cheshire cats. I'd figured they'd pepper her with questions or break out with some embarrassing childhood story bare minimum, but June piped up first.

"I'm so curious how you two got together, Callie." She watched her with eager eyes, already slipping into gossip reporter mode. "What made you decide to give this guy a chance?"

Wade chuckled at my side. "Karma's here to bite you in the butt."

I'd given June a hard enough time when she first got together with Ty, I probably deserved a little of it back. Didn't mean I looked forward to her teasing. Especially considering Callie'd had a rough go with making up stories on the fly for her friends so far. This whole pretend play might come crashing down in a few awkward answers.

"Well…" She dabbed her mouth with a napkin, glancing around the table but skipping me. "I think it was when we went on that big hike."

Okay, *not* what I'd expected her to say. I'd figured we were in for a fabricated recap of that night at The Broken Hammer, but the hike happened way before that.

"I liked how he had his eye on everyone, making sure nobody fell behind, checking in to be sure we were all drinking enough water. It was like he felt responsible for us, and I hadn't seen that side of him before. The hike was kind of a lot for me, and I had a hard time with the steepest part. He dropped back with me, telling jokes and pointing out weird-looking trees so casually, I didn't even realize at first how he was encouraging me along. He didn't say anything about me struggling or even talk about the hike, really, he was just *with* me, and that was enough to keep me going. I think that was when everything started."

My lungs shut down, my heart thumping away for the whole table to hear. I remembered the hike because it'd been a bear, and I remembered Callie because I'd always noticed her. But I hadn't thought something so small I'd done had stuck with her. If she'd said I'd looked good in my athletic shirt, I would have laughed it off, but the way she remembered *me* stole my words away.

When her eyes finally hit me, her smile held a trace of worry. Like she was afraid she'd said too much, or given too much of herself away and wasn't sure how I'd react. If she only knew.

I wrapped my arm around her shoulders and kissed her temple, gawkers be damned.

"Jed's got a big heart in there," Pop said. "He just doesn't always show it."

"All right, enough talk about my internal organs." I needed to steer this ship to safer waters before my poor heart expired from all the attention. "Start up some wedding talk."

"That's a really interesting change of topic." June smiled

innocently at me even as her meaning made my stomach flip. "Do you want to elaborate on that?"

Nope. I did not.

"I've been hogtied by conversations at this table a time or two," Ty said. "I'll have mercy on you, Jed. We're planning that shed clean-out for Thursday. I'll text you the details."

"Bless you, future brother-in-law."

"What shed clean-out?" Callie asked.

June explained about her reception plans for Ty's vehicle barn. "After they clear it, Marilyn and I and the girls will get it ready for the weekend."

Her eyes went soft, her shoulders relaxing, as if she'd forgotten she was getting married in a week. She looped her arm through Ty's and leaned into him, resting her cheek on his shoulder. He looked like he had everything he could ever want. These two would give cavities to everyone in the county if they kept this up, but I couldn't blame them.

"Do you need any more help with the prep?" Callie asked.

"She's got a good eye for that stuff," I said. "You want her on your team."

"We'd love more help." June nodded at her, but cut a look to me like I'd said something incriminating.

Probably had. When it came to Callie, pretty sure everything could incriminate me.

After dinner and cleanup, we all wandered out back, presumably to test the strength of Pop's new bug zappers in the yard. A soft pink glow filled the sky as it crept toward sunset, giving the evening a hazy quality. Dylan and Beau tore into the trees, and Wade handed Maisie off to Callie so he could chase after them.

I leaned my hands against the porch rail, drinking in the sight of Callie holding a baby like it was the most natural thing in the world. Maybe it was. Maybe she should always hold a baby in her arms. Not a very enlightened way to think, but my brain had snagged seeing her cuddling my niece.

If I could nail down a future I could trust, something I knew wouldn't break apart in my hands...I'd want that one.

June sauntered up next to me, an *I told you so* grin splitting her face.

I shook my head at her. "I can't look at you too long or I'll come down with smugness poisoning. Shouldn't you be sneaking off with your fiancé somewhere?"

"Oh, I plan to. The man is irresistible."

I thinned my mouth, regretting I'd asked. They were cute together, but I wanted zero details.

She nudged me with her shoulder. "I'm happy for you two. It's fascinating to see you so twisted up over a woman."

Tried not to think too hard about all the ways I'd proved it tonight. "I'm glad you're taking the high road and not gloating."

"I never promised to take the high road. This is golden. I'm not sure I've ever seen you so awkward before."

"I'm not being awkward." Would rather not define exactly what I was, but didn't think that one suited.

She laughed. "You so are. And you're so affectionate with her, it's adorable. You couldn't stop touching her all through dinner."

My hands had wandered during the meal, I admit, but not in any inappropriate way. Just little nudges to reassure myself she was still there, still fine, still with me. Hadn't thought anyone would be tallying up my touches to rub in my face later.

Although I probably should have.

"Is there a point to all this, or is it just payback?"

"It's definitely both." She quieted, following my gaze to where Callie stood with Maisie on her hip, talking with Pop. "Mom would have loved her."

I tried to swallow, but the lump in my throat made it impossible. Mom had been a little quieter, a little more subdued, but June was right. She would have adored Callie. Her warmth, her eager storytelling, the way she found the best in everything, like she needed to love the hell out of life. Mom would have claimed her as her new daughter from the first day they met.

"What's not to love?"

TWENTY-THREE

I REALLY HOPED there wouldn't be a test at the end of this impromptu lesson on peach tree history.

I wandered around in the orchards with Clint, Maisie shimmying away on my hip, Dylan and Beau dancing around beside us. Wade was off somewhere, and I hadn't seen the rest of the family in a bit, but figured we'd all circle back together soon. Mostly, I was glad I'd worn my sneakers, or this trip into the trees would have been a lot more uncomfortable.

Clint told me about the peaches they grew, heirloom types they could only sell at their roadside store and the local markets because they were too delicate to ship. He had as much pride in the trees we passed as if he were describing his own children, telling me how much they'd grown and all they'd accomplished.

"We've got a couple of varieties you can't find anywhere else. One I grafted intentionally a decade or so ago, the other sprung up by accident. But they're all delicious. They take good care of us."

"I love your farm. I think it's my new favorite place." Maybe I shouldn't have blurted that out, but it was a hundred percent true. From the smell of the peaches to the peace in the trees, I loved everything about it.

"I'm certainly glad to hear it." Clint's bright eyes sparkled. "I hope I'll be seeing you out here a lot more."

"I hope so, too." Yeah, definitely needed to quit sharing.

"Farming's not for the faint of heart. There's ups and downs, but it gets in your blood and sticks with you." He reached up to run his fingers over a big green leaf in a sweet caress, like he couldn't hold in his affection for the farm. "It'll demand a lot of Jed in the coming years, but it will give even more back, if he wants it."

Maisie kicked her little feet against my stomach, babbling in my ear. "He seems up for the challenge."

"I think so, too. But that doesn't mean it's not a lot to take on." He turned toward the house and exhaled soft laughter. "Here he comes. I wondered how long he'd be able to stay away from you."

I followed his gaze to find Jed striding through the trees, his long legs eating up the dirt between us. I couldn't stop staring, and heat crept up to my cheeks as I shifted Maisie to my opposite hip in a futile attempt at distracting myself.

"I've never seen him like this," Clint said softly. "It looks good on him, even if he doesn't see it himself."

"What looks good on him?"

He turned to me like I should have been able to fill in the blanks. "Being lost over a woman."

My heart spasmed around in my chest for a few glorious seconds before Maisie grabbed a hank of my hair with a shriek, snapping me out of my raptures. I'd just saved my hair from her little fist, to much unhappy burbling from her, when Jed reached us. His eyes moved from her to me.

"Maisie's giving you her customary welcome, I see."

"We were getting on fine." I bounced her on my hip, settling her down again. She babbled at Jed, swatting my back in her excitement. "I think the temptation just became too much."

"Oh, I'm with her there." He slipped his hand into mine, grinning away at me.

Could someone pass out from too much flirtation? Because sometimes, it felt like I might, the way my breath caught and my heart rate zoomed. A few more sweet smiles paired with saucy remarks, and I'd swoon right into the dust.

A little body wedged between us, and Dylan pulled Jed's hand out of mine, replacing it with his small one. He shot a dark look at Jed I'd rarely seen during the school year, but he wasn't messing around.

"She's *my* teacher."

Jed's eyebrows lifted. "She's *my* girlfriend, little man."

Clint chuckled, and I had to laugh, too. Out of all the unlikely fights over my affections, I never would have called this one. Or any, to be honest, but this one especially.

"Why don't I take the kids back to the house and let you two wander for a bit." Clint took Maisie from my arms and rounded up the boys. "Who wants ice cream and cookies?"

Dylan and Beau shouted their enthusiasm, and Maisie kicked her little feet as Clint guided them away, our magical pied piper giving us some time to ourselves. In another minute, Jed and I were alone in the trees with nothing but the sound of a breeze shaking their leaves. He took my hand again, leading me deeper into the orchard.

"Do you mind staying out here for a while?"

"Not at all, it's glorious out here and smells divine. I only have second thoughts over missing dessert."

"I wouldn't make you miss it, darlin'."

He moved us closer to a tree dotted with vibrant fruit. Releasing my hand, he found a perfect peach and plucked it from its stem. The red-gold color shouted out its ripeness, and my mouth watered in response. He rubbed it through his hands a few times, dusting off the light fuzz on the skin before he pulled a pocket knife from his jeans, ran the blade around the peach, and twisted.

He handed me the pit-free half with a flourish. "There's your dessert right there."

I took it greedily—I'd devoured every peach I'd bought from his farm store and knew what kind of deliciousness awaited me. I took a bite, the sweet-tangy flavors so good, I moaned.

Jed echoed the sound, but when I turned to him, he'd looked away, his throat working.

A more ladylike woman might have eaten her half of the fruit with a little less enthusiasm, but I didn't hold back devouring its juicy-sweet perfection. In another minute or two, I'd finished the last bite, and licked a dribble of juice off my thumb.

Jed made a strange sound. I found him watching me with enough heat to power a thousand suns, like everything in the world depended on what I did next. My stomach swooped and warmed, but I couldn't look away from his intense gaze.

"What?" I said with a touch more innocence than I felt. "I don't want sticky fingers."

"Tell me you're not doing that on purpose to torture me." His voice had gone all gravelly and rough, and it tugged at something deep inside me.

"Well, I wouldn't call it torture." I licked my thumb again just to be sure I'd got it all. That was the only reason. Not because I liked the idea of having this man weak in the knees over me.

A groan rumbled out of him as he closed the last scrap of distance between us, his eyes fixed on my mouth. "I promise you it is."

Maybe I should have called it good and stopped there, but I

liked the fire in his eyes as he tracked my mouth. I liked how he looked so on edge, as if he could snap any minute. And I liked most of all being the one that'd made him that way.

I dropped my voice low. "Staff Sergeant Evans, I would never."

His naughty grin was a lit match, and my insides went up like tinder, flames spooling out from my belly down to the tips of my toes and up to the top of my head. He swooped in and kissed me, his lips on mine before I'd registered they were coming. The kiss was sweet, like he'd cobbled it out of pure spontaneous affection. He smiled against my mouth, and my heart exploded into little stars.

Clint's words echoed through my foggy brain. *Lost over a woman.* I couldn't be sure he was really lost over me, but I was for sure lost over him. Smart or not, I was head over heels.

Before the kiss could get really good, a voice interrupted us. "Miss Callie, don't you want ice cream?"

Dylan's shout carried across the yard and into the trees, and I prayed he couldn't see me making out with his uncle at this distance. Jed released me, his expression still lit with an open affection that made my legs feel all woozy.

"Still need that dessert, darlin'?" he asked low.

"Holy crap, yes please."

His lips tugged into the smuggest smile. Because of course I'd gone and said that embarrassment out loud. I shoved away from him, rolling my eyes at my obviousness.

"We're on our way," he called to Dylan, his gaze stuck on me.

I swatted at him, managing to hit his pec, which surely made my cheeks flame a brighter red. "Stop that."

"Stop what?" His smile said he knew exactly what.

Stop making bedroom eyes and grinning that smug little grin and making my brain break apart with your kisses. Seemed just a touch too revealing to say.

I waved a hand in front of him, dangerously close to miming what I dearly wanted to do. "Stop *all this.*"

He laced our fingers together and headed us toward the house. "You're my girlfriend, Callie Lou. Better get used to *all this.*"

See, that was the trouble. I was used to it. At this point, I couldn't be sure I'd ever get *un*-used to it.

jed

SHOULD HAVE KNOWN BETTER than to think cleaning out any rancher's vehicle barn would be a quick or easy job.

Sure, Ty had it all arranged so everything could be found when he needed it, but we were talking a *lot* of stuff to get out of there. He'd hidden smaller items away in storage cupboards, and he'd already moved the ATVs, tractor, and trailers. Still left plenty of vehicle parts, sprayers, and Lord knew what else to clear away. He'd called a good-sized crew out here, though, and after an hour of shuttling items where he directed, we'd made good progress.

Couldn't envision it as a reception site yet, but good progress.

I grabbed a sixteen-foot ladder and hefted it to my shoulder, but June stopped me.

"That stays, we'll need it later."

I propped it back where it'd been. "You know, you could just rent a giant tent. Get you the same thing with less work."

She put her finger to her chin, looking remarkably like Wade whenever he got into a mocking mood. "Let me see, a plain white tent devoid of personality, or a fifty-year-old barn full of rustic charm and character. Tough call."

"I'll have to trust you on the charm and character." Looked like tetanus waiting to happen, but I figured saying so would get me evicted from the work party, and possibly the wedding.

Her glare didn't affect me all that much. She walked away, probably to find someone else to supervise.

Once she'd moved out of earshot, Ty walked up and leaned in close. "I suggested the same thing."

He shrugged, like *What can you do?*, before trotting outside with the old tool box he held.

Fools for love, I supposed. He wanted to make my sister happy, and I'd never fault that.

I glanced to one corner of the big old barn where Callie ran a shop vac going after the dust and cobwebs that had pretty much colored the unfinished wood walls gray. She'd pulled her hair into a short ponytail, but wisps of it had escaped, laying against her forehead and neck. She leaned up to get the vacuum nozzle as high as she could reach, her T-shirt riding up at her waist. My stomach tightened as my brain memorized that sliver of skin.

"Stop ogling your girlfriend and help us."

Wade's smirk just asked to be smacked off, but I had come here to work, after all. I dragged my eyes away from Callie, and he motioned me over to a wooden worktable where Booker and Ty waited.

"We're supposed to move this?" I asked. Thing looked like it could have been five hundred pounds.

"If we can." Ty's expression said he had his doubts, too, but he was willing to try, for June's sake.

Crazy kids.

I took a corner, and we all heaved. To my surprise, it came

off the floor. Took four grown men straining with every breath, but we had it.

"Where's it going?" Booker asked.

Ty nodded behind me. "Outside and around the corner."

Quick description, slow execution. We inched it along, my arms burning by the time we got it through the barn doors and situated where Ty—or more likely, June—wanted it. When we finally set it down in a more or less inconspicuous location, all four of us rubbed at our shoulders.

"I suppose there'll be a post-wedding work party to put the barn back together?" I asked Ty.

He winced as though he hadn't thought any further than the wedding. Couldn't blame the guy for not being able to think much past saying *I do*.

"If you wouldn't mind."

"Bright and early Sunday morning, then? Six a.m.?"

"If any of you show up on my property for any reason the week after the wedding, I'm throwing you in the manure pile."

Booker laughed. "He'll do it, too. The man deserves his honeymoon."

I held my hands up. "I'd never intrude on my sister's honeymoon."

Would not add I'd been pretty well set on never even *thinking* about my sister's honeymoon, much less crashing it.

Back in the barn, Callie'd switched off the shop vac and wiped a hand across her forehead while she examined her work.

I walked up beside her. "It's looking good."

She made a face. "It's getting there."

"June doesn't expect you to spray it down with wood polish, does she?"

"I don't think so, but a spray down wouldn't hurt." She

picked her floral water bottle up off the floor and drank the last gulp down. "Think Ty has a pressure washer?"

"I think a pressure washer would knock this whole place down." Seemed sturdy enough for the vehicles, but I sure wouldn't push it.

"We could use a toothbrush, then. Isn't that the way you cleaned things in the Army?"

She grinned up at me, and I gloried in her teasing. *Crazy kids.*

"Only really disgusting things. So, yeah, the barn counts." I eyed the way her hair clung to her forehead in sweaty tendrils. A bead of sweat worked its way from behind her ear down the side of her throat, and I wanted to brush it aside with my thumb in the worst way. "Are you holding up in the heat okay?"

Barn had no insulation, poor circulation, and the temperature hovered around a hundred degrees. June had rented giant fans for the reception, but those wouldn't arrive until the tables, chairs, and all the rest came on Friday.

"I'm okay. Is it too much for you?"

I winked at her. "Darlin', I've been through worse. Why don't you take a breather and I'll refill this for you."

I took the empty water bottle from her hand, letting my fingers glide over hers. Her lips parted in a soft little intake of breath that made my stomach jolt like I'd hit rough air. Or had suddenly become desperately hungry.

I needed to shut down that hunger. I'd promised her she could be in charge of the physical side of our fake relationship, and I'd broken that promise in the orchards. Kissing her had barely been a thought—it'd been an all-out need, and I'd acted on impulse. Did I regret it? No. Had I replayed that kiss in my head? More times than I could count. Should I do it again? Absolutely not.

Pretty sure with Callie, satisfying one need would only lead to others, a series of dominoes taking us to places I'd sworn we'd stay away from. No matter how much I longed to visit those places.

I swallowed hard, trying to clear my thoughts. All this over a finger touch? Maybe it *was* too hot in here.

I turned from her and found my beat-up stainless steel water bottle resting on the cross beam of the barn's side wall. "Anyone else need water refills? I'm headed to the house."

Turned out everyone needed refills, and I juggled six earth-friendly containers in my arms.

Wade took three from me. "I'll help you out with that."

"Thanks, guys." June looked about as wilted as Callie did, but she had a spark of determination to her, too, like this miserable heat couldn't possibly get in the way of the wedding reception of her dreams.

Wade and I strode off, crossing the gravel lot between the vehicle barn and Ty's house. He kept shooting glances my way, and I figured he had something smart sitting on the tip of his tongue.

I sighed. "Out with it."

"You're just so adorable, is all."

He laid it on thick, sounding like a teenager sighing over their crush.

"I'm always adorable. Didn't think that'd ever been in question."

"Checking in on Callie, watching her like your eyes are glued to her. It's a sight."

Why couldn't my whole family have got their gloating in over dinner the other night? One and done, bam, out of their system, and we could all move on. But no. Now Wade wanted a turn.

"You've seen me with women before."

"I actually haven't. Not since high school, and that's long enough ago now not to count. This is a novel experience."

"At least you're not giving me a hard time about it."

He laughed as we stomped the dirt off our feet on Ty's welcome mat. "I've only just begun."

We let ourselves into the house and over to the kitchen, where we filled up the water bottles in the sink. The cool air conditioning brought welcome relief from the stifling heat of the barn. I looked around as the faucet did its thing, taking in the clean lines in the kitchen, the wood flooring, the bright gray walls.

June had confided once that Ty had remodeled this house to suit her. Before they'd ever got together, before he'd even really had a chance with her, he'd made her a home. Either the most pathetic thing I'd ever heard...or the ballsiest.

"I can't figure out what took you so long."

I turned to Wade. "I don't follow."

"With Callie. She's exactly your type."

Had to laugh at that. "You just said you've never seen me with a woman. You don't know what my type is."

"Okay, then she's exactly who *I'd think* would be your type, is that better?"

Couldn't say it was, frankly. "How do you figure?"

"Is this what we're doing? I tell you all of Callie's great qualities so you can bask in the reflected praise?"

I hitched a shoulder. "I'm not against it."

"Okay." He capped the bottles as I finished filling each one. "You're not going for the subdued wallflower, you'd want someone like you. Someone outgoing and ready to join in anything that comes up, someone with a healthy sense of fun. Like Callie."

All true, but I didn't need to say so. He was enjoying this too much already.

"Plus, she's cute as hell."

"Agreed."

He chuckled low. "I'd seen you watching her for a while. Figured we'd get here one day. If she was interested, anyway. Seemed an awful big *if*."

"I wasn't *watching* her." Didn't like the creepy connotation.

"You keep telling yourself that."

But...I had been watching her, hadn't I? Long before our awkward coffee date, my attention had perked up whenever she walked in the room. I liked her smile, her laugh, the way she threw herself into everything she did. I'd gravitated toward her, not enough to be obvious—even to myself, apparently—but just enough to keep me in her sphere.

Wade grabbed up half the bottles but stopped when he caught sight of my face. "What's that look for?"

I just realized I've been crushing on Callie since I met her, and it's flipped all the switches in my brain. Couldn't very well admit that without blowing our cover, though.

"You don't think the age thing is too much?" I hadn't given the eight years between us a lot of thought lately, but I didn't have much to throw out there as potential incompatibilities anymore. We fit together better than I'd ever thought possible.

He shrugged. "She's what, twenty-five?"

"Almost."

"June's six years younger than Ty. We're going to their wedding in a couple of days. You do the math."

He headed out, and I followed, telling myself I absolutely would not do that math.

callie

I STOOD on top of the high ladder, running a spool of fairy lights around a ceiling beam. I liked the old barn, even if getting it ready turned out to be a bigger project than I'd expected. June's vision for the space included the lights to brighten it up and white fabric draped in sections across the ceiling to soften it. I'd never thought too much about wedding venues, but this barn would turn out gorgeous in the end.

I hadn't been as sure when Jed and I first got here. But after a couple of hours, we'd cleared out the floor space, cleaned up the walls, and now, June was sweeping the floor. It'd probably need a good mopping, too, but I couldn't be sure the worn cement wouldn't destroy anything that tried to clean it.

That pressure washer idea still sounded brilliant to me.

"That's perfect, Callie," June called. "You're spacing the lights exactly right. I can't thank you enough for helping today."

"I'm just glad to be here."

I really was. Maybe that sounded funny, but I liked being part of their celebrations and happiness. I liked being part of a big event like this. The real trouble was, I liked being part of their *family*. The camaraderie and the teasing, the way they all lent a hand when needed.

The only thing I didn't like was the thought that wiggled like a worm in my brain, reminding me this would all be over in another week. Maybe sooner. Once Gran was gone, Jed and I wouldn't need to fake anymore.

She hadn't said anything to me about it, but she'd started packing in earnest again. I'd found more boxes neatly taped up and labeled stacked along one living room wall. Her bedroom looked like a tornado had hit it, but she had fresh boxes packed up in there, too. The kitchen was missing everyday utensils she'd squirreled away, but I'd never dare complain. She was working like a woman who'd decided to be ready for the movers on Monday.

Monday. Five more days, and my relationship with Jed would crumble away.

That reminder curled my stomach in on itself. As much as I liked to think maybe this wasn't all fake, that maybe something real was building here, too, I couldn't forget how he'd said marriage wasn't in the cards for him. Like a chicken, I'd never asked why. And even if I didn't need it immediately, I'd like to know that marriage might happen someday down the line.

I wasn't sure I could date Jed in earnest for only a little while. Chances were good I'd want forever.

"Whoa, whoa, whoa."

I looked down to see he had returned with the water bottles and stood at the bottom of my ladder. He frowned up at me, a little storm cloud brewing behind his eyes.

"I'm gone five minutes, and you guys send Callie up into the rafters? Come down."

"What? No, I'm putting lights up." I shook the spool of lights, but that made him grab hold of my ladder as if it might fall down.

"Hardy can do this, he shouldn't be asking you to do it."

I didn't like the edge to his voice. He sounded even more upset than he'd been with Greg, because this time, there was no pretending at friendliness, just pure irritation on display.

"I didn't ask her to do it." Ty stood on another ladder on the other side of the barn, drilling holes into the ceiling to hold the fabric swags June wanted. "She volunteered."

"Because she's too nice to say no."

Jed's dismissive tone surprised me, not just for its fierceness, but for how it grated. I liked him protective of me, but this skated too close to patronizing, like I couldn't possibly have made this decision on my own.

"I volunteered because I wanted to," I said, glaring down at him. "It's not a big deal."

"It's a big deal to me. Come down."

"Not until I'm done."

"If June wants lights up there so bad, she can do it, and *you* can sweep the floor."

My warm, cozy feelings for this man iced over as my frustration reached its peak.

"Jed Evans, I am climbing down, and then you and I are going to have a talk."

Just inside the door, Wade whistled low. Jed whipped his head around to him, but Wade was smart enough to find something useful to do before he got involved here.

I climbed down the tall ladder, silently fuming as my foot hit every rung. Everyone else stayed completely still while my heart raced and my face had probably gone beet red. When I got to the floor, I passed June and walked out the big barn doors without even checking to see if Jed came with me. If he had any sense at all, he would.

I found a shady spot beneath an oak tree, far enough from

the barn we wouldn't be overheard, before I turned to face him. "What is your problem?"

He looked marginally less mutinous than he had in the barn, but no closer to giving in. "My problem is them sending you up that ladder."

"They didn't send me, I offered to do it."

"It's not safe up there."

"You climb ladders every damn day!"

His mouth twisted. "That's different."

"It is not."

"You don't have to do dangerous things just because they ask you. You should have told them no."

"There's no *should* about it. They didn't make me, and I can climb that ladder if I want to." I blew out a breath as we stared each other down. What a stupid thing to fight over, but I hated that undercurrent of doubt, like I didn't know how to choose for myself. I counted to ten in my head, willing my racing heart to settle. "You're not in charge of me, Jed. I'm not one of your soldiers to order around."

He shook his head, his brow furrowed like that didn't make sense. "That's not what this— I'm not trying to give you orders."

"It sure sounded like it."

His mouth fell open, and he paused a whole five seconds just staring at me like he needed to line his thoughts back up. Then, his shoulders dropped, and the air rushed out of him.

"I'm really an ass, aren't I?"

His voice had lost that hard edge to it, and he sounded more like himself. A little more contrite version of himself, but still.

"I mean, yeah. You were a whole ass just then."

He laughed, raking his fingers through his hair. He exhaled another hard breath, his mouth twisting. "I'm sorry, Callie. I was way out of line. I just didn't want you to get hurt, is all."

"I like the sentiment, but not the way you went about it."

"I was trying to look out for you."

"Yeah, but you made me feel like I can't be trusted to speak up for myself. Like I need you to do the thinking for me."

The epitome of what Gran wanted for me—and I for sure *didn't* want—and he'd gone and done it.

His face crumpled, the hard lines erased. "I know, I'm sorry. It doesn't excuse it, but I saw you up there, twenty feet in the air—"

"Sixteen."

His small smile said that clarification didn't make anything better. "Sixteen. And all I could think about was you falling onto that cement floor. I guess I kind of panicked."

I appreciated his regret, but I wasn't ready to just totally let him off the hook yet.

"And you expressed your concerns like a cave man," I said, coaching him along.

"I did. I shouldn't have talked to you like that. I just...if anything happened to you..."

He looked like he had all sorts of gruesome scenarios playing out behind his eyes. Reaching out, he took my fingers in the same uncertain gesture he'd made once before. "I don't think I could take it. I'm sorry. Truly."

My heart melted so fast, it had probably turned into a puddle at my feet. The man knew how to make an apology. "I forgive you."

"Thank you. Can I hug you?"

His voice came out just as hesitant as his finger-touch, like I might rather turn my back on him. I spared him a long wait by stepping closer and wrapping my arms around him. He released a jagged sigh as his arms came around me, pulling me close. He kissed the top of my head and laid his cheek against my crown, sending a warm, fizzy sensation through my heart.

Affection for this man—who, admittedly, didn't always put his best foot forward, but who ever did?—surged through me like an ocean wave. It rose up and up, higher than I'd originally thought likely or possible. Pretty soon, it'd fill me all the way up, and where would I be then?

In love.

Nope. I would pretend I hadn't just thought that. No way would I fall in love all by myself. Especially not when a goodbye already waited for us just a few days away.

I tilted my chin to look up at him and pinched his side. "Just so you know, I'm climbing back up that ladder and finishing the lights."

He sighed again, but this one had some humor to it.

"I figured. I might have to find something else to do so I don't go out of my skull the whole time you're up there."

I examined him a little closer. "Are you afraid of heights?"

"No. Just afraid of you falling from them."

The sweetness from this man had no end in sight. I patted his back and slipped away from his arms before I could be tempted to write up a change of address form and stay there permanently.

Back in the barn, nobody remarked on our absence, but every person inside shot us secret looks. A couple of raised eyebrows, and a smirk from Wade, but nothing too outrageous.

"How about I go get us sandwiches for lunch?" Jed said.

Ty looked down from where he sat perched on his ladder, screwing in a bracket. "I can take care of that."

"No big deal, I don't mind. I, uh—" His eyes cut to me. "I need the distraction while the lights are going up."

Wade laughed, but nobody else reacted as Jed left the barn. Outside, he tossed one last look back at me, raising his hand in that casual little wave I loved, before he got into his truck and drove away.

Booker looked up from where he was putting the brackets for June's fabric swag contraption together to pass up to Ty. "Now that is a man who has learned a lesson."

"We had a talk," I said, climbing back up my ladder.

Below me, June caught my eye. She winked and nodded before carrying on sweeping the floor.

I went back to wrapping the rafter with fairy lights, my heart positively beating out of my chest with affection—for Jed *and* his family. I didn't want these last few days with any of them to end. It would, I knew that. But I was determined to soak up this togetherness for as long as I could.

jed

PROBABLY TIME I just threw out that theory I was a smart man.

I'd spent about twenty of the last twenty-four hours replaying how I'd turned into a control freak with Callie. Not one of my finest moments, and I had no good excuse for my behavior. I'd seen her up on that ladder, and the image of her getting hurt had stormed into my head. My instinct had been to protect her from harm, and I'd gone about it in the stupidest way possible. Ordering her around like she was my—

Well, even if she were truly my *anything*, giving her orders would never be the way to go. My logical brain knew it, however tiny that side of me might have been in the moment. But my fearful brain had taken over, and I'd behaved like an absolute jerk, thinking I knew best. Probably did not deserve the forgiveness she'd so readily handed me.

At least my family hadn't given me a hard time about it.

No, wait, I must have been thinking of someone else's family. Mine had been rubbing my face in my mistake every chance they got.

"Now, I just want you to know, I'm about to climb this

ladder." Wade patted the steel rung next to him, making it clatter. "You might want to cover your eyes."

I socked him in the shoulder, but he laughed as he climbed up to arrange the fabric that now hung from the barn's ceiling at intervals. June had been asking for tiny adjustments all morning as the rest of us scrambled to arrange tables and chairs down below. Earlier today, we'd ferried benches for the guests out to the ceremony site, and she'd confirmed the location looked good, but in here, she'd been tinkering.

Probably the beauty of where they'd say their vows overpowered any urge to change things up. A pretty little piece of Ty's property beneath old growth trees and next to a babbling brook—not much to improve on out there.

June stared up at the ceiling, hands on her hips. "Bunch it up some more."

Wade did as she said, pulling the fabric together, waiting for further instructions.

"I'm okay up here," he called down to me, smug as all get out. "No need to worry, Jed."

"I hope you fall," I called back.

His chuckling grated on my nerves. Didn't really need the constant reminder I'd behaved like a moron yesterday.

"I thought it was sweet." June eyed the way the fabric hung as if lives depended on getting just the right look. "A little bit of an obnoxious overstep on your part, sure, but adorable to see you so worked up over her."

"Thank you, truly. It's great that we're all still talking about it, I'm really loving this back and forth. I hope it never ends."

She didn't seem that affected by my sarcasm. "Oh, relax. We've all been there. This one time, I was out riding one of Ty's horses by myself and he got so worried, he—"

"Jed doesn't need all the details," Ty cut in.

Her affectionate look showed every ounce of her love for the big, private guy. Or possibly she was undressing him with her eyes—it all ran together these days.

She turned back to me, wearing a much more normal expression. "The point is, we're happy for you."

"So happy." Wade's face twisted up as if in the middle of an ugly cry.

"That's it, I have to move," I said. "I can't stand y'all anymore."

"He can dish it out," he called in a sing-song voice.

Nope, I could not take it. Never thought I'd get so touchy. Not too hard to see the reason why. Callie and I had built up this thing between us just to set it at the edge of a cliff. A few more days, and we'd have to push it over, letting it crash and burn. A grim reality I'd been increasingly driving from my mind.

Instead, I'd begun to spin thoughts of an alternative option. One where we didn't go our separate ways, but went on spending our days together indefinitely. Wasn't all that sure what she'd think about that plan. I'd considered myself pretty skilled at reading a woman's signals, but I didn't like to assume anything with her, not when fake and real blurred together so easily.

Once we got past this wedding and her grandma's tail lights had disappeared off to Florida, we'd get a minute to ourselves. Then...well, we'd just see where things went.

"Make sure you bring Callie tonight," June said, edging closer to me. "Tell her *not* to bring food."

"She won't be too happy about that."

"It's the least we can do, after all her help."

Callie had been out here all day yesterday, even when I'd had to cut out for a while to get a few things done on the farm. She'd worked alongside June and Marilyn fixing up the table centerpieces, arranging flowers, and I couldn't guess what else.

"It's how she shows she cares."

"Yep. She's got a big heart." June smirked, taking me back to when we were kids and she wanted to gloat over the latest gossip about me. "Reminds me of someone else I know."

I headed toward the barn door. "All right, I've had about all I can take."

"Aw. But you could stay and talk feelings with us."

"I want to hear about your feelings," Wade echoed, saying the last word in a distinct baby voice.

I pointed where he sat perched up in the rafters. "The guy with a wife and three kids is one to talk."

"I'm not hiding anything, everybody knows how I feel. I am desperately in love with my wife. It's freeing to get it all out there. You should try it sometime."

"How about now?" June said with a grin.

I ignored my rotten siblings and turned to Ty. "You good here?"

"We're good." He nodded, releasing me from enduring more of this exultation. "But if you want to stay and discuss anything…"

"Dammit, Hardy, not you, too." I threw a hand up, walking away. "I'm out."

"Don't forget to bring Callie tonight!" June called after me.

"Like he'd ever leave her behind," Wade said, chuckling.

Man wasn't wrong, I just didn't need it thrown in my face every minute of the day. Wanting to be with a woman *indefinitely* was uncharted territory for me. Totally off the map. Their teasing only reminded me I had no clue what I was doing.

I'd just about reached my truck when a notification pinged on my phone.

Wade: I made it safely down the ladder
Jed: Blocked

Before I could get into my vehicle, my pop's truck rattled up the lane to Ty's house. He parked next to me and walked over.

"Where are you headed?" he asked.

"Going to join the guys picking for a while." Splitting my time between the farm and June's wedding had meant extra work waiting everywhere I looked. Tomorrow would be completely shot, but I still had a little left in me to finish out today.

"Don't go out there this late in the day."

I stared at him, trying to get those words to add up. *"Skip out on chores,"* said no farmer ever.

"Plenty of daylight left."

"Nah." He made a face. "You should take the whole weekend off. Treat it like a holiday."

Sure. A holiday. Something we never shot for during the summer months, knowing we'd have plenty of it in the winter.

"Okay, what's going on? Are you feeling all right? You haven't suggested I take a weekend off farm work since...forever." We'd both planned to take tomorrow off for the wedding, but I sure hadn't counted on more than that.

His blue eyes sparkled at me. "Then it's long past time you had a vacation."

"You want to just leave the crews to pick and sell without us, not even checking in? That's a lot to leave on their shoulders." And they could probably handle it, but to my knowledge, Pop had never been hands-off when it came to the farm. Didn't make sense he'd encourage me to be.

"I'll get some work done tonight and go in Sunday. The vacation's for you."

For me. Maybe I should have jumped at the chance. Harvest had been a bear this summer, and the extra hubbub over the wedding hadn't helped. But taking off and leaving him alone out there again felt like a step back. Like I wasn't even needed on the family farm.

I popped my mouth open to ask if he'd had second thoughts about me taking over, but didn't get the words out. Because if he had? The final hours before my sister's wedding probably wasn't the time to discuss it.

And, honestly, it would suck hard to hear. So I shut my mouth.

"Go have fun. Maybe see what Callie's doing on Sunday." He winked at me as he walked away, headed toward the barn.

Looked like I had more than one serious conversation tabled until after June said *I do*.

TWENTY-SEVEN

I SAT on the floor in my granny's bedroom, my lap loaded down with blouses, dresses, and slacks she thought I might like to keep for myself. We didn't have remotely the same taste in clothes, and I couldn't imagine myself ever opting to wear *slacks*, but I wouldn't dream to tell her so. I focused on the fact that after she'd packed up the last of her closet, she would be ready for Florida.

Only, I wasn't so sure I'd be ready for her to go.

I'd been gunning for this, for her and for me, but my throat had been tight all day, my heart heavy as I walked around the half-packed up house. I sat on the verge of a meltdown, and if I let myself think about her leaving too much, not even these polyester pants would stop me from crying big, gut-wrenching tears.

"This might be good for you." She held up a modest beige dress with long, ruffled sleeves I couldn't remember her ever wearing. "Maybe for school?"

"Maybe." I tried to sound as though I might wear it one day. Fashions changed so much. Ruffle sleeves might come back in, and I'd be glad I had it.

She tossed it on top of the pile in my lap, wafting up the scent of her perfume that clung to her clothes. Even that made tears prick my eyes, knowing she wouldn't be around anymore to spray too many pumps of perfume on her wrists before heading out to the post office or the grocery store. She could turn even the simplest errands into something fancy, and I already missed it.

"Oh." She pulled a black sweater from the closet. "I thought I donated this."

Now that, I did remember. My stomach turned, that lump in my throat doubling in size.

Holding it up, she looked like she was admiring it, but I knew for a fact she hated the outfit she'd worn to my mother's funeral. I'd felt the same way about my clothes, but I'd gotten rid of those the same week. I'd worn a colorful blouse and a somber wrap, and I'd never wanted to see either of them again.

She took the sweater off the hanger and put it in the trash bag destined for the donation center. Her eyes met mine as she sank on the edge of the bed. I could see the doubt written on her features, the hesitation she'd been battling for months now back full force.

"I promised your mom I'd take care of you."

Her sudden sadness poked a hundred tiny needles in my heart.

"You have taken care of me, Gran. You've taken the absolute best care of me for almost eight years."

Her soft smile didn't look all that convinced. Did she think she'd been anything less than the best grandma and guardian and trusted friend in all that time?

"You were always there for me. Whether I needed advice or a pep talk or just a kick in the pants." That perked her smile up a touch. "I couldn't have got through these last years without you."

"I don't have to go." Different from her threats to stay behind, this came out like a question, an offering she hoped I'd take.

"Gran." I paused, unsure I wanted to open this particular can of worms. "Do you *want* to go to Florida with the others?"

I'd never really considered the idea she might not want to go to Florida. She'd written off her misgivings as worry for me, and I'd accepted that without digging deeper. But she'd lived in Magnolia Ridge almost her entire life, had decades of friends and connections and memories here. Maybe she'd been dragging her feet because of her own doubts that had nothing to do with me.

"Of course I do."

Okay, maybe not.

"Those women are the sisters I never had. We've seen each other through weddings, divorce, grief, and loss. We can fight like cats, but we're bonded like family. We've been talking about Florida since before you were born." She twisted the wedding ring she still wore on her left hand. "Doesn't mean it's not hard to leave you. I feel like maybe I'm failing you somehow if I go."

"Gran." I fought against the clothes piled on me until I freed myself so I could sit next to her on the bed. I wrapped an arm around her waist and rested the side of my head against hers. "You're not failing me. But you can't take care of me forever."

"I know it. I do. Still isn't easy."

"You know I'll miss you." I kept my voice nice and soft so it wouldn't scare tears out.

"Oh, honey. I'm going to leave half my heart here with you. I'm so glad you have Jed now. I'll sleep a little easier at night knowing he'll be nearby."

My pre-emptive sorrow squeezed and twisted, turning into a slimy layer of guilt. I had to believe that in the end, getting her to Florida would justify the way I'd gone about it. Even if right this very minute, I felt like the worst granddaughter in the world for getting her hopes up about Jed this way.

And just a tiny bit like the worst fake girlfriend in the world for getting my own hopes up.

"But not too nearby!" she added.

I laughed, sweeping away my guilty confessions for later. "Mom would want you to have this, you know."

Her arm tightened around me. "Now, don't you make me cry."

"It's true, though. She would have booked the movers herself and packed your things when you weren't looking."

Gran laughed, wiping one hand beneath each eye. "Would have taken more trips to the donation center, too. Your mom never saw the need to hold onto things that weren't important."

Growing up, my mom's spring cleanings had been serious business. I hadn't developed the same Marie Kondo attitude when it came to pruning my stuff, but I tried to keep things neat and tidy, for her sake. And maybe it was silly, but thinking about my mom made me speak up.

Even if it was just to refuse old hand-me-downs, I needed to say out loud what I wanted.

"Gran, I don't want your old clothes." I pointed at the twisted bundle I'd escaped from.

She looked from the clothes to me. "You just said you did. You fibbed to me?"

Probably not the time to go into everything I'd been fibbing about—little *and* big. One confrontation at a time. "The truth is…I wouldn't be sorry to never see those polyester pants again."

Her sweet laughter broke free. "Let's bag it all up for donation right now."

We folded the clothes and tucked them away, relieving their burden both on Granny's room and my makeshift closet.

"You know," she said, carefully creasing those awful pants, "for as much as your mom could get rid of things that didn't matter, she sure held onto the ones that did and kept them close. That girl had so much enthusiasm for life, and spread her joy around freely. She never loved with half her heart.

"Now, some people weren't worthy of her devotion." Gran made a sour face, obviously thinking about my father. "But the ones who were got all her love. You're just like her that way. You love hard."

I liked to think so. Didn't make any sense to me to love things just a little. If I was going to love, I wanted to love big.

"What time is Jed picking you up?"

I snorted a laugh at her obvious thought process there. "A couple more hours. It's sort of a late evening thing."

June's wedding would be so small, they'd opted not to have a full rehearsal dinner. They'd invited a few of us to Ty's for some food and to unwind before the craziness of the big day. Very relaxed and casual, but not so chill I was allowed to bring a dessert. Jed had been pretty clear on that.

"Now, I want to tell you something."

My stomach twisted over her serious tone. I wasn't sure I could handle swimming in the depths of this conversation anymore. I tied my garbage bag of clothes and set it on the pile of items for the donation center. "Yes?"

She moved closer, her eyes bright and intense. "If you find out Jed—or any man—doesn't love you the way you deserve...if he doesn't love you back just as hard as you love him, I want you to know you can walk away. I don't want to see you love and love and love and get nothing in return."

She didn't have to worry there. I'd promised myself *one* was all the one-sided relationships I'd allow myself to have. Next time, I wanted the feelings to flow both ways.

"On the other hand...when you find a man who loves with everything he has, you hold onto him. A man who's there for his family, dedicated in his work, and true to you. Someone you can have fun with, who makes you laugh."

Truly, she was a master of subtlety. "Should I add *farmer*, *veteran*, and *good at Pit* to that list?"

Her cheeky grin shone out. "Wouldn't hurt if he kissed you so good your toes curled, too."

"Granny!"

"I'm just saying."

Truth was, Jed hit all her must-haves right out of the park.

* * *

Packing all day before June and Ty's evening get-together hadn't been the smartest. I wouldn't have missed their casual gathering for anything, but by the time we'd finished our barbecue dinner and moved into the yard for the bonfire, I was hiding yawns behind my hand.

"You've had a long day," Jed whispered. "We don't have to stay."

Couples were arranged in camp chairs and on picnic blankets around the fire pit, cuddling up as the evening sky turned an inky black. I'd opted for the ground, thinking being a little uncomfortable would help keep me awake, but Jed's big warm body right next to mine just lulled me into a deeper level of coziness.

"No, I want to stay. I'll perk up again in a minute."

"Sounds like the words of a sleepy person."

"I'm not sleepy, I'm just tired." I yawned again to really drive the point home.

His saucy eyebrow raise made my stomach swoop.

"I'd love to hear the difference."

"Sleepy is when your brain is shutting down and you can't keep your eyes open. Tired is when your body is sluggish and droopy. I'm only tired." I didn't have far to go to knock out both, but would not add that bit.

"Hmm. So, no chance you're going to make like Eliza? Because I'm okay with being your pillow."

Across from us, Eliza laid on a blanket, her head on Dean's lap while he rested back on one hand, stroking her hair with the other. And...yeah. The idea of doing the same with Jed was pretty tempting.

"Depends on how tired I get."

His mouth curled into a naughty smile. "Then I'll keep my fingers crossed the sandman shows up."

"Are we doing some kind of dinner train for you guys next week?" Eliza said to June, who sat snuggled in Ty's lap. "So you don't have to leave the house for anything?"

Hard to tell in the firelight, but pretty sure June blushed scarlet.

"That's not a bad idea." Ty pulled her even closer, nuzzling against her neck. "But just drop the meals and leave, no socializing."

"So, no different from a regular visit to your house," Booker said. Eden sat next to him in a camp chair, her legs draped across his lap.

"What if I feel a deep need to talk about horses or home decorating?" Eliza asked.

June looped her arms around Ty's as though any chance existed he might get away. "You heard the man. No socializing."

A breeze picked up, sending my hair into my eyes and a chill over my skin. I flipped up the blanket we lay on so it covered my lower legs, wishing I'd brought a sweatshirt with me.

"Are you cold?" Jed asked at my ear.

"Just a touch." The summer night wasn't anything like chilly, but the breeze could make me forget the heat of the day pretty quick.

"Do you want me to get you an extra blanket? Or would you rather snuggle for warmth?"

My eyes snapped to his. The heat in his gaze set my skin on fire, tingling down my arms and up my back. What was it with this man and hot looks? Had he learned them somewhere, or had he popped out of the womb knowing how to smolder?

He waited, his offer both flirty and genuine. I could have opted for the blanket. Stayed on the path of smarts and safety instead of veering off onto the risky road of PDA cuddles. Could have...but I knew what I wanted the second he'd asked.

"Snuggle, please."

His answering smile turned me inside out. In a second, he'd moved to sit behind me, his legs on either side of mine, his arms tight around me as I leaned back against him. His body blocked out the chill, and he ran his hands over my arms to chase away the goosebumps. Only now, the shiver that ran across my skin came from his touch, not the breeze.

"Better?" he whispered.

"So much better."

New dream house goal unlocked: backyard fire pit for cozy Jed snuggles.

"Callie, Jed told me about that tableau building game you like, with all the little animals," Harper said. "Please invite me to play sometime, I've been dying to get in on that one."

"The one with the tree where you send out armies of bunnies and hedgehogs?" Sam said at her side. "Mark me down for that, too."

"Oh, I haven't played it yet," I said. "I don't even have it, I just thought it sounded like a lot of fun."

Harper made a weird face. "But Jed said he bought it."

"Jed said he—" I twisted to try to face him, but we weren't positioned right for it. "You bought it?"

He shrugged. "I thought I'd have it ready for a date-night in sometime."

My poor little heart skipped and bounced around over his man. He'd bought the game I'd mentioned once in passing so we could play? I could have kissed his face off right then and there to show him just how I felt about that. But to do it, I'd have to spin around and pretty much sit spider-style in his lap —goodness gracious, yes, let's—but figured that would be just a touch awkward considering where we were.

I met my impulse in the middle, snuggling deeper against his chest and letting the back of my head rest on his shoulder.

"We'll have a game night sometime," I said to Harper. "It might take a couple of rounds to really figure out."

"It's crazy complex," Jed said. "I've been in military maneuvers with shorter instructions."

I tilted my head to try to see him better. "You've been reading the instructions, too?"

"After the way you shamelessly cheated at Pit, seemed like I should come to our next match better prepared."

The way he grinned down at me, spinning around to kiss those gorgeous lips was still on the table.

"Wait, how does someone cheat at Pit?" Wade asked.

"By someone, you mean Callie," Jed said, hugging me tighter to him. "And she does it by stealing all the cards."

"In my defense," I piped up, "my gran and her friends are usually ruthless, but for *some* reason, they were extra accommodating with Jed, and fell all over themselves to help him win. Someone needed to put him in his place."

Wade smirked. "Make no mistake, Callie, you've put him in his place."

Ty and Booker chuckled, no doubt thinking of our mini-confrontation in the barn. I hadn't given it a ton of thought in the moment, I'd just been mad and had no problem telling him. But now, I had to marvel a little that I'd held my ground. Normally, I made sure to avoid conflict, but with Jed, I hadn't even considered backing down.

Was it weird that I liked that?

The night went on, everyone joking and teasing and telling stories while I reveled in my cozy spot in Jed's arms. But eventually, the evening broke up, first when the parents left to pick up their kids from grandparents, and then everyone else made their own goodbyes. By the time Jed drove me back across town, I hovered on the edge of sleep, needing only one too-long blink to send me into sweet dreams.

He glanced over at me, a little smile playing along his mouth. "I thought for sure you were going to fall asleep back there."

"It was so tempting. Like seriously, that would be the best cure for sleeplessness ever. If I could turn Jed snuggles into a gummy supplement, I'd make a fortune."

His laughter rumbled to life. "Darlin', my snuggles are only for you."

Yeah, I liked the sound of that.

He pulled up to my house and helped me down from my side of the truck, locking my fingers in his, our palms tight together. Our feet made small sounds as we walked through the grass, the evening quiet and calm. The windows were dark, no grannies peeking out at us tonight.

"Goodnight, Callie Lou."

His soft, low voice sent my insides tumbling.

"Night."

He'd said goodbye but made no move to leave. We stood on the porch watching each other, the air around us stilling as though the world had held its breath. I was wide awake now. Every cell in my body had keyed into this moment and was taking notes for future generations.

We looked and looked like we needed to get our fill of each other's features, mapping out every line and curve. Like nothing had ever been more important than eye contact. The longer we stared, the more I filled up with a tingling electricity I wanted to convert into action until I positively crackled with it.

And then, we co-captained the ship.

We reached for each other at the same time, and his mouth finally met mine. Our first kiss had been abrupt and awkward, our second brief and sassy. But this kiss was luxurious, soft and slow, a gentle caress. Mouths, lips, hands moving in a leisurely stroll, the journey far more vital than reaching any destination.

Jed gave with every touch of his lips, the play of his tongue, the stroke of his hands over my back. Like he'd found the book of *How to Kiss Callie* and had studied up until he'd become a pro. Or maybe he'd written that book. My thoughts swirled in and out of focus, even as I tried to etch every second of this kiss in my mind.

My brain shut down, and my heart took over, confirming my affection for this man in every frantic beat. Sure, okay. Affection. Even unable to string together a coherent thought, I knew affection was too small a word. The word I wanted to use planted itself squarely in my head, written in sparklers until it burned my thoughts.

Love. That was definitely the word.

After minutes, hours, days, we finally broke apart. I opened my eyes, and—fool that I was—I sighed. His lips curved as he traced one hand from my temple behind my ear and along my neck.

"Me, too, darlin'."

I rolled my eyes at both of us. "Take that smirk on home, then."

He gave a crisp nod as though it'd been an order. "Yes, Cap'n."

Laughing, I shooed him off the porch. If he didn't leave soon, I'd pull him in for a repeat of that kiss and risk blurting out all the squishy feelings going on in my heart. As much as I might want to, I still wasn't sure that confession wouldn't shatter everything between us in an instant.

jed

BEING brother of the bride should not have made me nearly as nervous as I was. Hell, I'd been Wade's Best Man and I hadn't been this antsy, and I'd had to give a speech. Today, I'd only be a glorified chauffeur, virtually unnecessary, but nerves poked and prodded as if I'd be saying vows, too.

Yeah...maybe not the best analogy.

Wasn't sure how much sleep I'd got last night, only knew my brain had been full of Callie since our last kiss. Frankly, since long before that, but our mind-blowing goodnight had replaced all the background noise, my body lighting up with longing and need on every replay.

Probably a bad idea for me to be on the road in this distracted state. If I kept thinking about that perfect kiss, I could land the truck in the ditch. Would hate to see that police report. Cause of accident: daydreaming about girlfriend.

I knocked on Callie's front door, nerves creating a whirlpool in my stomach. By this point, I'd expected all the women to be there, ready to take pictures as if we were off to prom, but when Suzie opened the door, she stood there alone.

"Come on in, Callie's not quite ready."

"I'm a little early." I followed her inside, my eyes stuck on the other side of the room where my date would emerge any second now.

"Don't mind the mess," she said, side-stepping moving boxes. "We're down to the wire here."

"Are you ready for Monday?"

She turned to me, and I saw the stupidity of the question in her eyes. She might be physically ready, her things packed away all set to go, but emotionally, she wasn't ready to leave and might never truly be.

"I'm ready for the next phase of my life, but I'm not ready to leave my Callie behind. We've been through a lot, just the two of us. It's hard to go my own way." She nodded as if she needed to reassure herself. "But I can relax knowing you're here to take care of her."

I liked the thought, but it irritated, too, like an itchy tag in an otherwise soft shirt.

"Callie's a lot stronger than you give her credit for. She doesn't need me to take care of her."

Part of me wanted to rail against my own words and claim she did need me, but I was no fool. She wanted me, maybe. I thought so and hoped so. But that woman did not *need* me for a single thing.

"Everybody needs someone to take care of them," Suzie said simply.

Whatever argument my mouth dropped open to say died in my throat when Callie walked into the room. Her high-neck, sleeveless dress did a tight, bunching thing on the top, and fell from her waist in long, off-set tiers I couldn't have coherently described if I'd had a hundred years. All I knew was the fern green dress proved both elegant enough to make me feel under-dressed in my suit and tie, and casual enough to fit right in for a wedding on a farm.

"You look..." Yup, that was all I got out. I wanted to sweep her up into my arms, hold her close, and tell her how gorgeous she was, but instead, I barely squeaked out two words.

Killing it, Jed.

She crossed the room to me and spun a circle, showing off how those tier things swayed when she moved. The effect proved mesmerizing and did nothing for my completely absent brain. I needed a minute to recover my senses, but every view of her just sent me straight back to speechlessness.

"What do you think?" she asked. "Does it look good?"

Good didn't come close. *Gorgeous. Perfect. Brain-numbingly tantalizing.* Those fit a touch better.

I finally recovered a sliver of my senses. "I think I want to forget all about the wedding."

Her gran laughed, and I remembered we had an audience.

"You look handsome, yourself." Callie's eyes skated down my body and up again, and I caught a tint of color in her cheeks. "I like you in that suit."

I ran a hand down the pressed jacket. "Beige, though."

"Definitely not drab."

Her grin shone out, glorious and playful. That grin made me want to drive somewhere we could be alone, not surrounded by forty other people for the evening. And really, we didn't *have* to go to the wedding, did we?

The image of June hunting me down for skipping out on her wedding woke me out of that daydream. I held my elbow out to Callie, and she stepped up to loop her arm through mine.

"You kids have fun," Suzie said. "I'm going to do another walk through and make sure I don't forget anything."

"Are you ready?" I asked Callie.

She winked, and I think my heart exploded.

"Let's do this."

* * *

The only downside to having a wedding on a pretty piece of land in the center of Ty's property was that someone had to ferry guests out to the ceremony site. And by someone, I meant Wade and me.

They'd rented two six-seater golf carts for the occasion. While the primary wedding players got ready in the house, we shuttled back and forth as guests arrived. I would have much rather sat next to the stream waiting with Callie—would have much rather *anything* with Callie—but I'd accepted my duties.

Once all the guests were accounted for, I drove Ty, Booker, and the pastor across the property. In a few more minutes, Wade would bring June, Eden, Pop, and Marilyn, and then the big show would begin.

"How are you holding up?" I asked. Ty sat in the front with me, the only sign he was headed to his wedding the fancy suit he wore and the way his knee hadn't stopped bouncing. "Nervous?"

He shook his head. "I'm ready for June to be my wife."

I admit, the guy was adorable. Totally gone for my sister and not afraid to show it. Didn't mean I had to spare him a little teasing on his big day.

I parked the golf cart off to the side of the ceremony site and twisted around to face Booker. "Is there a betting pool for him crying when she walks down the aisle?"

Ty sighed and climbed out of the cart, brushing his hands down his gray suit to clear the wrinkles.

Booker leaned closer, his grin shining out. "Even he's not willing to bet he won't."

They walked up the aisle to take their places in front, and I took mine at Callie's side. Her hand slipped into mine automatically as she shone a look of pure happiness my way. Soft guitar music wrapped around us from somewhere, a sweet soundtrack to the peaceful place. Gathered together with family in this gorgeous spot with my woman right next to me—wasn't sure I'd ever had a more perfect day.

I knew better than to expect more, but today, I wanted endless days like this.

Eventually, Wade showed up with the bridal party, and the little assembly hushed. Marilyn made her way up the aisle to sit next to me and briefly squeezed my arm. Then Eden slowly walked up the aisle in a full-length sky blue dress, her eyes stuck on Booker who stood at the front keeping Ty's morale up as Best Man.

Finally, everyone rose. The crowd hushed, and the guitar music changed to a slow rendition of a country song. And there came June on Pop's arm. I couldn't have described her lacy dress any better than I'd done Callie's, I only knew it suited her. But the thing that suited her best was the huge grin she wore. Her love made her glow.

I snuck a peek at Ty and was pleased to see his eyes looked suspiciously shiny. He watched June with a raw look of love and longing, like his chest had been busted open and he had his heart on display for everyone to see. No shame, just a bald-faced need for her.

Had a feeling if someone pried my heart open, they'd find a similar sight.

Wasn't much to their ceremony. The pastor gave a blessedly short speech, and June and Ty said their vows. But out here in nature, that sounded just right. They didn't need anything more than each other.

The pastor declared them husband and wife, and Ty tugged June into his arms.

"Boom, done," he said, making them both grin before he gave her a celebratory kiss.

* * *

After dinner and speeches, we moved tables and chairs to the sides of the barn to create room for mingling. Maybe even dancing—music played from somewhere, and Lord knew all the couples here tonight were just itching for a slow dance.

Truth be told, so was I. It'd been a gorgeous ceremony, and I was happy for my sister, but I wanted to hold Callie in my arms. Wanted to know what that dress felt like beneath my hands. Wanted to tell her again how pretty she looked, how special she was. Really, I just wanted *her*.

She stood on the other side of the barn talking with Harper. Every now and then, she'd glance my way, and my heart pounded harder, urging me to cross the room. I would in another minute, but I liked watching her. She didn't hold back when she talked, gesturing with her hands and smiling with her whole face. She loved the crap out of life, and it thrilled me just to see.

"Well, we made it."

Pop appeared beside me, still puffed up from his proud papa moment of walking June down the aisle. His cheeks would be aching for days, he'd been smiling so much.

"It was a good wedding." Didn't have a long list of events to compare it to, but it'd fit them just right. The couple of the day stood off to one side, receiving congratulations and stealing moments together whenever they had a chance. Could see the sparkles in their eyes from here.

"I couldn't have picked out a better man for June, or a better fit for Ty." Pop's eyes sparkled, too, and I figured any minute, a tear or two would fall. "I'm happy to see them so in love."

"No denying that."

He turned to me, and that glint in his eye sent a strange sensation down my spine. The air suddenly felt dangerous, like

244

I'd walked into unknown territory and couldn't be sure of my steps.

"I'm happy to see *all* my children so in love."

My traitor eyes found Callie before I could think to deny it. She looked my way, and my heart seemed to inflate until it pressed against my ribcage, leaving me aching. I had no argument. This *was* love, filling me up to overflowing. Not just fun or friendship or even affection, but real, bone-deep love. My stomach dove like I'd missed a rung climbing down a ladder and wasn't sure when I'd land.

"I know it's soon," Pop went on, "but when you're ready, I have your mother's ring. She wanted you to have it."

The air rushed out of me like I'd finally hit the ground after that fall. "You never told me that."

"Didn't think knowing would have helped you any."

"Then why are you telling me now?"

He tilted his head in Callie's direction. "Because I have eyes. Callie's a forever kind of woman."

Forever. Heaviness crept through me like sand filling up my body. My lungs stung and ached before I realized I was holding my breath. The ambush I'd been waiting for had finally arrived, and found me utterly unprepared.

Pop clapped me on the shoulder. "Go dance with her, son."

He wandered away, leaving me crumbling down to dust. Somewhere in the last two months, I'd forgotten the key word in our fake relationship. Callie and I could only ever be temporary. Pop was right—she was a forever kind of woman. The kind that makes you think of houses and babies and a whole lifetime together.

Callie loved out loud—she gave and she gave without asking for anything in return. If I let her, she might love me. But I wasn't a forever man. I'd learned that long ago, proven it too many times to count. One way or another, I'd wind up failing her like I failed Zach. Like I failed Mom.

I couldn't be the guy to do that to her. I needed to stick to our original agreement. Fake date for the wedding. Get her grandma to Florida. And then...we'd let this fade away.

Sounded like the worst plan ever, but maybe for once, I could actually protect someone I loved.

callie

I'D NEVER BEEN to a more beautiful wedding.

Okay, thinking back, I had a very limited pool to compare it to. But I couldn't imagine a more perfect celebration for the bride and groom. From the gorgeous outdoor ceremony to the rustic reception, every little piece spoke of them and their love. They'd both teared up during their vows, but now smiled wide, like their hearts had found their other half. Even Ty couldn't stop smiling, which felt like some kind of personal record for him.

Me, I'd been smiling like a goof all evening, too. My heart felt weirdly buoyant, like it'd been filled with so much laughter and joy and hope, it might float me away into the clear night. But I had to place at least half the blame for that squarely at Jed's feet. I'd been sneaking glances at my date across the barn, admiring him in that suit. So handsome, he even made beige look good. I'd lost him, though, and couldn't spot his dark head in the crowd.

"Fair warning, I'm going to be a total bridezilla." Eliza squinted at Harper and me. "It's my day. It needs to be all about me, me, me."

Dean had recently proposed, but they'd been low-key about it out of consideration for June. Everyone knew, of course, but they hadn't thrown their own engagement party. I didn't think she'd have had a problem with them shouting their happiness, but it was sweet how all the girls looked out for each other.

Harper laughed. "I expect you to elope, bridezilla."

Eliza's eyes widened. "That's a genius idea. We're totally doing that. Where's Dean, I need to tell him about your eloping plan."

"Don't give me the credit, Mom would never forgive me."

"Sure she will. Only if *your* wedding is over the top."

Harper didn't look like she was on board with that, either.

Marilyn broke away from her daughters and joined us. "Girls, you all look so lovely today. Your dresses are too beautiful for words."

She leaned back a touch to admire us. I'd been pleased to see my dress fit right in with the boho chic theme of the day. Of course, nothing compared to June's full-length A-line dress. The cap sleeves and lacy tiers made her look like a country princess.

"You girls mean so much to June," Marilyn went on. "It's so special how close you've stayed through the years."

Harper and Eliza both gushed about June in return. I envied their closeness and just how much they meant to each other. Probably normal in big families, but I'd never quite known a relationship like that. Well...maybe until now.

Marilyn put an arm around my waist, wrapping me in a warm side-hug. "And we're so glad Harper introduced us to you, too. You're a perfect addition to our group."

I thought I'd used up all my tears during the wedding ceremony, but a couple more popped up, ready to spill. I hugged her back, my heart going haywire for this wonderful family.

She let me go. "Now, I'd like to invite you to visit me in the store sometime this week."

Next to me, Eliza shimmied, a wild grin on her face.

"Okay." I'd been in her home goods shop loads of times to pick up items for my house, and wouldn't mind another walk-through.

"I'd like to talk to you about your embroideries."

"My—what?" I hadn't thought she knew anything about them.

"June showed me a picture of the beautiful embroidery you made for Bee. And Eliza says you've made a lot of them?"

I nodded, trying to figure out where she was headed. Next to her, Eliza beamed at me like she might burst.

"I'd love to carry something like that in my store. Handmade, local, quirky—they'd fit right in."

"You want to buy my embroideries?" It just seemed so out there, I needed her to confirm it in actual words.

"Absolutely, I do." Her eyes might as well have twinkled, she looked so thrilled with the idea. "No pressure, of course, and this isn't the right time to talk business. But think about it. Come to my store this week and we'll chat, how does that sound?"

It sounded better than amazing, and I kind of already wanted to say yes. I loved making fun embroideries, but I'd given just about everyone I knew at least one—my latest sat wrapped in a box for June and Ty—and I'd pretty well maxed out my wall space with hoops. And let's be real, extra money never hurt.

"It sounds too good to be true." I matched Eliza's shimmy, imagining my embroideries for sale in Fine & Dandy.

"Honey, I know what my customers like, and they would snap up your work. But it's your choice. Think about it, and come down if you want to talk. Come down either way and just visit. Now, I'd better go find my husband so we can have a romantic dance." She walked off again, joining the others in the small crowd.

"I told you," Eliza said, bouncing around. "I knew you could sell them if you wanted to."

"It was only a matter of time," Harper said. "Marilyn loves helping out family."

Family. That cozy word cuddled me up in a big hug, my heart both squeezing and exploding for joy. For once, I didn't have words to say how much they meant to me, I just gloried in the moment. Friends and family and a man I couldn't get enough of—I could hardly contain all my blessings.

Couples started swaying together in the middle of the floor, taking advantage of the slow song that filled the barn with the sound of a steel guitar. Sam and Dean split off from the crowd to collect their dates, ready to dance.

"Mind if we—?" Harper hitched a thumb toward the couples, already inching away with Sam.

"Of course not. Dance it up."

They swirled into the crowd, and I backed up a few steps to give the growing dance floor more room. Still couldn't see Jed anywhere. Maybe someone had needed his help and he'd gotten sidetracked. Seemed like a Jed thing to do.

Figuring I could at least make a circuit of the building to look for him, I turned and ran straight into a towering man built of beige muscle.

Jed grabbed my arms to steady me. "Sorry. Didn't mean to sneak up on you."

"I was just going to look for you."

"Yeah?" He smiled down at me, all sparkly teeth and laughing hazel eyes. "Were you missing me?"

I shrugged. "Maybe. Want to dance?"

"Absolutely."

We moved over to the makeshift dance floor, and his hands went to my waist, mine to his shoulders. Swaying in time, I tilted my head to look up at him, probably grinning like a dang fool. It'd been a perfect night, but I wouldn't say no to a kiss to make it extra perfect.

"Are you having a good time?" he asked.

"So much. It was a gorgeous wedding, with good friends, and the best date."

"I'm glad."

"I love your family."

He nodded, his smile gentling down to normal levels. "They love you right back."

I felt the truth of it. They'd welcomed me into their big family, and everyone treated me like I belonged. I'd found a home in this group, and that knowledge had me as cozy and warm as I'd been at the fire last night. I loved them.

And I loved *him*. The words sat right on the tip of my tongue. I could pull him closer and whisper it in his ear. Or say it to his face and prove it with a kiss. All the ways I might show Jed how much I felt for him flashed through my mind until heat swam over my skin. He was right here, after all.

Yes. Good plan. I'd do it. I'd pull up my big girl britches and tell him how I felt. Just... maybe not while Clint and Marilyn were dancing so close to us.

They edged nearer, their smiles shining so bright, I needed sunglasses to protect me from their happiness.

"Beautiful wedding, beautiful bride," Clint said. "A great day to see all my kids so happy."

A thrill of pleasure shot through me like a comet, trailing a shiny tail of hope behind it for all his hints. I hoped Jed was happy with me. I thought he was. Maybe in a few minutes, I'd tell him how happy I was.

Soon.

Clint and Marilyn spun away, ready to spread their joy to someone else. They were so cute together. This family had no shortage of brand-new love.

For example, the one bubbling inside me like molten lava.

Jed's hands moved on my waist, pulling me closer. I met his gaze, and my stomach flipped, unleashing a swarm of delicate butterflies. His mouth tipped up as he leaned closer, bringing his face to my ear. Everything inside me stilled, straining to pay attention to whatever he'd say.

"I think we sold it."

My body kept swaying even as my brain shut right down. I sucked in two breaths back to back like I couldn't get enough air. Or like I was mid-sob. My ribcage felt too small for my organs, like I was being crushed by an invisible hand. No, no hand. Just a very poorly timed reminder.

Fake dating, Callie. You were fake dating Jed.

Hadn't I promised him I wouldn't fall in love? And then, I'd gone and done it anyway, falling so hard, I'd pancaked my heart when I landed.

Splatted, more like.

He pulled back and smiled down at me, proud of the way we'd fooled everyone. Oh, we'd fooled them good. So good, I hadn't been able to tell fiction from reality. My heart ached, my lungs weren't quite working, and my stomach churned until I thought I might throw up.

But running from the reception out into the night would have brought our little ruse to a crashing halt. I wouldn't take his win away from him. I could see this through to the end, even if my insides had turned into a vortex, sucking up all my joy and flipping it upside down.

Granny had told me to find a guy worthy of my heart. I'd found one worthy, all right—he just wasn't wanting.

I pasted on a big smile, like I'd cut it out of bright red construction paper and stuck it on. It wasn't real, but that didn't matter. Fake was good enough for us.

"We did it."

253

callie

IT TURNED OUT, having a broken heart and watching my gran move away were a terrible mix. Only scheduling a root canal in the afternoon could have made the day more miserable.

I couldn't even cry out all my tears, since Granny might have been suspicious if I'd spent yesterday bawling over every version of *Love Affair* the way I'd wanted to. Nope, I'd sucked it up and powered through, helping her hunt for forgotten items and prepping her boxes for the movers. I'd answered all her questions about the wedding and only fibbed a little when she asked how things were going with Jed.

"I think I'm falling for him." A complete fabrication, since I already knew I was totally, irrevocably in love with the man. Thank the sweet Lord she didn't ask what he felt for me.

In spite of Jed's original concerns I wasn't a good liar, I'd handled his arrival a few minutes ago like a Broadway actress. I'd texted him to come over, since saying goodbye to Gran seemed the right thing to do. One last show of our fake relationship to see her on her way. We'd fallen straight into our usual routine of flirty banter and affectionate touches, and if every sweet moment between us seared a little, well, I refused to let it show.

The movers pulled the truck's rear door down with a clatter and locked it in place. Gran signed off on the paperwork, and the truck rumbled away, headed to Florida.

The shine of tears in her eyes broke something in me. But if I cried now, I'd unleash my tears over Jed, too, and dissolving in a puddle of weepiness wouldn't help convince my gran to climb into her car and leave me behind. I held the tears in, making my breaths slow and awkward so I wouldn't sob. I could do this.

I hugged her like I could pour all my love into these last sixty seconds. I knew they weren't the *last* seconds, that we'd see each other again, and probably sooner than I thought. But that yawning unknown felt indefinite and murky on this side.

"Sweet girl," she said, stroking my hair. "I've got more love in my heart for you than I know how to say."

"I love you so much, Gran."

"I know you do."

We stood like that for a few minutes, embracing under the summer sun, Jed somewhere close by. After a while, she pulled back to cup my cheeks in her hands.

"You're going to be just fine, Callie Louise."

I nodded. I knew it, but right in that moment, it didn't feel like a sure thing.

"I've got to get on over to Linda's so we can get our caravan started."

I wanted to memorize her soft, sweet smile. She could be so tough sometimes, and maybe she'd had to be, helping us out after Dad left and through Mom's illness. But I loved those gentle smiles that spoke of more tenderness than she usually put into words.

I nodded, sniffling but not crying. "Call me when you get to Beaumont."

"You'll get sick of my calls, honey."

"Nope. Never."

She walked over to Jed and pulled him close for a quick hug. "You take good care of my girl."

Jed turned to me, his eyes full of...well, maybe I wasn't the best judge, after all. What I thought didn't really matter anyway, since this was all for Gran.

"She'll be just fine."

Loved his confidence. Also kind of hated it. Today, it sounded like a gentle goodbye.

Gran gave me one last hug and kissed my cheek. She double-checked the cooler in her front seat, making sure all of her snacks and drinks would be at the ready for her drive.

Jed came closer to wrap an arm around me, and I leaned into it. I wasn't sure if the hug was for Gran or for me, but I'd take the support right now. Lord knew, I needed it.

"You two be good," Gran said as she finally climbed into her car. She rolled the window down and leaned her gray head out. "But not too good."

I laughed as she pulled away, waving with one hand and holding on tight to Jed with the other. Her car winked out of sight, and I released a ragged breath. She'd really gone.

Knowing just what I needed, Jed gathered me up in his arms. Whatever his reasons, this hug was definitely for me, and I sighed into the embrace.

"It's okay," he whispered. "You're going to be okay."

And I would. I knew that. Yes, my heart ached like it'd been stomped on, and my body felt exhausted and wrung out, but I would be okay. I hated to see her go, but I needed this next stage, too. A nervous kind of excitement ran through me, just beneath the raw ache of saying goodbye. I'd be ready for whatever came next...

Except this.

I slipped out of Jed's arms, shoring myself up for this next goodbye. He looked almost as cut up as I did. Like when I'd shared about my dad leaving, he seemed to hurt because I hurt. He just didn't know he was a source of my grief, too. But could I tell him?

Absolutely not.

Just like Granny had predicted, I was torn between giving him my love and giving him his freedom, and it hurt more than I could say. I really wished she didn't have to be right all the time.

"Thank you for everything." Look at that. My voice didn't even crack. "You've been a great fake boyfriend."

I laughed awkwardly, which might actually work in my favor. Lean into the weirdness. Distract from the broken heart.

"Yeah?" He didn't look all that convinced.

"Oh yeah. Ten out of ten. I'd totally fake date you again." *No, no, Callie, too far.* "I'll tell all my friends."

He laughed, too, but there wasn't much heart to it. "When can I expect to get dumped?"

The reminder we'd have to officially end things at some point put a chill in the summer air. I couldn't even start thinking about that right now. I needed...something. Time. Clarity. Him. I could hope for two of the three.

I flashed a smile that felt so brittle it might crack at any second. "I can't give you fair warning, that's not realistic."

His mouth curved. "That's cruel, Callie Lou."

I could say the same of him, using his sweet nickname for me in this awful moment. I had to look away from his hazel eyes before I said something stupid. Pretty much everything in my heart qualified. But if he didn't know how I felt about him already, he didn't ever need to.

"Granny won't even get to their condo for a few days. They're taking the slow road and stopping at every interesting roadside attraction. Then she'll need some time to settle in. Maybe things will start to go south between us in a couple of weeks?"

"Text me whatever you decide."

His eyes stayed intent on me, but I couldn't figure out what he was waiting for. He'd gotten everything we'd agreed on, right?

"You let me know if you need me for anything else," he said. "With the house, the yard, or just...anything."

Right. Because he'd done this to help me. I appreciated it, but I only wanted one thing from him, and he wasn't offering. I couldn't ask, either. Asking for his heart when he'd told me from the beginning not to hope for more? I couldn't bear it.

"I can take care of myself."

He took a step back. "Okay. Well...I've got peaches to harvest. I'll see you around, Callie."

"See you."

He turned and walked away, headed for his truck. I shut myself up in the house before he reached it. I didn't want to see him drive away one last time.

Inside, I leaned my back against the front door, listening to the quiet. I'd never had to move on after a broken heart before, and I'd sure never had to go through something like this alone. But like he'd said, I would be okay. I could do this.

I just didn't know how.

jed

TIMES LIKE THESE, I wished I'd become a lumberjack instead of a peach farmer. Chopping down trees would have been a lot more satisfying than carefully pulling fruit off of branches. I'd spent extra hours in the orchards these last three days, working myself like a demon, trying not to think. Mostly, trying not to feel.

I'd done the right thing, but it sure felt wrong. Everything did. Couldn't sleep at night. Tried to paint, but I just wound up making a mess. Even being out here in the trees felt off, like I might bruise all the fruit just from being too close. Something inside me had shifted out of place, but if I looked at it too hard, I had a feeling it'd just wreck me more completely.

I set a full box of peaches I'd picked on the ground and grabbed an empty from the ATV's trailer. Off in the distance, Wade walked toward me through the trees. I sighed so hard, it rattled my teeth. This was not the day.

Pop had been relentless since the wedding, dropping hints about Callie and asking when she'd come to dinner next. Hadn't anticipated this part, after we'd gone our separate ways, but I couldn't act like we'd broken up.

Could you call it a break up if you'd never really been together? Whatever it was, I hated it. The smiling and pretending, coyly putting off Pop's questions as if every one didn't rake over my skin like razor blades. I'd finally convinced him he should take Marilyn to dinner and sent him off to town. But just when I'd got a minute to myself, my brother showed up. Late enough in the day he couldn't possibly have expected to get any work done, which meant he wanted to talk.

I did *not* want to talk.

"You should have left one of the ATVs at Pop's," he said when he reached me. "I had to walk out here."

He raked an arm across his forehead to prove his point.

I climbed a ladder, balancing the box on my hip. "How was I supposed to know you were going to show up?"

He stilled, his eyes heavy on me. Wasn't fair of me to say, I knew that. But I could get snippy when I hadn't slept well, and I'd had nothing but rough nights since things had fallen apart with Callie.

"What crawled up your butt?" He grabbed one of the empty boxes and climbed the ladder close to mine.

Too close, really, for good harvesting, but I wasn't in the mood to give him lessons on things he should have already known.

"Sorry. It's been a long day."

He nodded, still watching me warily. "Things okay out here?"

I shrugged and went on picking. Nothing had changed at the farm. Absolutely nothing. I hadn't had my talk with Pop. Figured one heart-wrenching experience a week was all I could handle. I had no more idea what he wanted from me than I ever did. Considering he was still doing all the background work and as much of the labor as he could get his hands on, sure didn't seem like he wanted me to run the farm, after all.

Maybe I hadn't been sure I could handle it, but damn, just now, I needed it. I needed to know I had something left to hold onto.

"Annie wants to have you and Callie down for dinner some night in the next week or two. You know the boys can't get enough of her. Just let me know when you're available."

I made a sound of acknowledgement but kept on picking. Callie and I would be unavailable for joint dinner dates indefinitely.

"Think she'd be willing to teach Annie how to do that needlepoint stuff she does? Annie's looking for a new hobby."

"Maybe." Callie'd probably love to show her how, but it wasn't my place to say so. We were only friends now. I didn't like it.

Yes, I wanted to be her friend, but at the same time, no part of me wanted that. I wanted *everything*. Just couldn't have it.

"What's got you so mum about her all of a sudden? Don't tell me June's wedding scared you off."

I climbed back down to the ground and set the box with the others. "Didn't scare me off, I just don't know what Callie's schedule is like. Annie should probably take that up with her."

"Huh." Wade climbed down after me. "So it did scare you off."

"How did you get that from what I said?"

"I've only known you my whole life."

I moved my mostly empty fruit box of the stack to the back of the ATV, even though driving anywhere with it would be a total waste of time. "Can we let this go?"

"Which part's got you panicking?"

"I'm not panicking." My heart rate begged to differ, but Wade didn't know it.

"Really? Because it looks to me like you're freaking out over finally falling in love."

"Drop it." I took a step nearer to him, dangerously close to turning this into something physical. "Now."

He stared me down, his eyebrows pulling together and creases forming around his frown. "Why are you acting like you want to fight me? We can, if that will make you feel better, but it might be easier if you tell me what's going on."

I sighed, backing away. He wasn't the one I wanted to fight. I'd been beating myself up for days now and hadn't gotten nearly enough hits in. Admitting the truth would hurt in all new ways, but maybe I needed that pain.

"It was all fake with Callie." I couldn't get the words off my tongue fast enough.

That only made him frown harder. "What do you mean? What part?"

"All of it. We were never really dating."

"I don't follow. You went out. You brought her to June's wedding. How is that not dating?"

From his blank look, I had to guess firemen didn't experience the same marriage of convenience phenomenon that soldiers did.

"It was all for her grandma. Before that night at The Broken Hammer, Callie asked me to pretend to be her boyfriend to get her grandma off her back. You saw the kind of guys Suzie and her friends were setting her up with. She thought if she had a boyfriend, her grandma would move and ride off into the sunset, I don't know."

"Okay, that's her reason. What was yours? Why would you just pretend to date her?"

"Why wouldn't I want to help her out? She's a ray of sunshine in human form. Her heart's too big for her own good, and she's not afraid to show it. She's always going out of her way to help the people around her. Wasn't hard to want to help her a little in return, take care of her for a minute, soak up any time she'd give me."

"Yeah," he said, his voice quiet. "Sounds pretty fake to me."

I glared. "Don't. I can't do this right now."

My heart felt like it'd been through a blender—I couldn't stop to examine all the broken bits, too.

"Help me understand, then. It started out fake, what's to stop you from carrying on for real? You obviously care about her."

"I can't give her what she deserves. You've seen me with commitments. I don't let anything stick. I don't have plans for next month let alone years down the line. Pop doesn't even think I can handle the farm, how can I promise her anything?"

"Do you want to be with her?"

The question burned through me, its answer just as painful.

"More than I can say. But what I want and what I get aren't the same."

He just kept watching me with that calm curiosity, picking me apart with his eyes. Kind of wished I'd chosen the fistfight.

"I don't think you're looking at this right."

"Good thing I'm not paying you to think, I'm paying you to pick fruit." Rude, but this conversation had only served to pour a healthy splash of lemon on my flayed heart.

"You're not paying me at all." He assessed me, and honestly, I didn't want to know what he saw. "I feel like there's more going on here."

Nope, that was the end of the conversation. Thank you, goodbye. Would not try to explain about Zach and Mom. He'd just use his logical brain on me, and I wasn't in the mood to hear it. I picked up the fruit box again and headed up the ladder.

Wade's phone rang in his pocket. "You're going to run from this?"

"There's nothing to run from. It's already over."

Those words left me broken and raw, but I couldn't see a way past it. Callie deserved forever, and I couldn't be the one to give it to her.

"We're not done talking about this." He brought his phone to his ear. "Hey, Marilyn. What's—" He paused, listening, everything in his body language going stiff. "When?"

My instincts kicked in, and I climbed back down. Dread unfurled in my ribcage like a black flag pointing to danger. *Please, God, no.*

"Okay. Okay." Wade had gone pale. "I understand. We'll be there as soon as we can."

He thumbed off the phone. When he looked at me, I knew.

"Pop's had a heart attack."

* * *

I sat in the Magnolia Ridge Medical Center waiting room, one foot tapping on the floor. Marilyn didn't have much information, only that Pop had experienced some distress in town and they'd called for an ambulance. Doctors hadn't said much more than to wait. So we did.

Marilyn spun beads on a bracelet until I thought she might rub their shine clean off, stopping now and then to text her daughters what little we knew. Annie had dropped the kids with her parents and turned up not long after Wade and I. He had his arm around her, pulling her in close like he needed the anchor.

And me? I sat alone, eaten up whole by dread. Tried to call on my training, my experiences in combat when I'd had to face desperate uncertainty, but I found myself clinging to a rock wall, and fear kept slamming into me in waves, dragging me down.

I hated this place, mentally, emotionally—even literally, this place where my mom had passed away. I'd been on the other side of the world, but she'd died right here. For the last three years, I'd hated myself for being away from her, but I found I hated being here in person just as much. And now, I might lose my Pop.

I couldn't think that way, but I couldn't seem to rein those thoughts in. The noise they made proved deafening, a clanging echo that wouldn't quit. They ran and scattered like spilled BBs, and nothing I did could bring them under control.

"Your dad's a fighter." Marilyn nodded over at me. "He's going to come through this."

I wasn't sure how she could believe that when she'd lost her first husband to a heart attack, too. Maybe she had to believe, because the alternative would be falling to pieces the way I wanted to.

"There's coffee in the cafeteria. Do you need anything? Wade? Jed?"

I shook my head. I didn't need anything. Nothing could soothe my rattled nerves right now. Except...maybe a hand in mine offering comfort. An arm around me to hold me together. A spark of sunshine to cut through the gloom.

Turned out I did need something. I needed Callie.

I stood and walked to the other side of the waiting room, pulling my phone from my pocket. I tapped a contact, my heart racing like a motor revved to the breaking point. She answered on the second ring.

"Callie." It came out more plea than greeting.

"Jed? What's wrong?"

The concern in her voice squeezed my lungs, and I needed a second to fill them again.

"My pop's in the hospital."

"Oh no."

She made a sound of dismay, and I hated spreading my anguish, but the one thing I needed right now, the one thing that might help, was *her*.

"Could you...could you come and just be with me? Please?"

DÉJÀ VU HAD NEVER CUT QUITE SO deep. I'd lived out this scene in the medical center a dozen times before. Jed and his family huddled together, waiting for news. I knew that worry, too, the grief that loomed over them just waiting to strike. Jed sat slumped with his elbows on his knees, his hair skewed every which way, his head bowed down.

I walked farther in, and Wade nudged him. Jed looked up, and when his eyes met mine, his sigh echoed across the room. He rushed over, gathered me into his arms, and tucked his head down against mine. I held him close, trying to transfer whatever strength I had into him. I hugged him with all my might, giving him everything I could.

"Thank you for coming," he whispered.

"Always," I whispered back.

We rejoined the others, and I hugged each one, sharing what words of support I could.

"I'm glad you're here," Wade said when he'd released me.

I sat next to Jed, our hands clasped tightly together as Marilyn brought me up to speed. Clint was in surgery, but they didn't know what type or how long it would take. The nurses had been kind, but hadn't shared anything more. We'd just have to wait it out.

"June isn't here yet?" I asked.

Wade and Jed exchanged a look.

"We didn't want to ruin her honeymoon until we knew anything for sure," Wade said. "It'll shake her whole foundation."

"It's going to shake her no matter what."

He winced, his mouth thinning. "I guess we don't want to hurt her until we have to."

I could appreciate the depth of love and affection they had for their sister, and how badly they wanted to protect her from heartache, but that sweet impulse had led them to a stupid conclusion. "It will be worse to find out you kept something like that from her, no matter how good your intentions are. I'm sure she'd rather you were honest with hard truths than find out you'd kept her in the dark."

Oh.

My turn now to share a look with Jed. Wasn't that what I'd been doing to Granny? Keeping her from the truth so I wouldn't hurt her feelings about the house or the set-ups or Jed? Wanting to spare her a little hurt was all well and good, but how much more would it hurt when she found out I'd lied about everything?

I ticked my head in a tiny nod at Jed. I needed to come clean to Granny. Not spin a break-up story, but tell her the whole truth.

"You're right," Wade said, standing. "I'll give her a call."

He walked away, and Jed squeezed my hand tighter. I wasn't sure if it was for me deciding to tell Gran, or for convincing them to call June, or what, but I squeezed him right back.

"How are you liking living solo?" he asked quietly.

Sure didn't seem like the right time to talk about my sad state in the house, but the look in his eyes said he needed to think about something other than his dad. I could understand that.

"I rearranged the furniture in the living room, and I've got color swatches taped up in the dining room. I think I'll paint that this week."

"What color?"

"Maybe seafoam green. Something soft and cozy."

"No booger gray?"

I laughed but almost burst into tears at his little joke. I couldn't believe he had any humor in him right now at all, but here he was, sharing it like he needed to cheer *me* up? My heart held nothing but love for this man.

Faster than I would have thought possible, June and Ty arrived. We went through another round of hugs, trying to keep each other's spirits up, hoping for the best news.

June sat down and shuddered. "I hate this damn place."

She shared a soft look with me. They'd spent plenty of time here with their mom, too.

Time stretched and thinned, dragging out as if any one of us wanted to memorize the moment. The next hour passed like twelve, but finally, a doctor came out to speak to the family. He explained that they'd treated Clint's heart attack with an angioplasty, and he'd need to stay in the hospital for a few days. Most importantly, they expected him to make a full recovery.

The collective sigh between us might have been choreographed, everyone slumping in relief. The cloud that had been hanging over us lifted, and our smiles peeked out again in our hope.

"He's got a road to get there," the doctor said, "but he's awake and able to have a visitor for a few minutes. I suggest one for tonight."

The family looked to Marilyn, but she urged Wade to go. "Tell him how much we love him."

He nodded and followed the doctor through the ICU doors.

Jed pulled me into his arms, and we held each other tight. I said a silent prayer of thanks Clint would be okay. Then I offered up a second in gratitude Jed had asked me to join him here. I hated the idea of him needing me and not asking, here with his family but suffering alone. I needed him to know he never had to shoulder his burdens all by himself. Not if I could help it.

Not long after, Wade came back out. His faint smile gave me even more hope than the doctor's words.

"Pop's looking worse for wear, but he's strong. Doesn't want any of us to worry, but I told him he's stuck with us, worries and all. They want to let him sleep tonight, and we can visit tomorrow."

"I wonder," Marilyn said, patting her hair with shaky fingers, "if one of you would drive me home? My car's downtown, and I don't think I..."

Annie wrapped an arm around her. "We'll drive you home. In fact, would you like to stay with us tonight?"

"I think I would. Thank you."

"My truck's at the farm," Jed said.

"I can drive you home," I told him.

Marilyn stepped closer to give me a great big hug. "Clint and I are so grateful Jed has you."

We headed out of the hospital, those words knocking around in my brain. Jed did have me. Not just now, walking to my car hand in hand, but...more. All of it. And I wouldn't be afraid to tell him anymore. I hated the idea of putting it all out there and getting nothing in return, but I couldn't risk keeping quiet about something this important. I would speak up and share my heart, and see if he felt the same.

Sometime later, when his dad wasn't in the hospital recuperating after a heart attack, and everyone's emotions weren't already dialed up to tens.

But soon. Because this man had my heart, and I wasn't about to let him go if I could help it.

jed

MY BRAIN finally kicked in on the drive to my house. I phoned our pickers and the couple who usually ran the store to let them know about Pop. Asked them to cover what we normally would have done, at least for the next couple of days. I figured after that, I'd make a new plan. Not just for a few days or a few weeks, but years on into the future if I needed to.

My heart crumpled at the thought. I would take on the farm —*wanted* the farm—but I didn't want to have to do it on my own yet.

Callie parked at my house, and we walked up my steps, her hand locked in mine. Wasn't sure I'd let her go for more than a few seconds since she'd showed up at the hospital. She'd saved me there, giving me the strength to pull myself together before I'd tumbled straight over the edge.

I opened the door and let us inside.

"Are you hungry?" she asked.

Like it'd been waiting for someone to remember it, my stomach growled. Almost nine at night, and I hadn't had a bite since noon.

"I could eat. There's not much in the fridge, though."

Wasn't much in the house at all. Strange time to notice, but this place didn't feel like a home. Not the way Callie's did. Always thinking I'd be on the move again one day, I hadn't made it mine. No life, no color, no heart.

All except for the woman who watched me with something like love in those big brown eyes.

She ran a hand over my upper arm, comforting and reassuring. My breath slowed like she'd worked magic on me.

"Why don't you take a shower, and I'll order us some food. Chinese okay?"

"Okay." I walked toward the short hallway between bedrooms, but turned back like I needed to be sure she hadn't left already. She smiled and set to looking something up on her phone. Probably dinner. I followed her instructions and took a shower.

I let the water run over me longer than I normally would have. Soaped up, lathered my hair, scrubbed. Cried a little, too —relief and exhaustion and just straight up emotional overwhelm needing a minute of release.

Pop had a heart attack.

But he's going to be okay.

But he had a heart attack.

The hot water soothed my muscles, and if it couldn't soothe my heart, at least it cleared my head a bit. The greasy dread from the hospital washed away, and my thoughts rearranged into something less ominous. It wasn't much, but for now, that would be enough.

I dried off and slipped on a pair of basketball shorts and a T-shirt. In the kitchen, Callie pulled plates from a cupboard. The house smelled of noodles and beef, and I spotted two takeout containers on the counter.

"That got here fast."

Her smile hit me in that achy part of my chest that'd been

through the wringer today, working like a salve to soothe the fears that fought to rise up again.

"I don't think it's their busy time. I wasn't sure what you'd like, so I ordered noodles and rice with two kinds of meat." She opened the containers, releasing even more of their delicious smells. My mouth watered, and my stomach twisted in its eagerness to be filled.

"Sounds perfect."

I sank into a dining chair in a semi-daze, watching her load up my plate like that was the limit of what I could do. Should have helped her, should have offered to do anything at all, but I sat like I'd been glued down. She set the plate in front of me and squeezed my shoulder.

"Eat."

Her soft command got my limbs moving, and I did as she said. I shoveled in food, barely stringing two thoughts together while she served up her own meal and joined me. I'd almost finished my plate before the meat and carbs started to bring my brain back online.

"Thank you." Wasn't flowery, but my brain wasn't so fired up I could be more elaborate.

"You're welcome."

When we'd finished eating, she took care of the dishes and put the leftovers in the fridge. I stood from the table, but paused like I didn't know the next steps. Panic still hovered over me, and I wasn't sure how long I could keep it at bay.

She ran her hands up and down my arms. "What do you need?"

Just you. Not the time to say it, but the only right answer.

"I should probably sleep, but I don't know if that's happening."

I'd already been sleeping poorly, but tonight, I had zero expectations.

"Then let's get ready for bed."

She locked the front door and turned out the lights. Then, she took my hand and led me into my bedroom, my brain spinning like a computer that'd frozen up. At my bedside, I tugged on her hand to stop her.

"Callie? What are we doing?"

"We're going to sleep. You've had a rough day." She pulled her lower lip into her mouth, worrying it. "I won't stay if you don't want me to—"

"I want you to." I never would have asked, but given that she'd offered? I could have fallen to my knees in gratitude.

"Then I will. Do you have something I can sleep in?"

I grabbed the first thing I saw in my T-shirt stash in my dresser and handed it over, still a little dumbfounded by this impromptu sleepover.

"I'll just get ready," she said, and slipped into the bathroom.

She came out a minute later wearing my shirt and not much else. I kept my gaze eye-level as we traded places, and I got busy brushing my teeth, trying to settle my unruly thoughts. When I came out again, she sat under the covers in the middle of my bed, the red sriracha sauce shirt billowy on her. She looked perfect and cozy and at home, and the moment felt significant. Monumental.

I prayed my brain was functioning at a high enough level to file this memory away.

Careful not to touch her—or stare too hard at her—I climbed in next to her. She slipped lower into the bed, stirring up her citrus scent. I snapped off the lamp, willing myself to not ruin this whole moment by doing something stupid.

She curled up against me, one hand resting on my chest, her legs tangling with mine. "Is this okay?"

"Better than okay."

This...this just might wreck me. Sleeping in my bed, Callie's perfume everywhere, her wearing my clothes. She'd knocked me out, and I wasn't sure I'd ever get back up again.

We laid together in the dark, breathing in time with each other. The weight of the day found me again, flattening me out, but I held her close. Like she'd become my talisman, my defender, and could keep those thoughts at bay.

As I drifted toward sleep, she whispered against my chest.

"You don't have to be alone."

jed

PIECES of the night before came to me before I fully awoke. The hospital, my pop, the crush of fear. My arms tightened instinctively around Callie, and I remembered the rest. Her sitting with me, bringing me home, feeding me. Taking care of me.

My head felt clearer in the morning light. Wasn't saying a lot, considering the daze I'd been in last night. I'd always been pretty good in an emergency in the Army, but I guess that didn't apply when it came to my pop. Panic had dug its claws right in, driving out my usual calm.

Callie sighed in her sleep and rolled over, her face a breath from mine. That I'd slept the night through past seven a.m. was a testament to her good heart. If I'd been alone, I suspect I would have lain awake all night letting grim thoughts gnaw at me in the darkness. Instead, she'd held me close and given me her peace. She was sweet and soft and wonderful, and I most definitely did not deserve her.

My phone rang on my nightstand, jolting me out of the last tendrils of sleep. I pulled away from Callie, but my heart beat a frantic pace when I saw the name on the display. I sat up, swallowing down my fears. "June?"

"Hey. Everything's fine, I didn't mean to worry you."

Oh, thank God.

Callie had woken, and she sat up, too, her eyes round as she watched me.

"It's okay," I said to both of them. Callie visibly relaxed, her shoulders easing back down, and her hand slipped into my free one.

"I'm headed over to see Pop, and I thought you might need a ride. Figured your truck was still over at the farm."

"That sounds good, thanks."

"I'll be there in fifteen."

Not a lot of time to prepare, but she probably didn't need to know that. We hung up, and I raked my fingers through my hair. Nothing like terror to get a person wide awake. I explained what was going on to Callie.

"That'll be good. You'll probably feel better once you see him for yourself."

While she slipped into the bathroom to get dressed, I changed into a pair of jeans and walked out into the living room to find my boots. Didn't even remember taking them off, much less where I'd left them. I'd been such a mess last night.

Maybe I should have regretted being so exposed in front of Callie, but I didn't. It felt just right. Wouldn't have wanted anyone else with me in a time like that.

When she reappeared, she grabbed her purse from the table. "I should—" She waved at the door. "You'll keep me updated?"

I nodded. "I can't thank you enough for everything last night."

She shook her head as if single-handedly holding me together wasn't that much. "I'm glad you called me."

"What are you doing today?"

"Maybe painting the dining room."

"Sounds like a good plan."

I leaned down to hug her goodbye, and I meant it to be normal, friendly, even, but hugs had never been that with her. They were whole body embraces that made the shattered pieces of my heart reform and weld together, leaving me stronger than I'd been pre-hug.

A lot to put on a woman's arms around me, but she succeeded every time.

I watched her drive off, not knowing if I deserved her, not knowing if I could give her everything she needed in return, but knowing without question I didn't want to lose her.

* * *

June and I sat in the medical center's waiting room, trying not to watch the clock as the minutes ticked by. Wade had brought Marilyn in to see Pop first thing, and he'd taken a walk outside to pass the time while they visited. Maybe I should have joined him—being back in this awful room sure didn't qualify as soothing.

"I'm sorry about your honeymoon," I said. Callie had been right—keeping the news from June would have been unforgivable, but it'd put a damper on what should have been a week of celebrations. Not that I wanted to think a whole lot about those celebrations.

"We didn't miss out on anything."

I smirked. "I'll be sure to tell Hardy you said that."

She lightly pinched my arm. "You know what I mean. We weren't going anywhere, we can take a few days off another time."

The way Ty ran his one-man horse training business, he

couldn't very well take a week off to go traipsing around the country. June had a one-woman business, too, but I figured her decorating clients would be a lot more understanding about vacation time than the horses would.

"He feels bad about it, you know." Her voice had gone soft, her gaze stuck somewhere in the middle distance, like she saw something other than the nurses' station. "That we're not going on a big honeymoon. I told him he can make love to me just as good here as he could under palm trees somewhere."

"All right, all right." Didn't need the whole thing spelled out for me.

She laughed. "I don't care where we are, as long as we're together. The honeymoon's nothing to me as long as he's my husband."

"I truly am happy for you."

"I'm happy for me, too." She grinned and stretched out for a second in the hard-backed chair but thought better of it and sat up again.

"How did you know Ty was the one for you?"

Something in my voice must have given me away. She turned her eyes to me like she was looking through a microscope, searching for everything I'd been hiding. Today, I couldn't be sure it wouldn't all be visible to the naked eye.

"Ty loves me for who I am, not some version of me he wants to see. I never felt so safe to be myself, the good and the bad. We butt heads sometimes, but it's a whole heck of a lot better than a relationship where you never really scratch the surface."

She laid a hand on my arm like she thought I might scramble away if she didn't hold onto me. "Opening myself up to him can be scary sometimes, but that's how the love gets in."

Maybe she'd been right to hold onto me. Kind of wanted to bolt, just wasn't sure where to. My instinct had me mentally checking out and heading for the hills...but my heart wanted to sprint straight to Callie. Being with her wasn't the ambush, it was the safe haven.

"Damn, Junebug, you didn't have to go that hard with the love talk." I touched a fingertip to the outside corner of one eye, begging it not to get all leaky on me. It'd be hard enough to see Pop in a few minutes, I didn't need a pre-game cry.

She squeezed my arm and let it go. "Just trying to look out for my big brother."

Marilyn walked out of the ICU hallway, and June and I went to her. She still looked a little wrung out, but she seemed encouraged by the visit.

"Your dad's doing really well," she said. "His color's good, and his spirits are up."

"Can we see him, or should he rest?" June asked.

"Oh no, one of you should get on in there. He wants to see you, and you know how stubborn he can get. Seeing you will help him get better."

June turned to me. "You go. I'll head in after."

"You sure?" I knew she was as eager to see him as I was.

"Yeah. Build up the anticipation for the favorite child." She flashed a teasing grin.

"Wade's got you beat there. He gave Pop grandchildren."

June conceded defeat, but I had a feeling it wouldn't be long before she joined him in those ranks.

I followed Marilyn through the double doors and down a hallway.

"This one's his." She nodded, squeezed my arm, and turned to go back to the waiting room.

I took a deep breath and pushed the door open. Pop sat propped up in the big hospital bed looking better than I'd expected. Marilyn was right, he looked good for what he'd been through, a little pale maybe, and more tired than I'd ever seen him, but still himself.

He stretched a hand out. "Come sit with me, son."

I did as he said and sat beside his legs to take his hand up in mine. Machines and monitors beeped around his bed, and tubes snaked out from the back of his hand and the openings in his gown. But I focused on how big he smiled and how tightly he gripped my hand. Both good signs.

"How are you doing?" I asked.

"Better every hour. The event itself was frightening, I admit."

Event. Was that what we'd be calling his heart attack now?

"I didn't like being awake for the procedure—" He gestured at his groin, indicating something I didn't even want to guess at. "But I'm doing better. I don't want you to worry about me."

"Too late for that."

He nodded, understanding as well as anyone we couldn't stop the worry. "How are you holding up?"

"I'm okay."

Yeah. Okay. I didn't know what I was doing with the farm, my father'd had a life-threatening *event*, and I was messing up my relationship with the one woman I'd ever loved. Pretty okay.

His gaze cut right through me. "How are you really?"

"I'm scared." The words came out small and soft, baby animals that didn't want to frighten me into admitting just what exactly I was scared of. I sat on the edge of losing it all —the farm, Pop, Callie. And I didn't want to let any of them go.

"I'm scared, too."

I must have flinched, because he rushed to soothe me. "Not about this. I don't like this, but I believe I'm going to get through it. I mean I've been scared *out there*."

He nodded toward the door like something lurked in the

hallway. I hadn't thought of my pop as being afraid of much of anything. He sure hadn't showed it often.

"I think I confused you, asking you to take over the farm and then not letting you. Maybe you thought you'd done something wrong, or I didn't want you to have it."

"Something like that." Didn't need to go into details, especially not here and now.

"I was afraid I'd pushed it on you too fast. For years, I thought I might wind up having to sell when I retired, and then you came home from the Army, and we were back in business. But I never really asked you if you wanted it. I just took it for granted that you would."

"I do want it." No doubt in my mind. I wanted the farm he and Mom had loved into existence, built from the ground up. Fears still lingered, but I couldn't see myself doing anything else. "I don't know how to do it all, but I want to carry on the farm, Pop."

He clasped my hand tighter. "The closer I got to stepping away, the more afraid I became of being useless. I was afraid of losing what I've been doing for forty years. I clung to it tighter, and in turn, I pushed you out a little bit."

"I never wanted you to leave." It didn't line up with the way I'd been hounding him to get out of the orchards and into his comfy house. Exactly where he hadn't wanted to wind up. "I thought you wanted to retire."

"I know. I've been of two minds about it. Maybe this is God's way of telling me to step back a bit."

He laughed, but his smile strained. It hurt just to see all the things taped to his chest—it couldn't feel good to move around with them on.

"What do you think? Can we find a way to keep me busy and still let you take the reins?"

I nodded, and for a minute couldn't speak for fear the crush of emotions of the last twenty-four hours would come tumbling out if I did. "I'd like that."

"Good. Now get on out there and give Callie a hug for me."

The happy moment fizzled. "Pop, Callie and I…we aren't…"

I couldn't even say the words. Didn't want to agitate him by confessing the whole thing had been fake. Although, looking at it now, I couldn't say for sure just what between us hadn't been real. But his eyes sharpened like my hesitation gave him all the information he needed.

"I know you've got fears there, too. Maybe losing your mom was part of it, maybe something you experienced in the Army. But I see you living your life like it's all going to be stolen from you. Like you're living on borrowed time, so you don't look very far into the future in case it gets taken away."

My heart spasmed so hard in my chest, I probably should have hooked myself up to one of Pop's machines. I'd never been very good at planning ahead, but since Zach and Mom's deaths, it'd felt wrong to try. They'd died and I'd lived, and expecting more would just make me presumptuous and greedy.

"I don't know if I deserve a future." Couldn't even be sure he'd heard me over the beeps, my voice came out so tiny and afraid. Hard to admit the thing that'd been dogging me for years.

He ran a hand over my head the way Wade sometimes did with his kids. That sweet gesture finally brought my tears out. They made Pop blur out of focus, but they felt cleansing, too, like I'd held onto them far too long.

"Jed, you deserve a whole lifetime of happiness. Full stop. You know better than most that we don't get guarantees in this life, but that doesn't mean we can't love the life we have for as many days as we get. You've been my fearless boy for so long, I hate to see you afraid to act."

I hadn't thought I had been…but looking at my life now, I

could see the fear written across it in bold indecision. My empty apartment, the land I wouldn't build on, the company I hesitated to step up and run. I'd been afraid to settle in too deep, thinking someone would realize I wasn't worthy and snatch it all away.

"Now, there are some things in this life that you won't want, and that's fine. But if there are things you *do* want..." Pop's razor-sharp eyes hit mine. "Then go after them. The only guarantee you'll lose them is if you don't try."

Could I try to go after what I wanted? I'd been so afraid of looking to the future in case I lost it...but if I tried to imagine it? If I looked ten or twenty years down the road, what did I want to see? A vision of the orchards...a wife...babies. A lifetime of happiness with Callie sounded exactly right to me. I might not know how to get there, but I wouldn't deny anymore what I wanted.

"I'm proud of the man you are, and your mom was, too. You are a joy to me, son."

The word *joy* came out reverent and significant, keeping me choked up.

"I'm kind of a pain in the ass sometimes." I needed to lighten this up a touch before I fell sobbing into his arms.

"That you are, but you're our pain, and we wouldn't trade you for the world." He smiled wide, eyes shining. "You know, your mom would have loved Callie."

He knew how to hit me where it hurt. In the best way, but it still hurt. "That is the going opinion, yeah."

He flashed a sly look. "And you?"

Didn't require much soul searching. I nodded, the words seeming to fill up my chest cavity, pressing against my ribcage as they fought to work their way out. "I love her, too."

I loved every part of her, from her tender heart to her surprisingly sturdy backbone. And I wanted every part of her, too, the good days and the bad, the joy and the sorrow. I wasn't sure yet if Callie was mine, but without a doubt, I was hers. Totally and completely.

Pop's grin came with the soundtrack of faster *beep-beep-beeps* on the machine, driving home his happiness.

"Then go get your woman."

THIRTY-FIVE

I WASN'T sure how this conversation would go, but I knew I had to have it, and I wouldn't put it off any longer.

Granny picked up after the first ring. "Callie, my girl, you have perfect timing. We just got to our condo, and we're all on the lanai looking at the beach."

I giggled a little over that. *Lanai*. They'd been there half a day and were already full-fledged Golden Girls.

"Are you heading down to put your toe in?" I asked.

"We'll go down in a little while. The movers should get here tomorrow, so we'll stay in a hotel tonight."

"Sounds good."

I paced around the living room, my eyes stuck on the color swatches I'd taped to the dining room wall. I could do this. She would be better off knowing the truth. Just had to get through the tricky little part of telling her.

"Gran, can you find some privacy for a few minutes? I need to talk to you."

"Of course. What is it?"

The background sounds of the other women faded out, and I heard a door close.

"I need to tell you something about Jed and me."

"I'm ready."

Oh dear, she sounded like she thought I was about to deliver *extremely* good news. Maybe I should have planned better wording, but I'd never been the best at that. "Can you sit down?"

"If I get on the floor, I'm not getting up again. What happened?"

"Okay. So..." I exhaled until my lungs emptied out. "What I have to tell you is that Jed and I were never really dating. It was all fake."

I imagined all sorts of expressions flying across her face in the silence that followed, none of them good.

"I'm going to need you to explain this to me," she said. "What do you mean, it was all fake?"

"Gran, I hated all those set-ups y'all were sending me on. The guys weren't the greatest, and there was all this pressure to find a man or you wouldn't move to Florida. So I asked Jed if he would pretend to be my boyfriend."

I paused, but she didn't say anything, so I charged on. "He didn't really want to, but then he saw me on one of those dates, and the guy was really handsy, so Jed stepped in and said he'd do it. I know I shouldn't have lied to everyone, and I never meant to hurt you, I was just...afraid to tell you the truth, I guess."

"Which guy was handsy?" She sounded like she could have throttled him herself.

"It's not important. The point is, I should have just told you the truth. I tried, but I didn't try as hard as I could have. I wanted you to move with your friends and be happy, and I could never have asked you to move out if you'd stayed."

"You wanted me to move out?"

Now her voice had a layer of hurt to it. I should have kept

my thoughts somewhat in order, but as usual, they'd all jumbled together and come out at the wrong time.

"No, it's not that, I really loved living with you." Another pause while I gathered up more courage. "But Gran, I want to sell the house. Maybe not immediately, but I want something of my own. I want something out in the trees that's secluded and peaceful and cozy and mine."

Might have just described Jed's property. All except for the *mine* part.

"How long have you felt this way?"

"For a while. I've never really loved the house, after everything that happened in it, but I should have been honest with you. I didn't want you to stay because of me, but I didn't want you to leave because of me, either."

Made no sense whatsoever, but both things were absolutely true.

She sighed. "Maybe I shouldn't have pushed you so hard to find a man. I just hate the idea of you being alone. We've only had each other for so long...and...I thought if you had someone, I wouldn't feel as guilty as I do for going off to Florida without you."

Huh. So we'd both been trying different versions of the same thing. Easing our own guilt and making the other happy in our own convoluted ways.

"You don't need to feel guilty, I'm glad you're with your friends. But I'm sorry I lied to you."

"I'm sorry I made you feel like you had to. I just didn't want you to be alone."

"I'm not alone. I have my friends, and work I love, and a good life." I really did. I didn't want to move out of Magnolia Ridge in any scenario.

"What about Jed? You're trying to tell me everything between you two was a sham?"

I stopped my pacing and lowered onto a dining chair. The same one I'd commandeered while Jed was still in it. So basically, my favorite chair.

"After a while, it wasn't fake on my side. But I don't know if he feels the same way."

Hope and *know* felt worlds apart right now. I'd promised myself I'd tell him my feelings, but that didn't mean I'd totally convinced myself he shared them.

"Well, I don't buy it for a minute. I refuse to believe that man isn't head over heels for you. If that was all an act, he sure put everything he had into it."

Especially the way he kissed me, but I wouldn't add that.

"He's a really good guy. He was just trying to do me a favor." I didn't completely believe that anymore, but at this point, I wasn't sure just how much was real and how much was fake.

"That's not the kind of favor most men agree to if they're not interested. The way he looked at you, Callie Louise...there's no faking that."

"I think he feels something, but this isn't really the best time to confront him about it." I explained about Clint's heart attack and how the whole family had been turned upside down. "I need to give him some time."

"And then?"

"Then...I'm going to tell that man I love him."

A little earthquake rocked through me at the image, but I could face my fears. I needed to try, however things turned out. Whatever he said, at least I'd know I'd been honest with him and asked for what I wanted. And the only thing I really wanted was him.

"I promise you he feels the same. And he's going to come to you first, you mark my words."

I had to laugh. "I love your optimism, Gran."

* * *

Another drawback to being fun-sized? I had to climb all the way up the ladder every time I needed to roll the top parts of the walls when I painted. We didn't have high ceilings, either. I'd slowly made my way across the main dining room wall, painting from the top down in small sections, and still only had half of it done. It was already worth it, even if my legs burned from the workout. Painting over the mustard yellow with this soft green made the whole place feel lighter.

I was loading the roller with paint for another run when a knock sounded at the door. A quick glance out the front window showed me Jed's hulking truck out front. My heart did this jumpy kind of flutter as I set the roller back down and went to the door. I scolded my heart to be patient, but it never had paid all that much attention to me when it came to Jed.

He stood in the doorway with a pizza box and the sweetest grin. "Hey, Callie Lou. Did I miss the painting party?"

"I'm right in the middle." I waved him on in. "How's your dad doing today?"

"Better. He sends you his love."

"Aw. You send him mine right back." We picked our way across the living room, still out of order from Gran's packing spree. "It's a mess in here."

"I'm all about that Callie chaos."

I snorted a laugh that made his eyes light up. That, in turn, set my insides on fire, a never-ending chain reaction when I was around him.

I'd covered the dining table and chairs with a drop cloth and tucked plastic sheeting up against the baseboards to protect the hardwoods, but we could make it work. He set the pizza on the table, and a bunch of slick brochures slid off the top.

"What are these?"

I spread them out. Each one had a drawing of a different house front and back, with a floor plan laid out in tiny grids. A Craftsman with an ornate entry, a modern one-level with a sloped roof, a farmhouse with a wraparound front porch and full-length back porch.

"I need your opinion. I think it's time I put a house on the property, but I wasn't sure which one you'd like best. I have a hunch, but I need to be sure."

I looked up at him, that fluttery feeling in my heart turning into a banging drum. He gave me a small, hopeful smile that careened through me, zapping all my tender spots from my head to my toes.

"You want my opinion on your house?"

"Yeah. Only, I want it to be your house, too."

I couldn't speak—I wasn't even sure I was breathing. I could only manage to listen and stare.

"I realized I hate the quiet when you're not around. I miss how you snort when you laugh. I miss the way you always jump in heart first. I miss the way you love with everything you have. I miss my girlfriend."

He moved a tiny step closer, like a question, and I answered by taking my own step toward him. He took hold of my fingers in that sweet little gesture I'd come to love.

"I don't know if you need me, Callie, but I sure as hell need you. Turns out, I love you. I think I loved you from the beginning, it just took me a while to realize it. And yeah, we started out in a pretend relationship, but there's nothing I want more than to make it real."

Did he just—did Jed Evans just tell me he loved me?

I launched myself at him, throwing my arms around his shoulders and kissing his face, his jaw, his mouth. And boy, oh boy, did he ever kiss me back. His hands made a slow map of my back while he absolutely ruined me with the kiss, my body turning to mush in his arms.

I was so thoroughly his, I didn't know how I'd ever thought we wouldn't wind up here.

I broke the kiss, and if he could see the hearts in my eyes, so be it. "Obviously, I want the farmhouse with the big back porch."

His mouth tipped up. "Called it."

I drew my hands up to cup his face. "And I love you, too. I am embarrassingly, completely in love with you. I said I wouldn't fall for you, but I did."

His smile stretched wide. "I forgive you."

I rolled my eyes at his teasing. "I just told my granny we're not together. Seems no matter what I do, I end up lying to my gran."

He tilted his face closer to mine. "Then you'd better call her back, because we are together. I'm in this for the long haul, Callie."

Oh, Gran would have a field day when she found out her prediction had come true.

Jed's smile dimmed a touch, but his hands stayed locked on my waist. "I've never done the long haul before. I think I've been afraid to look to the future, feeling I didn't deserve these extra years when people I loved didn't get the same."

I stroked a hand along his temple, and he leaned into it in a move of such tenderness, my heart squeezed all over again. I loved my sweet man's gentle soul.

"We can do everything as slowly as you want to," he said. "You're still the captain. Of the house, the relationship, the...*everything*."

His eyes heated, and my belly dipped in response. *Everything* sounded good to me.

"But I want a future with you," he went on. "Days and months and years of it. As much as you'll give me."

"I want that, too. But I have one condition."

His resolute little nod sent sparkles over my skin. "Name it."

"We co-captain all the ships."

He grinned and bent down to kiss me again. "Co-captains, it is."

epilogue

JED

TEN MONTHS *later*

I'd been through brutal Basic Training, dangerous scenarios, and even watched my niece and nephews for a whole weekend while Wade and Annie went out of town for their ten-year anniversary, but I wasn't sure I'd ever been so nervous.

Driving my truck up the lane, I tapped my fingers on the steering wheel, my nerves on full display. Didn't matter, though, since Callie couldn't see my antsiness.

"Are you peeking?"

She laughed. "How could I peek? I'm wearing two blindfolds and a baseball hat tugged over my eyes."

"You're sneaky."

"I know where we're going," she said softly. "I think I do. Maybe it's something else, but I'm pretty sure."

We'd been out here together after they laid the foundation, and again to see the progress as the walls came up. But once it started looking like a real house, I'd asked her to steer clear. She might have helped pick out everything about it, but that didn't mean it couldn't be a surprise.

I parked out front and stepped around the truck to Callie's side. I swung the door open, tamping down my chuckle at the sight of her perched in the passenger seat, eyes covered, hat angled low.

"Now for the fun part." I put my hands on her waist and turned her to me so I could lift her down out of the truck. She made a soft little sound as I lowered her to the grass, her hands tight on my shoulders. Having her in my arms had become my favorite part of every day, and if I went out of my way to find excuses to get her there, I was only human.

I guided her into position and took off the hat. "Are you ready?"

She grinned so wide, her dimple showed and—well, I had to stoop down to kiss it.

I moved to stand behind her and untied both bandanas I'd put around her head. I stuffed them in my back pocket and placed my hands on her shoulders. "You can look."

The sound she made when she opened her eyes was just what I'd hoped for. Part gasp, part squeal, all delight. She spun around, sparklers shining in her eyes.

"Is it finished?"

"It's all done."

The one-story white farmhouse sat in the middle of my property, its covered front porch beckoning us inside. It looked modern but classic, the perfect fit out here in the sticks. The perfect fit for us.

She took a step closer. "Can we—?"

I handed her an Evans Orchards keychain with a single key on it. Her grin flashed right before she swiped the keychain from my hand and darted onto the front porch.

Her nonstop *oohing* and *aahing* provided the soundtrack for our tour of the house. I'd been through it already on a final walk-through with the builders, but seeing it with her made everything more special. We'd focused on putting together a comfortable, inviting home, skipping most of the luxury options in favor of a functional, classic style. Open floor plan, warm wood kitchen cabinets, hardwood floors. White walls, so Callie could cover each room in her favorite bold colors. An office with perfect lighting for painting and embroidering. Porches in front and back.

She ran from room to room, testing out cupboards and flipping on lights, double-checking everything we'd picked. In the primary bedroom, she spun a small circle, but when she stopped, her lower lip wobbled.

Tears weren't where I wanted her to go. Not yet.

"This is going to be our home," she said quietly.

"Don't sound so happy about it, Callie Lou." I took her hand and ushered her out. "You haven't seen the best part."

Although, to be honest, our future bedroom ranked right up there.

I opened the door that led out to the big back porch. She stepped out and sighed as the view hit her. Beyond the grassy lawn, sycamores and ashes and oaks surrounded us, sheltering the house. A little ways beyond that sat the acres of orchards, and a trace of their summer scent reached us on the breeze.

"It's perfect," she breathed.

It was. This cozy house, in the middle of the orchards I loved and worked with my pop. Only one thing left to make it extra perfect.

While she gazed out at the trees, I moved behind her and pulled the ring I'd been carrying around all day from my pocket. Lowering down on one knee, I held my breath, said a prayer, and lifted it up.

"Callie Lou."

She turned and gasped again, clamping her hands over her mouth when I liked nothing more than hearing those sweet sounds.

"I'd like to proposition you."

She laughed, tears squeezing from her eyes already.

"You are the sunshine of every one of my days. I love you more than I ever thought I could love anybody. The only thing I want in this world is you. I want us. Will you marry me?"

"Yes!" She swiped her hands across her cheeks and dropped to the floor with me, wrapping her arms around me.

I slipped the simple solitaire ring with a filigree band on her finger, pleased to see it was a perfect fit. I'd asked Harper to help me figure out the sizing. If Callie had suspected anything when they'd tried on rings 'just for fun' at the farmers' market a few months ago, she'd never said.

"It was my mom's." I'd got through my whole proposal okay, but sharing this brought out a crack in my voice. "She wanted me to give it to you."

"Oh." She ran a hand over my cheek. "But she didn't know me."

"No. But she told my pop to have it ready for when I found the woman I couldn't live without. And that's you."

Her mouth twisted, smiling as she fought tears. "I love you so much, Jed. This house is amazing, the ring is beautiful and so special, but I don't need any of that. I just need you."

"You've got me." I pulled her to me, arranging us so she sat in my lap on the bare porch. "Today, tomorrow, for as long as we get. *You* are my forever, Callie."

I kissed her, echoing my promise in every touch of my lips, every stroke of my hands. This was it. A lifetime of togetherness and laughter and babies and farming and loving the heck out of each other awaited us. And I was ready for every minute.

She pulled back, the sassy light in her eyes making my stomach flip.

"I'm so glad I fake dated you."

I laughed and kissed her on the nose. "It was all real."

THE END

magnolia ridge

Find out how June got together with grumpy horse trainer Ty in Say the Words.

Read how free-spirited Eliza fell for buttoned-up Dean in Have a Heart.

Find out how overworked Harper got back together with adventurous Sam in Stay this Christmas.

Get the novella of Eden and Booker's whirlwind romance Take the Shot free when you sign up for my newsletter.

acknowledgments

Thank YOU for reading Jed and Callie's book! I fell a little bit in love with Jed when I wrote the first draft of Say the Words in 2019, and it was a joy to finally bring his story into the world. I hope you fell in love with him, too.

Thank you to Claire, Amanda, and Allison for feedback that always makes my books better! I'm especially lucky to have two military spouses in my corner to help make sure Jed's story rang true.

Thank you to my ARC team for taking the time to read and hype my books, it means so much!

Thank you Zee for your editing insight on this series. You always find ways to push me deeper into my characters and I'm so grateful!

So many thanks to Melody for this cover! These two are everything, and I'll never get over this artwork!

Shout-out to my family for inspiring the book's game nights. You're all cut-throat and you beat me at everything, but I love you anyway.

Genny Carrick is a sucker for an HEA, especially if there's a whole lot of laughter along the way. She writes romances and rom-coms about stubborn women and the men who fall for them.

When she's not lost in swoony reads, she's probably up to something crafty or trying to get her dog and two cats to love her.

Genny recently moved to Texas after a lifetime in the Pacific Northwest. She brought her brilliant husband and two hilarious kids with her.

Stay up to date with book news at gennycarrick.com

www.ingramcontent.com/pod-product-compliance
Lightning Source LLC
Chambersburg PA
CBHW061518210726
48287CB00006B/1726